Twelve Lives

A Threat to Millions But This Time It's Personal

by

Nigel Seed

The Sixth Book In The Jim Wilson Series

www.nigelseedauthor.com

Copyright © 2018 Nigel Seed

The right of Nigel Seed to be identified as the author of this work has been asserted.

All rights reserved. No part of this publication may be reproduced, stored in a retrieval system, or transmitted, in any form, or by any means (electronic, mechanical, photocopying, recording, or otherwise), without the prior permission of the publisher. Any person who does any unauthorised act in relation to this publication may be liable to criminal prosecution and civil claims for damages.

This is a fictional work and all characters are drawn from the author's imagination. Any resemblance or similarities to persons either living or dead are entirely coincidental except where they are detailed in the factual chapter.

ISBN-13: 978-1987553376

ISBN-10: 1987553373

For Sofi and Toni
With thanks for their
remarkable hospitality
at Cases Noves in Guadalest, Spain

Acknowledgments

We are all travellers in the wilderness of this world and the best that we can find in our travels is an honest friend.
-Robert Louis Stevenson

I have been blessed with a number of honest friends who have helped me by reading my book at the embryonic stages and giving me useful criticism. They know who they are, but they deserve a mention for putting up with me. My grateful thanks to Pam and John Fine, Glenn Wood, Brian Luckham and Peter Durant.

The biggest debt though is to my wife who has lived this project with me and been supportive throughout, especially when I was struggling

Chapter 1 - Cyprus – One Week Ago

Ivan stood quietly behind Geordie watching him move carefully forward and take a position behind a small bush from where he could see the large white villa. He smiled slightly as he walked silently forward and dropped to the ground next to him.

Geordie rolled left and stared at the apparition that had appeared next to him. "How the hell did you get here? How did you know where I would be?"

Ivan grinned. "And good morning to you, too. How's the plan working out?"

"What plan? And, come on, how did you find me?"

Ivan raised his head slightly and looked at the villa then turned to Geordie. "Not too difficult, really. I saw your face when we found out about the GPS tracking pendant these people fooled you into wearing and I could see you were planning something. Then you spent so much time on the computer in Gibraltar I knew you were up to no good. So I went and checked your browsing history when you went off to get a shower."

"Does the boss know you are here?"

"No, mate. He thinks I'm on my way to a parish in Wiltshire to check in and he thinks you are staying in Denia for Carmen's funeral. How did Manuel take it when you took Carmen's body home to him?"

Geordie sighed. "Not well. That girl was his pride and joy. He just sort of crumpled when he saw her. The rest of the family came round and they were pretty devastated too. They bought the story about the car accident, though. I told Manuel the truth and somehow that helped him a bit, that she died for a reason. I told him that I loved her and he said that she had confessed to him that she had feelings for me."

"Pretty rough then?"

"Yeah, pretty rough, but now I pay the bastard back who caused it."

Ivan looked down at the distinctive wooden-stocked Dragunov sniper rifle that lay in front of his friend. "I take it that Mike Donald got that for you?"

"Yeah, he's a good guy. Even took me out to the ranges at Dhekelia to zero it in. It's ready now and so am I."

Ivan picked up the powerful binoculars and scanned the house. He could see the wide open terrace where they had eaten lunch, when they first met Christophides, the arms merchant who had caused the death of a lovely Spanish girl. He tracked to the right and spotted the uniformed security guards climbing the hillside outside the walls of the extensive garden. He looked back at the villa and could see no other security people.

"So how have you managed to convince the security force to chase up the hillside?"

Geordie gave a tight little smile. "If you look up near the top of the hill you might see some goats wandering about."

Ivan lifted the binoculars again and scanned up the slope. He saw nothing for a moment and then a scraggy goat wandered from behind one of the shady pine trees. Then another, until he could see seven or eight of them eating the scrubby grass.

"I've got them. So what?"

Geordie lifted the rifle and focused the telescopic sight before he answered. "If you see a black one with really curly horns, that's our decoy. He's got a very nice pendant of Saint Anthony round his neck. I relied on them keeping a check on where I was with that tracker."

Ivan chuckled. "They're going to be so irritated once they catch up to it."

Geordie nodded. "I picked a skittish one; I had trouble catching him, even in the pen. I guess he is going to keep moving away as they get closer to him. Should lead them a merry dance while I do what needs doing."

Ivan laid the binoculars down and looked at his friend who was still looking intently through the scope. "Are you sure about this?"

"Never been more sure about anything in my life."

Geordie stiffened as Christophides walked out on to his terrace. He saw the Greek arms dealer raise a pair of powerful binoculars to watch his security people scrambling up the hillside beside the villa. He watched him lower the binoculars halfway and turn his head towards the French doors just as Calanthe, his beautiful daughter, came through wearing a simple white dress and carrying two glasses of something cold. Through the powerful sight optics he could see the condensation running down the glasses.

He adjusted his position to make the rifle steadier and controlled his breathing. The range was around six hundred meters. Well within the capabilities of the weapon.

Christophides turned and reached out for his glass just as Geordie fired. The potent 7.62mm round punched through the arms dealer's back, directly between the shoulder blades. He dropped like a felled tree as his blood spattered across the white dress in front of him. Geordie could hear the girl's shocked scream from where he lay.

Geordie lowered the rifle and Ivan could see his shoulders sag. Ivan waited a moment or two and then patted his friend on the shoulder.

"OK, he's had his payback. Now it's time we weren't here."

The two men slithered backwards into the cover of the trees behind them, then hiked through the wood for two kilometers to where Geordie had left his car. As they got closer Ivan could see that his own hire car was still there, parked neatly behind Geordie's.

The Welshman turned to Geordie. "We'd better get that rifle back to Donald so he can put it well away before the police get called. When are you booked to leave?"

"I'm on the morning flight out of here tomorrow."

"That's handy, so am I. And it's your turn to buy the beer."

They sat in Donald's living room later that evening watching the football on the TV and not speaking, when Ivan's friend came into the room.

"Good thing you two are leaving so soon."

Ivan turned. "Why's that?"

"Just had a call from a friend of mine, asking if I want to make some money. It seems the lovely Calanthe has taken over her dad's arms business right away. She's using you to put out a message to her own people and her rivals. She's put a contract out and you two, plus your friend the Major, have got a price on your heads and it's a big one. To make it absolutely clear to everyone that she's a bad bitch to mess with, the contract includes your families."

Chapter 2 – Norwich, England

Brian Mason slammed his mobile phone down on the desk in irritation as soon as the call ended. He heard the screen crack and turned it over. 'Bloody perfect' he thought. An urgent summons from his wife to come home to see his sainted brother-in-law and now a smashed phone. But, with no clients to see, he might as well go home a bit early tonight. With that thick East Anglian fog swirling outside his office window it would be a slow drive anyway if he was not to end up in one of the water-filled dykes beside the road.

He packed his few papers into the smart leather briefcase his son, Simon, had bought him last month for his birthday and stood up. Simon was a fine boy, but even he hero-worshipped his damned uncle. How the devil could he hope to compete, in his own son's eyes, with a decorated Army officer who went off for months on end on secret missions? And now Major Jim bloody Wilson wanted to see him and he had to drive through this lot to get there urgently. What the hell could be so urgent after hardly a word from him since he left the army and moved to British Columbia to live in a godforsaken cabin in the forests?

Brian stood up from behind his now empty desk and left his office. There was nobody to tell that he was leaving early as his insurance business could not support any other staff. He locked the outside door and walked to where his car should be. He drew his coat closer around him as the damp, cold fog swirled around him.

The standard family saloon appeared out of the darkness just where he had left it. Of course, nobody would want to steal this piece of junk. Not like Jim's fancy sports car that took up half the room in his garage. The red and white Austin Healy 3000 was another thorn in his side. His wife, Sandra, insisted that they had to look after the car for her brother Jim, since it was the only inheritance he had got from his father once the debts were paid off. And now Jim had written to Simon and said he could have it once he was old enough to drive.

With the car door slammed shut, Brian started the engine on the third try. He sat and waited for the air vents to clear the misted windscreen, though heaven knew, there was not much to see out there. He put the car in gear and started the long crawl home through the fog.

He drove slowly with the headlights almost more of a hindrance than a help as the light reflected off the grey swirling moisture. Other cars moved around him and every now and then a pedestrian loomed out of the murk. The streetlights helped, but that stopped as he left the town and drove along the East Anglian country roads. Thankfully, there was not a lot of traffic on a filthy evening like this. He could just make out the white lines in the middle of the road as he followed them, with his foul mood getting worse by the mile. What the hell could be so important that he had to go through all this?

He carried on driving at what felt like crawling speed, with the headache and the ache in his neck from concentrating growing all the time. He saw the waving flashlight ahead and slowed even more. He braked to a halt as the police officer loomed out of the fog with the big red flashlight in his left hand. The officer tapped on the window as he reached the car and Brian opened it.

"Good evening, officer. Is there a problem up ahead?"

The police officer smiled pleasantly. "Not really, sir, but could you tell me your name, please?"

"What? It's Brian Mason. Why do you want to know?"

"Oh, it wouldn't do to stop the wrong person, sir."

Brian saw the policeman's right hand come up from behind his back. He couldn't believe his eyes. The officer was holding a pistol. The muzzle swung round and pointed at him, the large caliber weapon looking like the top of an open rain barrel. He heard the metallic click as the hammer was thumbed back and then two heavy rounds tore into his chest, throwing him back in his seat and across the gear lever.

The police officer gazed down at him for moment or two and Brian tried to speak to ask why, to try and say there had been a terrible mistake, but the blood bubbling up in his throat wouldn't let him. He felt the hand removing the wallet from inside his jacket pocket. He saw the policeman remove his driving licence and then casually toss the wallet back at him. He raised his head as the policeman aimed his weapon again and carefully shot him in the forehead.

The police officer smiled as he turned away from the car and slipped the pistol into his jacket pocket. He slid the high visibility police vest off his shoulders and dropped it into the ditch at the roadside. The police cap he threw into the deep, water-filled dyke that ran along the other side of the road.

Chapter 3

Jim Wilson drove into the driveway in front of his sister's house and parked to one side to allow his brother-in-law access to his garage. With the news he was bringing, the last thing he needed was to start off with another argument. The drive up from London in the hire car had been tiring, the fog having slowed him as soon as he reached the edges of the East Anglian fens and had continued, even thickened, as he came to the Norfolk Broads. If things had been less urgent he would have left it until the next day. He supposed he could have phoned, but he felt he owed it to them to explain why their lives were in danger face to face.

He pulled down the sun visor and checked in the small vanity mirror that he looked presentable. The blue eyes were still clear and didn't need glasses yet. He still had his full head of hair, but he did notice that there were more grey flecks starting to appear as well as the small patches at his temples. The suntan he had picked up in Spain during their last mission for the Prime Minister hadn't faded completely. He opened the door and uncurled himself from the seat, obviously designed for someone shorter than him, then eased the kinks out of his spine before he walked across to the front door.

In the evening gloom, with the windows alight and the fog curling around, the cottage looked more convincing than usual. People often marvelled at how well a five hundred year old cottage had lasted, until they were told it had arrived on the back of a truck in kit form only six years before. Still, it was a nice house and his sister loved it.

He knocked on the carved oak door with its small leaded light window and it was swung open almost immediately by his nephew, Simon. Jim paused and looked at him for a second or two. He was a good-looking boy. Tall for his age and obviously fit. He had inherited the blue eyes and fair hair from his mother and virtually nothing from his father, which was a blessing.

"Hi, Simon, you're looking well."

"Uncle Jim! We've been waiting for you. Mum says it's something important. Sorry, come on in. We're letting all the heat out."

Jim gave the boy's shoulder a squeeze as he walked in and looked around. As usual the house was immaculate, with all the pictures hanging exactly level and fresh flowers in the vases on the side table. His sister came through the door from the kitchen wiping her hands on a red checked towel. She gave him her usual wary smile.

"Hello, Jim. Brian not with you?"

"Hello, Sandra. No, I haven't seen him. Are you OK?"

"I'm fine. I just thought he would be here by now. He said he was leaving the office over an hour ago."

"Don't worry; the fog will have slowed him down. Any tea going? I've got a mouth like the bottom of a parrot's cage."

"Go into the sitting room with Simon. The kettle's just boiled. Do you want anything to eat or do you want to wait for dinner?"

"I'll hang on for dinner. Come on, Simon, come and tell me what you've been up to since I last saw you."

Jim and his nephew walked into the sitting room and each took a chair beside the fire. Simon had hardly started to speak before there was a firm knock on the front door.

Sandra called through from the kitchen. "Simon, can you get that? I'm finishing the tea."

Simon sighed and got up out of his chair. He walked through and opened the door enough to see the unexpected caller. A policeman stood on the step in front of him.

"Is this Mr. Brian Mason's house? We weren't sure in the fog."

"Yes it is. What's the problem?"

"Is Mrs. Mason in? We need to speak to her."

Simon stepped back and, with the first tremors of anxiety starting in his stomach, swung the door wide. "Come on in, I'll go and fetch her. If you go through there and take a seat, I'll have her right with you."

The sergeant nodded to Jim as he walked into the room and took the other armchair, but didn't speak. Jim was about to ask him what was going on when Sandra bustled through with the tea tray. She set it down on the coffee table and sat on the edge of the sofa.

"Right then, help yourself to tea, Jim. Now, sergeant, what's the problem?"

The sergeant looked between the two of them and cleared his throat. "Erm, who is this gentleman?"

"He's my brother, Jim Wilson. Why do you ask?"

The sergeant looked at Jim keenly before he continued. "I'm afraid I have some bad news for you, Mrs. Mason. There has been an incident involving your husband."

"An accident? Is he all right?"

"Not an accident, I'm afraid, Mrs Mason. There's no easy way to say this, but on the way home this evening he was shot. I'm sorry to have to tell you he was pronounced dead at the scene."

Sandra's hands flew up to her mouth and tears rolled down her cheeks as she slumped to her knees on the thick carpet. She looked at Jim, then turned to Simon who was standing aghast in the doorway with his hands limp at his sides and his mouth hanging open. The boy stepped forward to put his arms around his mother, holding her while silent sobs wracked her body. The tears were rolling down the boy's face as he tried his best to comfort his mother. He glanced at Jim, who pointed up the stairs and nodded encouragement. Understanding, Simon turned her to the door and guided her upstairs to her bedroom.

Once they had gone from the room, Jim looked across at the sergeant. "There's more to this, isn't there?' he said. 'What have you not told us?"

"Very perceptive, sir. It's the way he was shot. Two in the chest and one in the forehead. All at close range, by the look of it, although the experts will have to confirm that. If this wasn't Norfolk, I might say it looked like an execution-style hit."

"Oh bloody hell! It's my fault. I'm too late."

The sergeant's eyes opened just a little wider. "Too late, sir? Just what might that mean?"

"Until very recently I was in the army and on a special job for the Prime Minister, with two of my men. There was an incident that has caused a foreign criminal to place a bounty on our heads. She has put a contract out on us and we also feared it included our families. It seems we were right about that. I didn't realise it would start so soon. I came here tonight to warn my sister and her husband."

The police officer looked hard at Jim and sat back in his chair. "That seems a little far-fetched, if you don't mind me saying so. Can you prove any of that?"

"I can. When whoever is running this investigation gets here I will give him a phone number that he, or she, can ring to verify what I have said. In the interim, I'll get my sister and her son to pack a bag. We'll be leaving as soon as we can."

The sergeant shook his head slowly. "You won't be able to leave, sir. I'm afraid you have a lot of questions to answer before there's any chance of that."

Jim gave the sergeant a small smile. "We'll see. Once your senior officer rings that number he won't want to delay us, I promise you."

Chapter 4

Jim, Sandra and Simon walked slowly up the air bridge from the British Airways aircraft that had brought them to Vancouver. There was no point in rushing through the crowds only to stand waiting at the baggage carousel. Sandra had been quiet, almost monosyllabic, since they left the house. Simon had spent a lot of time staring through windows; first in the car and then in the aircraft. Jim had decided to let them deal with the numbness of grief in their own way. He would start to try and bring them out of it once they reached the cabin and safety.

Once the baggage handlers had finally unloaded the aircraft the transit through Canadian immigration formalities was fairly painless. They picked up a taxi outside the terminal and drove north to Coal Harbour. Jim paid off the taxi and walked them around to the front of the flight centre on the harbour edge and down the slope to the floating jetties with a number of single engine floatplanes tied up alongside.

"Uncle Jim, I'm confused. Where are we going? I thought you were taking us to a hotel?"

"No, Simon, we are getting out of town and heading up to the cabin straightaway. It's safer that way."

Simon stopped and put down his suitcase. "So you think we are in real danger? Mum and me? And it's all because of something you did?"

Jim nodded. "I'm afraid the danger is all too real and, yes, it's probably my fault, at least in part."

"When are you going to explain it all to us? We've gone along with you so far, but I think it's time you told us all of it."

Jim picked up his own luggage and Sandra's. "Let me explain it all to you when we get to the cabin. Then I don't have to explain it all over again for Megan."

"Megan doesn't know?"

"Not yet, she doesn't, and she's probably going to be furious when she finds out. Maybe she won't set the dog on me if you two are there."

Simon shrugged and picked up his own bag, then followed Jim towards the yellow and white high-wing aircraft that sat on its floats against the jetty. Jim opened the large rear door and flung the luggage in. He turned and took Simon's bag and tossed that in as well.

"Do you want to take the co-pilot's seat? The front doors are a bit small, so it might be awkward for your Mum in that skirt."

Sandra walked past them and without a word climbed onto the nearest float and then into the back of the aircraft.

"Don't you want to sit up front with the pilot, Uncle Jim?"

"I do. I'm the pilot."

"I never knew you could fly. Why didn't you tell me?"

Jim grinned. "Nah, where's the fun in that? I got my pilot's licence just before I went on my last job and one of Megan's friends brought the plane down and left it here for me."

Simon scrambled in through the front left-hand door and across into the co-pilot's seat. He looked around wide-eyed while buckling himself in. The levers and dials were old-fashioned compared to modern glass cockpits, but all the more exciting for it.

"So what kind of plane is this? Is it yours? How much did it cost? Where do you keep it? I thought you lived in the forest?"

Jim smiled. The healing had begun, at least for Simon. "She's called a Beaver. They were built by De Havilland of Canada and they are one of the finest bush aircraft ever made. I don't own her, she belongs to the university that I work for. They decided we needed one up at the cabin in case of accidents, so we could get the students out to medical help quickly. The cabin is in the forest alright, but just on the edge of a waterway with a ramp up to a hangar that we use during the winter for storing the aircraft and our boat. Now give me a minute to get her started and then we can be on our way once the jetty guys push us off."

Jim set the propeller pitch controls to the right position and started the nine cylinder Pratt and Whitney Wasp engine. The airframe trembled as the large engine roared into life and the propeller became a blurring disc. Jim signalled to the jetty support crew, who cast off the mooring lines and pushed the aircraft out into the water. As the throttle advanced the aircraft moved smoothly forward, causing a small wake behind the floats.

Jim took the old aircraft out into Vancouver harbour and lined it up for take-off. With the throttle pushed to its maximum stop, the Beaver surged forward and rapidly soared up and away over the edge of Stanley Park and over the Lion's Gate Bridge, before starting a gentle turn to the north-west to skirt the edge of Vancouver Island.

As they flew Jim pointed out the massive rafts of tree trunks being moved down the coast towards the city. He looked for any sign of killer whales to try and lighten the mood, but saw nothing this time.

He spotted the inlet he needed in amongst a maze of islands and waterways along the coast, and flew low across it to make sure none of the local fishermen had their boats out in the area he needed to land. Satisfied it was clear, he lined the aircraft up and eased back on the throttle to put the Beaver into a gentle descent. The floats kissed the water smoothly and the spray erupted from under the floats as he brought the plane in for a perfect water landing. He taxied back to the bottom of the concrete slipway that led down to the water's edge from a large shed tucked into the forest border.

As Jim cut the engine he looked round at his sister. For the first time she was taking an interest in her surroundings. He opened his door and climbed down onto the float, then passed the mooring lines around a ring set in the concrete to hold the aircraft in place. He waited as Simon helped Sandra down out of the aircraft and then helped him with the luggage.

"Come on, you two. The cabin is just through those trees there, in the next bay. Megan will have heard us land and have the coffee on by now."

Chapter 5

As they walked towards the large cabin set back in the trees, the front door opened and an over excited Border Collie dog raced towards them. Jim dropped the cases and bent down to greet the wriggling mass of black and white fur. Once Jim was suitably greeted the dog dashed to Sandra and then on to Simon, who fell to his knees to cuddle it.

Sandra walked to Jim's side and watched her son fondly. "He's always wanted a dog, but Brian would never allow it. Nothing to stop him now, I suppose."

Jim looked down at his sister. "It will get easier, I promise."

Sandra looked up at him and smiled sadly. "It wasn't a good marriage, but I would never have wanted it to end this way. Brian did his best, but …" She shrugged.

"Are you people going to come in here before the coffee gets cold or do I have to bring it out there?" Megan called from the veranda of the cabin, with a smile in her voice.

Jim gave her a wave and turned to Simon. "Come on, young man, there's somebody else wants to meet you. Don't worry, Bracken will follow us in."

They walked up the short wooden staircase onto the wide veranda and then into the cabin. Simon's mouth dropped open as he saw just how big the cabin was inside. He looked around at the rustic wooden furniture and the massive rough carved wooden table with benches either side. The large roof beams were hung with examples of native artwork and as he turned he saw, over the front door, a rifle mounted on a wooden rack.

"Wow! Where did you get the cowboy rifle?"

"What cowboy rifle?" Megan asked.

"That one over the door. It's the one they use in all the cowboy movies. It must be a hundred years old."

Megan looked up and then grinned at the boy. "No, that's a Winchester 94. They're so good they carried on making them until very recently. For all I know, they may still be making them. Most of the time we use it to scare off any bears that wander too close. Every now and then we hunt with it, if there's an injured deer or something."

"Can I have a try with it? I've never fired a gun."

Megan nodded. "I'll get Jim to teach you how to use it, but first let's get you settled down. There's plenty of room as all the students have finished their summer fieldwork and gone back to the university."

Jim led Sandra and Simon through to one of the bunk areas and then showed them where the bathrooms were before shepherding them back to the main room. As they arrived Megan had the coffee pot on the table with three mugs and a bottle of soda for Simon. Jim sat down on one of the bench seats next to Megan and waited until Sandra and Simon were settled across the table. He cleared his throat.

"Now then, I've got a story to tell you all about what I have been doing and about why Brian died. And why I brought you here to the backwoods of British Columbia."

He paused and took a sip of Megan's signature strong black coffee. He'd really missed that while he was away.

"You know I left the army and came to live here with Megan, working for the university and studying for my doctorate? That all ended when I was called back into the army by the Prime Minister himself. He needed me and two of my soldiers to do a special job for him. We had done some previous tasks for the former PM and he had recommended us to his successor. I'll cut out some of the details for now, but just say that we made an enemy of an arms dealer during the task and she put out a contract on us."

Simon looked up from his drink. "Sorry, what do you mean by a contract? Is it like they say on the TV shows and what did you do to make her want to kill you?"

"Unfortunately, yes. A rather beautiful Spanish girl was killed by the arms dealer's thugs and my friend Geordie went after him for revenge. His daughter took over the organisation and she has put a price on our heads and anybody who wants to be paid, and paid well, needs to kill us. But it gets worse. She is also using our deaths to establish her control over her late father's criminal organisation by showing what a bad bitch she is. She has extended the contract to cover our families as well. That's why you are here; to keep you safe until I can sort this out. I was a bit too late getting to you and I'm truly sorry that Brian paid for that."

"So if you were working for the Prime Minister, that's why that police inspector got really polite after phoning the number you gave him?"

"Correct. I gave him the number of the duty officer at 10 Downing Street, who put the PM on the line. I've told him what's going on and he is going to see what the government can do to help us stop this thing before anybody else gets hurt."

Chapter 6

The Reverend Sarah Mansfield stood in the pulpit of her church and looked out across the empty rows of pews. She always found that standing up here with the massive church bible in front of her gave her inspiration when searching for a theme for the Sunday sermon. She silently turned the familiar pages and scanned across the words she loved.

The sound of hammering to her right distracted her and she looked down at the man who was on his knees repairing the front pew. She admired the broad shoulders of the man she was going to marry one of these days. Ivan Thomas had come to her at a particularly difficult time in her life and each had recognised deep personal suffering in the other. Together they were working through that and together they were starting to rebuild their lives.

It was strange, she thought, how a man like him had adapted so well to the quiet life of this parish in rural Wiltshire after such an active life in the army. The scars of his physical wounds were healed now, but he would never tell her how he got them. Just like he would never tell her about the jobs he had gone away to do with Major Jim Wilson and their friend, Staff Sergeant Geordie Peters.

She watched him as he stretched to ease his back and then looked up at her and smiled. He really was everything she could wish for. He was a big man and his strength was remarkable. She was often startled by the size of the wood beams he carried in when repairing the old church. She had persuaded him to let his hair start to grow longer than the very short buzz cut he had worn as a Squadron Sergeant Major. It suited him and softened his face, which was a blessing, as having him look so stern when singing with the choir worried the parishioners, even if they did admire his deep Welsh baritone.

Ivan bent to his work again and she turned back to look down the aisle of the church. It really was quite beautiful with the coloured sunlight shining through the stained glass windows and illuminating the dust motes slowly dancing in the air.

She was about to return to her bible when she noticed the dust motes suddenly start to swirl. That was odd. She watched as they returned to their lazy floating once again. Ivan's hammering disturbed her and she was about to ask him to stop when she felt rather than saw movement to her left. She froze and waited to see if it was that damned cat again.

It was no cat. As she watched, a man emerged from the shadows and walked slowly and silently towards Ivan, who was intent on his work and did not notice him. She was about to ask him what he wanted when she saw the gun. The newcomer had a large black automatic pistol in his hand and he was slowly raising it to aim at Ivan. She had no idea what to do: if she cried out the man would fire, if she did nothing the man would fire. She searched her mind feverishly and then a bible verse came to her. "In the Mount of the LORD it shall be provided" (Genesis 22:13, 14).

She looked down at the massive bible in front of her as the man paused below her to take aim. Silently, she lifted the book and held it out in front of her before dropping it on the intruder. The book landed fair and square right on the man's head and he went down like a stone to the floor of the church, his pistol clattering away from him. Ivan spun round at the noise and, moving remarkably rapidly for a big man, he crossed the church to where the attacker was starting to struggle to his feet. Ivan took in the gun and realized instantly what was happening. His massive right fist struck the man and lifted him off the ground before he fell to the stone floor, unconscious.

Ivan picked up the pistol from where it had fallen and unloaded it before turning to hug a tearful Sarah who ran to him from the foot of the pulpit. "All over, *cariad*. Nothing to be upset about," he told her as he stroked her hair.

"But he was going to kill you! Why would he want to do that? Who is he?"

"I'm going to have to tell you a story about the last job I was on with Jim Wilson, aren't I? It didn't all go quite to plan, you see. But first I need to see if I can find out who our friend here is. You go back to the house and make us some tea and I'll be along in a couple of minutes."

Unused to violence, she sniffled and nodded. He watched her walk unsteadily out of the church before turning his attention to the attacker. He quickly went through the man's pockets, tossing everything he found into a small pile. Once he had it all he sat down on the stone step before the altar to go through it. He examined the pistol. That could have really ruined his day. He put the gun and the two magazines to one side. He opened the man's wallet and was surprised to find his own face staring back at him from a small photograph. He opened a small pocket in the wallet and drew out a piece of paper. Unfolding it, he found it was a list of eleven names. Jim was top of the list with his own name second, followed by Geordie Peters. Then his face grew more serious as he read the rest of the list.

The mobile phone in his pocket started to ring and he drew it out. The caller ID screen told him it was Jim Wilson calling, so he thumbed the green button.

"Hello, boss, how's life treating you?"

"Ivan, we've got a problem. Calanthe was serious about that contract she put out on us. It's started."

Ivan couldn't help but chuckle. "Your timing is a bit off this time, boss. I've just had a visit from some thug with Calanthe's list in his pocket."

"Are you and Sarah OK? Where's the killer now?"

"We're fine and the thug is lying quietly having a little sleep down by my feet. He's brought me a very nice Browning Hi Power in case there's another attempt later."

"Thank heaven for that, but what's this about a list?"

"Eleven names, boss. You, me and Geordie, of course, but everyone we care about too. My two kids are on there, but thankfully not Sarah. Megan and your ex-wife Janet are there and so is Geordie's wife, Sam. Your sister and husband, plus their son, are here as well. Eleven in all. You'd better warn them."

Ivan heard the sigh from the other end of the call. "Too late, they already got Brian, shot him execution style on his way home. Simon and Sandra are here with me in Megan's cabin."

"Good thinking. Nobody is going to find you there."

"I hope you're right. Look, can you contact Geordie and warn him while I try and get hold of Janet?"

"Consider it done. Now, what would you like me to do with laughing boy here?"

"I'll call the Number 10 duty officer and get Police Special Branch down there to collect him. We'll probably hold him on terrorism charges. That should keep him on ice for a good while and then I have to have a difficult conversation with Janet."

Chapter 7

Jim sat in the window of the cabin looking through the thin screen of pine trees down to the rocky beach and the waterway. He could hear the various connections clicking in his ear as the phone call was routed through to his ex-wife's villa, halfway up a mountain in Spain. He heard it ring and ring until eventually she picked it up.

"*Digame.*"

"Hi, Janet, what does that mean?"

"Jim, I wasn't expecting it to be you. What do you want?"

Jim looked up at the rough beams above him; this was not going to be easy. "That's not very friendly, but no matter. Janet, listen, I've got something to tell you and you're not going to like it, but stay with me."

He heard her sigh all those thousands of miles away. "Go on then. I'm listening."

"Alright, you know I've been on some classified tasks I could never tell you about? Well, after the divorce I got involved with some even more classified ones and one of them has come back to bite me."

"How does that affect me? What do you need from me?"

"It's not like that; you need something from me. During one of these tasks we fell foul of an arms dealer who seems to be borderline mafia of some kind. Long story short, they have put a contract out with a generous reward for anyone who kills me."

"Oh Lord! How can I help?"

"That's not the problem, Janet. The contract also includes my family and Ivan just got hold of the kill list. Janet, I'm really sorry about this, but you are on that list."

There was a silence as Janet absorbed what she was hearing. Jim waited, not speaking.

"Jim, is this some kind of joke? Because I'm not finding it funny."

"To be honest, I wish it was a joke, but no, it's deadly serious."

"What am I supposed to do now?"

"Is there somewhere you can go where people don't know you? I'll be there as quickly as I can and we'll work something out, but you just need to be out of sight for a while until we can. Don't say where, in case someone is listening."

Janet thought for a moment. "How long till you get here?"

"A couple of days at most. I need to stop over in London to see if I can get all this stopped from there."

"Alright. There is somewhere I have been meaning to visit anyway. I want to do some painting up there. It's a village that was in the big painting on my wall. You saw it when you came here. Do you remember? Call me on my mobile phone when you get there. You still have the number?"

"I have the number and I remember the painting. I'll be with you as soon as I can, but don't hang about. Go there now and tell nobody where you are."

Chapter 8

Staff Sergeant Geordie Peters stood quietly to one side of the men while Squadron Sergeant Major Tom Silk briefed them on what they were to do that day. They had been up in Scotland on the Blair Atholl estate for a week now, building a Bailey bridge across a ravine to replace an ancient stone bridge that had collapsed during the winter storms. Normally, Royal Engineers would not have been used for such a task, but it provided a useful training opportunity and the bridge was needed for a royal visit to the estate in a couple of months' time.

The soldiers had enjoyed the challenge and the local people in the pubs around the area had been friendly and welcoming. Now, it seemed, they were to be rewarded by the estate with the chance of some shooting. The deer herds had outgrown the available food and needed to be thinned out, so the old and the sick were to be humanely culled. The game wardens would lead the soldiers and show them which animals they could shoot, at least the officers could. The rest of the squadron were to act as beaters under Geordie's control as the SSM had decided he would join the officers in the shooting party. At least the soldiers had been promised barbecued venison that night.

Briefing over, Geordie watched as his men climbed into their trucks to be taken to the start point and the officers were driven to the firing points in a Land Rover. He waited as the SSM walked over to join him.

"Geordie, keep the lads under control. I'll keep an eye on the officers to try and make sure they only shoot deer. The game wardens are going to keep an eye on things as well."

Geordie nodded and gave the SSM his brightest smile. "Right you are, sir. Just as long as none of them have to read a map."

The SSM smiled back to acknowledge the old joke about army officers and their map-reading skills. He turned and walked back to the second Land Rover to join the rest of the squadron officers.

Geordie checked that all his men were on board the trucks and gave the signal to start engines before he climbed into the cab of the lead vehicle. They drove down the narrow winding road until they came to the parking area where two game wardens waited to show them what to do and where.

As Geordie watched his men jump down and form into their sections, each one under the control of a corporal, he looked around at the weather. The crystal clear day they had woken to was a thing of the past and the misty drizzle was sweeping across the hills in waves. By the time they had finished chasing the deer out of the gorse bushes and onto the guns, they were going to be soaking wet and seriously fed up. The best thing was to get them moving before they got too cold and grumpy.

Geordie spread the game wardens and his sergeants among the men to ensure they did not get too close to the firing points, and then started them moving forward. To his right was Corporal Turner, an intelligent young man from Birmingham. His mixed race parentage had given him the same colour skin and hair as Geordie and gained him teasing from the squadron as the love child of the big Geordie. He took the teasing in good part and gained respect by doing so. The two men chatted quietly as they walked forwards.

The herds of deer must be moving, as they heard the occasional rifle shot from in front of them as the animals earmarked for culling came in range of the firing points. Geordie stopped and looked along the line of men to ensure nobody was moving too far forward. The next rifle shot sounded closer and he was sure he had heard the high-speed round crack past him. There was a second shot and he heard Corporal Turner gasp, then saw him fall to the ground.

Geordie was on his knees beside the downed man in a second. The round had smashed into the Corporal's left shoulder and exited through his back. Blood was pumping from the wound and the camouflage jacket was already slick with it. Geordie grabbed the handheld VHF radio to contact the SSM.

"Check fire! Check fire! Man down! Man down!"

Geordie returned to his injured man. The section was around him now with two men working on stopping the bleeding and one already on the phone to call in an ambulance. Corporal

Turner looked up at him and grimaced with the pain.

"So much for the SSM controlling the bloody officers, eh, Staff?"

As he spoke, the SSM and the squadron commander, Major Irwin, came running down the slope. The major was still carrying the scoped hunting rifle he had been using.

Geordie turned to face them, his usual smile missing. "So which of the silly bastards shot him then, Sergeant Major?"

"None of them. They're all further down the other side of that hill. The Major here was the closest to you and he hadn't fired yet."

As he spoke another high-speed round cracked past Geordie's head. He spun round to look up the slope and saw a man in hunting clothes further up the hillside taking aim again. There could be no doubt who he was aiming for. Geordie was conscious of rapid movement at his side as the squadron commander snapped his rifle up into the aim and fired. The assailant further up the slope was jerked backwards and fell into the low gorse bushes.

Geordie turned to order some of his men up the slope, but they were already on the move, spread out and moving rapidly. They had a score to settle. Geordie and the squadron commander followed them as quickly as possible. They reached the circle of angry men and looked down.

"Nice shooting, sir. The bastard's as dead as a doornail."

Major Irwin shrugged and put the sling of his rifle over his shoulder. "Check his pockets, please. Let's find out who this son of a bitch is, then we call the police in."

In the breast pocket of his hunting jacket the sappers found a photograph and a list. They passed them to the Major, who looked at both and then at Geordie.

"I think you've got a fan here, Staff Sergeant. It seems he was after you in particular. Would you care to explain that?"

Geordie nodded slowly and took the mobile phone out of his pocket. He checked the screen and found there was a weak signal. Lucky, up here in the Scottish hills. He handed the device to Major Irwin.

"I'm guessing it's all to do with the last job I went away on with Major Wilson. It's probably best if you let him explain while I chase up the ambulance and police."

Chapter 9

Jim drove the hire car north along the Spanish coastal motorway from Alicante airport. He was still seething about how ineffectual the Prime Minister had been, despite promises of help if they ever needed it, after the last task he had completed for him. The explanations about how difficult it was to do things legally and his troubles with his departments had been tedious at best. Damned politicians' promises. He should have known better. Now he had to get everyone safe and then find a way to sort this out himself.

He reached the signs for Benidorm and turned off the motorway and away from the seaside holiday town into the hills that rose rapidly up behind the coastal plain. The road climbed steadily through industrial developments and what seemed to be an unnecessary mass of traffic roundabouts until he eventually came to the sign for Guadalest and turned to the left. The road became narrower, but continued to climb with a series of hair-raising bends around the edges of the mountains, with spectacular drops into the valley just beside him.

He came upon the village surprisingly quickly as he rounded yet another bend. He drove slowly in behind a large tourist coach and followed it into one of the car parks. Parking the car, he climbed out and looked about him at the steep, rugged mountains that surrounded him. The village itself seemed to be clustered around an old castle perched on top of a set of impossibly jagged cliffs.

He walked slowly towards the village that was obviously geared up for tourists with numerous cafés and shops selling souvenirs.

Jim found himself a café overlooking the dramatic valley that fell away to the Mediterranean Sea, just visible in the distance and pulled out his mobile phone. He called up Janet's number and waited for the connection to be made. He waited while it rang and then she answered.

"Hello, Jim. Where are you?"

"I'm in a café in the village looking up at a small white bell tower on a rock pinnacle."

"Really? Well look a little to the left of that at the castle wall. I'm just there. Can you see me waving?"

Jim looked up again and saw her arm waving as she leaned over the low stone wall on the next pinnacle of rock.

"Shall I come up to you or are you coming down?"

"Order me a *café con leche* and I'll be there before they deliver it."

Jim called the waiter over and ordered for Janet. True to her word, she walked onto the terrace just as the waiter returned with the coffee. She sat down and looked at Jim before pouring the small packet of sugar into her cup and stirring it.

"When did you start taking sugar?"

"Ever since I moved here. The Spanish like their coffee strong. It's very tasty, but I really do need the sugar to take the edge off."

"Not like the swill you get in the coffee shop chains then?"

She sipped the coffee and then looked at him again. "So exactly what have you got me into with your secret adventures this time, Jim?"

He told her as much as he could about their involvement with the Cypriot arms dealer, Niklas Christophides, during their last task for the Prime Minister and then told her that his daughter Calanthe had taken over the business and put a contract out on them. Janet sat back and drank her coffee slowly, taking it all in.

"So who was it actually shot this Christophides? It doesn't sound like something you would do. And then, what the hell are you going to do about it?"

Jim looked at her steadily. At least she was taking this calmly; he had always admired that about her. "It was Geordie who actually did the shooting. He felt he had to, after the thugs Christophides sent after us killed a Spanish girl he had feelings for. He certainly shouldn't have done it and I guess he knows that now, but we have to deal with the situation he's caused. And what I think I have to do is to get you to somewhere safe, while I try and get this contract cancelled."

"And how are you going to do that?"

"To be honest, at this moment I have no idea, but I do need to get you to where they can't find you."

"Where's that going to be, or don't you know that either?"

"How about coming back to British Columbia with me? We're a way out of the city, so it can be a bit basic, but the cabin is warm and there's plenty of room now the students have gone back down to the city."

"Who's we?"

"We? Oh, I see what you mean. I live there with Megan."

"So you want me to come and hide with you and your new girlfriend? That should be comfortable."

Jim shook his head sadly. "She has agreed to it and it's not about all being pals together, it's about keeping you alive while I sort this out. Sandra and Simon are there already."

Janet put down her cup and sat back in her chair. She looked down the valley to where she could see the sun reflecting off the azure blue Mediterranean. She looked around at the lemon trees waving gently in the breeze and sighed.

"Take me back to the hotel. It's called Cases Noves. We'll see if they have a room for you and we can discuss it some more after dinner. We'll be eating with an English couple I met yesterday, Pam and John. I think you'll like him especially. He tells silly stories about when he was in the Army in Aden."

Chapter 10

The flight Jim booked from Alicante to London Gatwick, where they would transfer to Heathrow for the flight to Canada, was not due to leave until late afternoon so they took their time and had a late breakfast. Toni, the owner, was his usual bubbly self, making a production out of serving each small part of the breakfast in turn and explaining what it was. It was an enjoyable performance. Jim noticed Toni's wife Sofi standing in the door of the kitchen. She was staring at him with an odd, cold expression on her face. She had been doing the same thing last night during dinner. He was going to ask her what was wrong when she turned away and he thought no more about it.

With most of the day to fill before they had to leave for the airport, Jim suggested Janet show him around the castle. The village was quiet now before the tourist buses arrived. They walked through the tunnel carved through the living rock that was the entrance to the castle and the older parts of the village. They paid their entrance fee to go through the museum called *Casa Orduña* and then up the ninety-three green metal steps of the staircase set on the rock at back of the building that led up into the castle itself.

The staircase took them past the iconic bell tower and on up to a walkway graced by white and blue pillars, each with an image on tiles inset in them. Jim realized they were the Stations of the Cross. Probably set here back in the days when the castle had a garrison and maintained by the villagers ever since. They climbed past the small cemetery and up to the highest point of the ruined castle; the view from there was exceptional. Down below they could see the tourist coaches arriving and the herds of people spilling out of them. Their quiet time in the ruins would soon be over as the tour groups shuffled along behind the tour guides, with their piercing voices and their silly flags on sticks.

Jim helped Janet down the steep stone stairs and they walked along beside the blue and white pillars to a viewpoint looking back up the valley, away from the sea. Over the low safety wall the cliff dropped away to a ragged array of vertical stone, with a small path meandering beyond.

Jim turned to find a man standing silently behind them maybe twenty feet away. How had he got so close without being noticed? The man smiled slowly and Jim saw a glint of gold in his mouth where a tooth had been replaced. The man reached to his belt and the sun reflected off the knife he produced from under his jacket. The smile disappeared as he moved towards Jim with the knife held low.

Janet turned and whimpered slightly as she saw the knife in the hand of the threat made flesh. She staggered a little as Jim grabbed her arm and propelled her across the path and into the cover of a small patch of bushes. She stopped and watched the attack develop as the man moved carefully closer to Jim.

The knife flashed forwards and outwards, tearing through Jim's jacket sleeve and slicing deep into his arm. A cry escaped Jim's lips at the unexpected burning pain. The grinning assailant paused before coming forward again. The silence of the attack was unnerving, but Jim was ready for him now. Making a show of cradling his injured arm and hissing with the pain, he waited his moment.

The man attacked again and Jim spun away from the thrusting blade. The razor-sharp steel slashed his jacket, but didn't cut him this time. The assassin didn't pause, but continued the attack. Jim's unarmed combat training kicked in and he struck the man in the chest with a roundhouse kick that sent him staggering back. The attacker smiled and nodded in silent acknowledgement of Jim's skill. He moved slowly forward.

The knifeman smiled again, confident of his ability to kill. He lunged forward with the knife, making a lightning-fast thrust towards Jim's stomach. At the last second Jim stepped to one side, grabbed the man's jacket with both hands and accelerated him forward. Taken by surprise, off balance and unable to stop, the attacker flew out over the low stone safety wall and down out of sight. Jim glanced at Janet standing behind a bush, white-faced and trembling, then walked to the low wall and looked down.

Between the nearest stone pinnacle and the base of the castle lay the body of the attacker. Judging from the damage done to him, he had hit the rough stone pinnacles on the way down. The pool of blood around him ebbed slowly down the slope away from his torn and battered corpse. The gleaming knife, still bearing Jim's blood on the blade, lay on the ground by the low parapet. Jim looked across to the car park; the horde of tourists forming up into their groups had seen nothing. He kicked the blood-stained knife into the patch of bushes where Janet still stood. He kicked the knife to the back of the area and pushed dirt over it. No point making it obvious that there had been an attack. Just an unfortunate accident.

Jim walked back to Janet and took her arm. "We need to get out of here before some tourist looks over the edge. He's shielded from the path by bushes, but he's obvious from here if anyone looks down. We don't need the *Guardia Civil* delaying us."

Janet swallowed hard and allowed herself to be led out of the bushes. "What about your arm? That looks deep. We'll have to stop that leaking before we try and walk through the village."

Jim looked down at his arm. She was right. The sleeve was soaked in blood and as he stood there a pool of it was growing by his feet. Janet started to unwrap a scarf from around her neck to use as a bandage.

She gave him a weak smile. "Don't worry, it's only one I got from a tourist stall yesterday. If it had been that Hermes one you bought me years ago, I'd have let you drip."

Jim was forced to smile. The old resilient Janet was back and he needed her to be strong right now. This was never going to be the end of it.

"Just make a quick job of it. We'll get something better sorted out when we get back to Cases Noves."

He paused and walked slowly back to the safety parapet. He bent down and picked up the assassin's shoe that had been knocked off as his foot hit the wall. Stepping to the wall, Jim tossed the shoe down to its owner, who lay on his back staring at an uncaring sky through dead eyes.

Chapter 11

Toni met them as Janet helped Jim through the front door. The shock had kicked in now and he was feeling sick and unsteady on his feet. The hotel keeper paled when he saw the blood and steadied himself against the door before helping them into the dining room where Jim sat with his arm resting on the table while Toni went in search of bandages.

Jim looked up to find Sofi standing in the doorway, her eyes wide with horror and her hands up to her mouth. "*Dios mio!* It is my fault. I did not know anyone would be hurt."

"How can it be your fault?" Jim asked.

"Yesterday when you arrive, I remember I have seen a picture of you on the Internet. It says 'have you seen these people?' There is a phone number for calling and they say there is a reward if I call."

Toni stepped back into the room with bandages and a first aid kit. "Why would you do such a thing?"

"We need the money, of course."

"We will speak of this later," he said to his wife.

Sofi turned and left the room, her face expressionless, while Janet and Toni slowly unwrapped the wound. It looked a mess, but once cleaned Jim could see it was not as deep as he had feared. He gritted his teeth while Janet used her nursing training to put eight stitches into the wound edges to hold it together. She applied disinfectant cream from the first aid kit and then bandaged the injury.

"I will call the doctor now," Toni said, standing up from the table.

Jim raised his head and looked the man in the eye. "No. We are leaving right now. If you would get our bags down from our rooms that would help."

Toni hesitated, then nodded and headed for the stairs up to the bedrooms.

"You need a doctor, Jim."

"I know, but I also need to get you out of Spain as soon as possible. Thanks to Sofi there, we know that the killers know where we are. That one is not going to be the last. You'll have to drive. Leave your car here and we'll take my hire car and get the hell out of Dodge before the police block the roads."

Chapter 12

Jim walked into the departure hall at Heathrow Airport with his left arm now supported by a proper sling. The doctor had insisted he take it easy, but then he didn't know about the death threats. He and Janet were travelling light, having decided not to return to her villa for extra clothes before they left Spain, and Janet was carrying both of their bags.

"Must be nice having a personal porter, boss."

Jim turned to find Geordie smiling broadly behind him. Just behind him and to one side, he saw the four very obvious soldiers that Major Irwin had sent with the Staff Sergeant to ensure his safety.

"Hi, Geordie. Are your companions here coming with us?" Jim asked, gripping his friend's hand.

"Nah. They've been told to get me to the security gate in one piece and then they can have the rest of the day off. With the promise of beer in London for them if I'm safe, I must be the safest person in the airport today."

Jim grinned back at Geordie. "Well, let's not keep them away from their beer any longer," he said, as he turned towards the security area.

The three of them walked across the wide open concourse floor with the four soldiers forming a loose screen behind them.

"Are they armed?" Janet asked, glancing at the serious-faced men behind her.

Geordie shook his head. "No, bonny lass, but they're all in the regimental rugby team and you wouldn't want to argue with any of them."

They reached the start of the security check area and Geordie turned back to his escorts to shake their hands and wish them a fine afternoon in the pubs of London. Once through the security checks, they negotiated their way through the ambush of sales people trying to spray them with overpriced perfume, and made their way to a booth in a burger restaurant where they could talk without being overheard.

"So then, boss, what's with the arm? Lifting too many heavy beer glasses?"

Jim smiled at Geordie and Janet jumped in to the conversation. "He was knifed by someone trying to kill us. Can't you people ever be serious?"

Jim put his good hand on her arm. "We can, but we usually choose not to be. It's a coping mechanism. You should remember that from the old days."

Geordie grinned at Janet. "So did he get away?"

Jim nodded. "You could say that, but he won't trouble us anymore. What happened to you? Major Irwin said you'd been shot at when he called me, but he didn't give me any details."

"I was lucky. It was a bit misty and he mistook Corporal Turner for me. He's got virtually the same skin colour as me and all us blacks look alike, as you know."

"Not a fair comment there, Geordie."

"Sorry, boss, still a bit wound up about it. Turner's a good lad and they aren't sure yet how much damage it's done. The bullet went right through, up in his shoulder. If it restricts his movement that could be the end of his career."

"Yes, so we'd better work out how to stop this before more innocent people get hurt or worse. There's at least twelve lives on the line and we've got one down already."

Geordie looked puzzled. "I spoke to Ivan and he said there were only eleven names on the list."

"There's the baby that Megan is carrying."

Janet's head snapped round to look at Jim. "Megan's pregnant? Oh, that's going to make this even more comfortable, isn't it?"

Chapter 13

Ivan was waiting in the arrivals hall at Vancouver's International airport as the three travellers came through from the Air Canada flight. With no heavy baggage to wait for, the immigration procedures had been simple and quick, letting them through ahead of most of their fellow passengers. The taxi ride to the Coal Harbour airport to pick up the Beaver floatplane waiting there was quiet, as none of them wanted to discuss anything where the driver could hear them.

They walked along the jetty and boarded the yellow and white aircraft without incident, though Jim noticed that both Ivan and Geordie were keeping a close eye on the people around them. The flight was a joy, in the clear air above the impressive scenery of the British Columbian coast. Geordie and Ivan had been to the area before, during a previous classified task on behalf of the US Government, so Geordie kept Janet occupied by pointing out things of interest to her.

The landing on the waterway was executed to Jim's personal satisfaction and they moored the aircraft at the foot of the ramp before walking through the screen of trees to the cabin. As they walked up towards the open wooden stairs to the veranda they saw Simon and Megan coming in the other direction. The boy was carrying the Winchester rifle in one hand and a target in the other.

"Hi, Uncle Jim and Aunty Janet. Megan's been teaching me to shoot," Simon said, excitedly.

Jim looked at Megan. "Is he any good?"

Megan smiled at Simon before looking back to Jim. "It must run in the family. He's a natural. I've got a couple of the locals coming over tomorrow to take him out and start to teach him hunting the proper way."

"The Heiltsuk?"

"That's right. They've said they'll teach him to handle one of their seagoing canoes as well."

Janet looked between the two of them. "Who or what are the Heiltsuk?"

Jim looked at Simon. ""Do you want to explain, while I get these bags inside?"

Simon nodded. "The Heiltsuk are the native people around here. What the Canadians call one of the First Nations. They've lived along this coast for about ten thousand years, way before the Europeans arrived. They're expert hunters and fishers and they make these great seagoing canoes called 'Qatuwas' and they do some amazing wood carving." He pointed down to the rocky shoreline. "That's one of the totems they make, but Megan just uses it as a marker so the students can find the cabin when they come up here during the summer."

Jim stopped on the veranda and looked back, smiling at the enthusiasm of his nephew. "Come on inside. You've got a rifle to clean and this time it has to be to a Sergeant Major's standard."

Janet was wary of Megan as they met, but the Canadian woman's broad smile and obvious concern melted any ice between them. While Megan showed Janet where she was going to be sleeping and where she should hang her few clothes Jim called the men to the big wooden table. The three men and Simon sat down and they field-stripped the Winchester for cleaning. Each of them took a part and began to clean it as they talked.

"OK, Ivan, so how's Sarah?" Jim asked, as he checked the barrel of the rifle.

"Not a happy camper. It's good she wasn't on the kill list, but she didn't like me coming over here. I did explain it's not to hide, but to get some breathing space while we work out our next move."

"What happened to your attacker's pistol?"

"Oh, that. Well, I may have forgotten to give it to the police and they were very understanding when I explained things, so they forgot to ask for it. I've shown Sarah how to use it, just in case, and told her how to check in case she's being followed."

Geordie put down the cleaning cloth and looked across the table at Jim. "So what's the plan, boss? Do we just hide here and hope it all goes away?"

"I don't think that would do us a lot of good." Jim took a sip of the coffee that Megan put down in front of him and waited until the others had theirs. "You remember that the Prime Minister promised that if we needed a favour after the last job we did for him, we only had to ask? Well, I called in on my way to Spain to fetch Janet. I did manage to get in to see him, after some trouble with the bloody civil servants. It turns out it was pretty much a politician's promise. He really couldn't see what he could do to help, though he would consult his experts of course."

Ivan put down his coffee mug. "You've missed a bit there, Simon. Rub harder." He looked up at Jim and then Geordie. "So we're on our own as usual?"

"Maybe not completely. We do have one really big ace in the hole that I haven't tried yet."

"What's that one?" Geordie asked.

"You remember the first time we were round here, that job turned out to do a real big favor for the USA and the President in particular? I get the feeling that Randolph Baines is a good deal straighter than most politicians and again he did say we should call on him for help, if we ever needed it."

Simon had been listening to all of this with his mouth hanging open in amazement. "Uncle Jim, are you talking about Randolph Baines the President of the United States? The vice president who took over when the President got sick?"

Jim nodded and smiled at the boy. "That's not quite how it happened, but yes, that's the one we're talking about. A very nice man and as honest as the day is long."

"And you can just call him up and ask for help?"

"Probably not quite that simple, but if we can get to him then we can ask for his help."

Ivan nodded slowly and looked at the rifle before them. "This seems clean enough for now. Let's see you put it back together, young man." He looked at Jim. "If we are going to ask for help, we'd better work out what the hell we are going to do and then what we are going to ask him to do to help us."

Chapter 14

Jim and Simon sat in the coffee shop waiting for Megan and Janet to finish touching every item in the dress shop across the road. The two women had bonded quickly over the need to get Janet some suitable clothes and were well on the way to becoming friends. They had been to the food store in the local small town to stock up on essentials for the unexpected influx of visitors to the cabin. Simon looked around and then whispered to Jim.

"Have you seen that guy in the corner?"

Jim managed not to turn around and look. "What about him?"

"He hasn't touched his coffee for a really long time and he keeps looking at you."

Jim smiled indulgently at his nephew's keenness. "Are you sure he's just not checking out the very attractive waitress?"

Simon bridled a little at being patronised. "Yes, I'm sure. It's you he's checking out and there's something just wrong about him."

"Wrong? In what way?"

"It's the way he's dressed. He's wearing the stuff everybody round here wears, red check shirt, jeans, boots, big leather belt, but everything he has on is brand new. There's not a scuff on his boots, his jeans aren't creased or stained and there's even a price label hanging off the back of his shirt collar."

"Maybe he just bought new stuff ready for winter?"

Simon leaned forward. "Uncle Jim, I'm serious. It looks like he's playing a part in a play and his hair is just too neat. It looks like a city haircut. The guys round here are all just a bit shaggy."

Jim saw the two women come in through the front door, carrying their trophies from the dress shop wrapped in plain brown paper. "Come on. Time to get back."

Jim stood and picked up his heavy jacket from the back of his chair. He glanced at the corner of the café just in time to see the stranger quickly avert his gaze. Simon could be right; the man did look out of place in this working town. They left the coffee shop and walked across to Megan's pickup truck in the car park. Jim kept an eye out behind them and noticed the stranger in his new clothes leaving the café just after them. Interesting.

Jim drove along the highway and then turned off down the rough track that led eventually to the cabin. Just round a bend he pulled over and waited, but nobody appeared to be following them. He shrugged and drove on. They pulled into the clearing behind the cabin and busied themselves moving the supplies inside and stacking them on the open shelves in the storeroom.

Simon volunteered to help Megan with the cooking and Jim decided to take a walk down to the waterside to check his fish traps. As he walked through the door he picked up the battered .38 Webley revolver he kept there as a bear scarer. The old Brown Bear had been wandering around there lately, looking for food before hibernating, and could well be interested in the fish traps. Jim didn't want to hurt the old animal so carried the noisy pistol to warn it off if it came too close.

He walked across the rocky beach to where the lines from the traps were secured and pulled them in one at a time. There was nothing in any of them, so he started to reset them back in the waterway. He kept a wary eye out for the bear in the direction it normally came from, but saw nothing to worry him.

Back in the cabin the meal was almost ready and Megan sent Simon out to call his uncle in. The boy reached the door and stepped out onto the veranda. He raised his hand and shielded his eyes against the sun. He could see Jim was just about finished, so waited to call to him.

Simon felt the hair on the back of his neck rise. He looked around carefully. The Heiltsuk hunters had taught him never to ignore something like that. His eyes swept the woods around him slowly, until he spotted the movement in the trees to the right of the cabin. He stood stock still, waiting to see what sort of animal it might be, probably one of the caribou going down to drink.

The red check shirt showing between the fir branches told him this was no animal. Then the sunlight shone back to him from the barrel of a rifle held in the man's hand. He could see that the stranger was sneaking through the trees intent on Jim, down by the waterside. He took three slow steps backwards into the doorway of the cabin and looked up. The Winchester 94 was there in its rack. He knew Megan kept it loaded.

Simon reached up and lifted the weapon down. His throat was dry as he quietly jacked a round into the chamber, then took one step forward to where he could see the red checked shirt still moving slowly. As he watched he saw the man stop and drop to one knee. The rifle came up and there could be no doubt it was aimed at Jim. With no time to call for help Simon brought the Winchester up to his shoulder, controlled his breathing the way Ivan had told him and took aim. He swallowed hard at the thought of shooting at a person, then squeezed the trigger.

The padded butt slammed back into his shoulder, but the 30-30 round flew straight and true. The bullet smashed into the stock of the rifle in the assassin's hands and shattered it. As the rifle spun out of his hands, the wooden fragments of the damaged stock flew and ripped a deep slice into his cheek. The man stumbled to his feet and blundered through the trees, away from the cabin. Simon racked the cocking lever and fired two more rounds after him, to speed him on his way, but deliberately aimed wide.

Jim ran up onto the veranda with the Webley in his hand. "What the hell are you shooting at? I thought I told you not to shoot close to the cabin?"

Simon turned and smiled at his angry uncle. "Maybe we'd better go and see? Come on."

Simon walked down the open tread wooden steps and then went towards the treeline. Jim followed him, puzzled. They reached the spot where the killer had been kneeling and looked down. The splash of blood across the stones was dripping slowly onto the pebbles beneath.

"What did you hit, Simon?"

Simon pointed to where the ruined rifle lay up against a tree trunk. "The guy who was aiming that at you. He ran off that way. And by the way, I'm pretty sure it was the one from the coffee shop in the new clothes that you thought I was imagining."

Chapter 15

Jim picked up the broken rifle and unloaded it. He turned to look at Simon and patted him on the shoulder before walking back towards the rocky beach where Ivan and Geordie were just pulling the boat ashore.

Ivan looked at the rifle in Jim's hand. "We heard gunfire. Everything all right?"

Jim handed the damaged rifle to the big Welshman. "Not really. Some clown just tried to shoot me with that. Simon stopped him. One round from the veranda to that treeline and knocked the weapon out of the scumbag's hands."

Ivan looked from the veranda to the place where Jim had pointed, then at Simon. "Nice shooting with just iron sights. This rifle is buggered, but the scope looks untouched. Maybe it will fit the Winchester? Then you can get really accurate, eh, Simon?"

Simon said nothing as the four of them turned and walked back up the gentle slope to the cabin. Geordie put an arm round the boy's shoulder and patted his arm.

"You may not know it, but that was really high praise from Ivan. Did you hit the gunman?"

"I'm not sure what happened. I hit the rifle, but there was blood on the stones over there so he's injured. He kept on running when I put another couple of rounds through the trees."

"But you didn't try to hit him again?"

Simon looked up at Geordie. "Should I have?"

"Killing a man is serious stuff, mate. I think chasing him off was probably the right choice. If he comes back the choice may go another way. We'll have to see."

The four of them reached the cabin and walked into the big open room. Ivan put the damaged rifle down on the big wooden table and gestured for Simon to do the same with the Winchester. Geordie walked off into the kitchen area and came back with four mugs of coffee. Simon looked at him quizzically.

"Mate, you just saved your uncle's life. I don't think we can treat you like a kid anymore."

Simon smiled and felt the warm glow of pride. Being accepted by these three men was something very special to him. He sipped the coffee and spat it back into the mug. How could anybody drink that muck?

Ivan detached the telescopic sight from the attacker's rifle and examined it. As far as he could see, it was undamaged. The Winchester already had scope mountings, factory fitted as standard, and the scope was quickly attached. He handed the rifle back to Simon.

"We'll go and zero the sights in for you this afternoon. That should make you even more of a force to be reckoned with."

Jim smiled to himself at the way these two men were treating his nephew. The praise would help the healing process after his father's death.

"So then, boss," said Geordie, cradling his coffee mug. "What's our next move? Now that one of these bastards has found us there'll likely be more of them. It'll be like flies round moose dung."

Ivan nodded as he put his mug down. "That's right. If we do nothing we might as well just paint targets on our backs."

"You're both right, as usual. We need to find somewhere for the rest to live until we three have sorted this out. Obviously this won't do, since anybody can come along one of these logging trails right to the cabin without being seen. Any ideas?"

"I do," said Simon. The three men turned to look at him and he continued. "David Red Cloud took me fishing a couple of days ago in one of his canoes and we passed a group of small huts, on one of the outer islands. He said it was a fishing camp his people use when one of the big shoals of fish is due to come round."

"Do you know what state it's in?"

"We didn't land, but David will be able to tell us."

Jim nodded. "It's a possible. Ivan, will you go round to see David this afternoon and see what the score is? Tell him what's going on. I'm pretty sure he'll help."

Simon perked up. "Can I go with you, Ivan? I'd like to talk to David."

Geordie smiled and chuckled. "That wouldn't have anything to do with a certain very pretty daughter of his, would it?"

Simon blushed. "Mary is teaching me to speak sign language."

Ivan nodded. "Yes, you can come. I'd forgotten about Mary being deaf. I'll teach you some signing as well on the way, but her signs will be a bit different to British signing."

Simon, pleased to be allowed to go along, said, "I didn't know you could sign, Ivan."

"My little sister was deaf so all the family learned it. We'll leave as soon as we finished whatever that is I can smell coming from the kitchen."

"There's another problem," Jim said. "What about your kids, Ivan? I don't think we can assume they are safe down in Florida. And then what about your wife, Geordie? I know you and Sam have broken up, but she is still on that list Ivan found."

"I've warned my kids' grandparents. They may not like me, but they are both highly capable people. They've taken them off to Orlando in the RV for a starter. Hiding two kids in Disney World amongst hundreds of others seems like as good a place as any to start with."

"True, but that won't work long term."

"Once the kids have had enough of that, they are going to drive the RV cross-county towards Seattle and then up here, stopping to do the sights on the way. That should keep them out of sight for a good while and maybe we'll have fixed this mess by the time they get here."

"What about you, Geordie?" Jim asked. "What have you done about Sam?"

"Not enough. I called her and told her what's happening, but she won't have it. She thinks I'm lying to try and get her back."

"So where is she now?"

Geordie shrugged. "On holiday somewhere in the Caribbean, with her new man. She didn't let the grass grow under her feet once she'd dumped me."

"Right then, Ivan, while you are talking to David, see if he can get us any useful weapons just in case they manage to find us in this fishing camp."

Chapter 16

Despite having been married to Geordie Peters, Samantha had kept her own surname, Lanton, famous as it was as a part of the renowned family of actors. It made things less difficult now as the divorce was grinding its way through the legal system. She thought about Geordie as she lay on her beach lounger working on her suntan.

Her new man wasn't quite as handsome as Geordie and certainly he was not as obviously masculine, but he was there for her. Geordie had been away far too much, on the strange tasks he would never talk about. Eventually, she could not stand the separations and secrets anymore and called time on their marriage. Still, it had been good while it lasted.

Apparently Geordie had thought the same, trying to get her back with his ridiculous story about her being on some kind of hit list and hunted by contract killers. He must have thought that she would fall for his theatrics, because she lived in that world. It was a nice try and she was pleased he had at least attempted to get her back, but her mind was made up and Geordie was now just part of her backstory.

She watched her new companion, Julian, emerge from the sea and walk slowly up the beach towards her. He had made sure his hair was back in place before he left the water. She could see him looking around casually to see who was checking him out. He really was very self-centred, but he would do for now. It was just a shame he didn't have Geordie's physique or he really would have been nearly as beautiful as he thought he was.

Julian picked up the towel from the lounger next to hers and started to wipe himself dry. She noticed he didn't dry his hair. Heaven forbid there should be a hair out of place. She watched him check for admiring glances once more before he lay down and turned to her.

"Swimming in the Caribbean is so much more pleasant than swimming in the English Channel, don't you think?"

She looked out across the azure sea to where the gleaming white cruise liners docked. "I'm sure it must be, but at these prices I'm glad you're enjoying it."

"So where shall we go for dinner tonight? The hotel is a bit boring. Maybe we should go and experience a bit of native culture, such as it is?"

"I don't think the islanders would like to be called natives, do you? Maybe we could go along the beach a little way? There's a bar set on the edge of the trees about half a mile away that the receptionist says is good if you want fish."

"All right, I think a little time here to make sure my tan is even and then we can take a walk down there. Unless you want to go back to the room for a while first?"

She turned and looked at him under the brim of her sun hat. The constant stream of suggestive comments was getting really old. It wasn't as if he was that good in bed anyway. And there was another thing she missed about Geordie.

She sighed gently. "No, I'm happy to walk along and get an early dinner as the sun goes down."

"And then we'll have to see what else goes down, eh?"

She sighed again and returned to her book. She was going to have to find a replacement soon. This guy had been a mistake.

They walked through the soft white sand as the sun began its dive to the horizon. The bar was just in front of them peeping out of the palm trees and looking very inviting when she became aware of the man approaching them. With his leather shoes and long-sleeved shirt he looked completely out of place on a Caribbean beach.

They were about to walk past him when the man spun and punched Julian in the stomach. Julian was winded, but more startled than hurt. He drew himself up and looked at his assailant before spinning on his heels and running towards their hotel. Sam stared after him open-mouthed, then looked at the attacker.

"You picked a great one there, Miss Lanton. Such a shame he didn't want to protect you."

She was about to ask what she needed protection from when she saw the knife in his hand. He took the one step he needed towards her before he plunged the blade into her stomach and thrust upwards. It was a killing blow and she had no time to cry out before the man twisted the knife. As she lay dying on the beach, he took a small camera from his pocket and took three photographs, then turned and walked away, leaving her to bleed into the pure white sand.

Chapter 17

Jim stood next to David Red Cloud and looked slowly around the fishing camp. The small huts were sound and would keep out the weather, but with the savage winds and rain of winter coming, this could only be a temporary solution. The few trees on the island would do little to shield the small settlement from the cold that scoured these coasts as the season changed.

They walked down the pathway to where Geordie and Ivan were unloading one of the three big painted canoes they had used to bring supplies. Jim watched them for a moment as Geordie lifted the pump action shotguns out of the first boat and took them across into a hut, while Ivan unloaded cardboard boxes of tinned food. David and Jim walked across to the second canoe and started to unload that one.

With all the three boats unloaded and the stores put away, the four men returned to the beach. They lifted one of the canoes clear of the water and carried it between them up to a shed with a wide door, locking the door with the boat inside.

"Are you sure your people can keep them safe until we get back, David?" Jim asked.

"These are our islands and Megan is one of our own," David said, his face expressionless. "Your people are guests here and we look after them as such. You forget, my people have been hunting these lands since before time itself.

Hunting intruders who wish to hurt us, or our friends, is easier than taking on the bear."

Jim nodded his thanks, reassured by the calm confidence of this man, who was helping them with no thought of reward. He only hoped none of his people would be hurt.

He looked around one last time. "OK, folks, let's get back and start moving people. I guess I'm not going to be popular when they see this place."

They paddled the remaining two canoes back to the main cabin. As they curved into the beach they could see Simon waiting and watching to one side with the Winchester in his hands. Jim smiled to himself; the boy was taking his responsibilities seriously.

"Any problems, Simon?"

"Nobody has been anywhere near us while you were gone."

Jim gave the boy a wave and carried on up to the cabin. As he walked in he could sense that things had not gone well in his absence. Megan was sitting in the window seat with her packed bags by her feet. As he looked at her she shrugged and nodded her head towards Janet, who was standing by the large stone fireplace even though the wood burning stove was no longer alight.

"I don't see why we have to go and hide in some scruffy shack on a barren island while we've got this place," Janet said, flushing.

Jim sighed; he had anticipated something like this. "Janet, I explained it all last night. It's too easy for someone to sneak up on this cabin through the forest. On the island there is less cover and anybody trying to do you harm will be spotted."

"Well, you can just stay here and look after us. They aren't going to try anything with three armed men to guard us."

"Simon will be here, as will some of the local hunters. You'll be safe, but moving to the island makes it just a bit safer and we should have you away from there before the winter kicks in."

Janet sucked in a breath. "A child and some Red Indians are hardly the same thing as having soldiers here."

Sandra walked into the room with her bag over her shoulder; she paused and looked at Janet. "If you've finished being a silly bitch, can we get going? If Jim and the others stay here, guarding your moaning backside, this will never end. They've got to go and sort it out and, by the way, that child, as you call him, has already saved your ex-husband's life."

Jim was delighted to see the old Sandra back again. The fiery temper had vanished during her marriage to Brian, but she seemed to be finding herself out here in the forests.

Janet stood open-mouthed and then turned to Megan for support.

"Don't look at me, Janet. Those Red Indians, as you call them, are my people and we've never been anywhere near India. Now we're going, so get your stuff or stay here on your own, I really don't care." Calling her dog, Megan walked to the door.

Chapter 18

The three men were preparing the Beaver for the flight down to Vancouver when Geordie's mobile phone rang. He pulled it out of his pocket and answered. Jim and Ivan saw his face fall as he listened and then he sat down heavily on the aircraft's starboard float. He closed the phone down and sat staring into space. Jim, startled, saw a tear roll down his cheek.

"Geordie, what's happened?" Ivan asked, moving towards him.

Geordie looked up, his eyes swimming. "The bastards have got Sam. Knifed her on the bloody beach and left her lying there. The new boyfriend ran like a jackrabbit as soon as it started. Oh God, I should have gone for her."

"How did they know to contact you?"

"I'm still in her passport as the emergency contact; she hadn't bothered to change it."

Ivan looked across at Jim and shrugged. Jim shook his head and indicated they should leave Geordie alone while they finished checking and refuelling the aircraft.

Geordie eventually stood up from the float. "This is all my bloody fault. I shot Christophides and started everything. I should have shot his bloody daughter at the same time, then we could have just got on with our lives. And I should have forced Sam to take notice of me."

Jim stepped forward and rested a hand on the big man's shoulder. "You couldn't know Calanthe would do this and you did what you could with

Sam. You could hardly have dragged her off that beach. She made her own choice and it's a tragedy, but you are going to have to work past this if we are to stop it. Geordie, I need you on top of your game."

Geordie drew himself up and looked at both Jim and Ivan. "I'll be OK. I just need a while, but I need you to promise me something."

"What's that?" Jim asked.

"When the time comes, and if it comes down to it, I want to be the one who drops the hammer on Calanthe. Can you promise me that?"

Jim shook his head. "We're a long way from that, but I'll keep it in mind. That's my best offer."

Chapter 19

The United Airlines flights from Vancouver to Washington got them into Baltimore airport just before midnight. They had eaten during the two-hour stopover at Chicago O'Hare airport, so once they had picked up the hire car there was nothing to delay them getting into the Holiday Inn on Wisconsin Avenue. At least they knew their hotel would be comfortable and would serve them a fine breakfast. It was also very convenient for getting to the British Embassy through the scrubland at the back.

Jim had phoned ahead and Lieutenant Commander James Delaney from the military liaison staff in the British Embassy joined them for breakfast. He was an old friend, having helped them twice before during the secret tasks they had been allocated. Luckily, that meant he assumed they still had the authority to ask for his assistance this time.

They settled around the table and placed their orders with the attentive waitress and waited until she left before speaking.

"Well, gentlemen, it's always exciting when you three turn up in DC. What do you need this time?"

Jim paused as the coffee arrived and then, checking he could not be overheard, he said, "What we really need this time is to speak to the President."

"Hell's teeth! You don't want much, do you? I know you got to speak to him when he was the

Vice President, but that was with the Prime Minister here to facilitate the meeting. You can't just call up and ask if you can drop in to the White House for tea and buns."

Jim looked at Delaney and smiled slightly. "James, last time we were here we did him and the USA a big favour. Now, he is a rare beast, an honourable politician. He told us that if we ever needed anything, we should call on him and now we need to do just that. We just have to hope he recalls his promise."

Delaney sat back in his chair and studied them. "You're serious? You really think you three can get in to see the President, just like that?"

"It depends on the Ambassador helping us. If we ring up out of the blue, we won't even get past the switchboard, but the Ambassador is a different kettle of fish. Is it still the same one as when we were here last, or has he moved on?"

"No he hasn't gone yet; Sir Peter is still in post. Interestingly, our relations with the White House warmed up considerably when the President changed, according to the diplomatic staff. Was that something to do with this?"

"It could well be," Jim confirmed. "So can you get us in to see Sir Peter? Sometime today would be best for us."

Delaney recovered from his surprise. "I'll try, but I can't guarantee anything. Where will you be if I need to come and get you?"

"That's all we can ask of you, but I think you will find Sir Peter wants to see us this time. We'll be here all day. We have to work out a plan to solve a nasty problem."

Chapter 20

The three men sat in the minimally decorated lobby of the hotel, far enough back from the walkway so nobody would overhear them. Jim waved a waiter over and ordered coffee.

"Right, gents, we know the problem and we know what we are going to ask the President for, but what the hell else can we do to get this contract lifted?"

Geordie shifted around on the wide sofa he was sitting in. "I know it didn't work out so well last time, but what would be the objection to dropping the lovely Calanthe? She's the one who has put the contract out on us, so once she is out of the picture nobody gets paid for hitting us."

Ivan shook his head. "It'll be the same problem again. Somebody in the organisation will step up and take over. Just like Calanthe, they will need to put down a marker to the rest of the gang that they are not to be messed with and the best way is to get us publicly slaughtered."

"I suspect Ivan is right, as usual," Jim said. "Attractive as the idea is, I don't think it's one we want to risk, unless everything else fails. Any other thoughts?"

"Not to be repetitive, boss, but how about we make Calanthe think we are going to kill her if she doesn't lift the contract? We don't actually have to do it, just as long as she believes we will and are capable of it."

"She knows you are capable of it. That's what got us into this in the first place."

Geordie shook his head and sipped his coffee. "Not that, I mean if she believes we are physically capable; that we can get at her. What is it the snipers say? We can reach out and touch her."

Jim wrapped his fingers around the coffee mug. He could feel the warmth building in his hands as he thought about Geordie's suggestion. Would it be enough? Would she frighten that easily?

"It's a good thought. If she is still at the villa it might be possible. Ivan, can you contact your friend in Cyprus? What was his name? Mike Donald, wasn't it?"

Ivan sat up straighter. "I can, but what do you want to know?"

"Simple one to start with. Is Calanthe in Cyprus and still at the villa? Then, if he can, where does she go? Does she go out to clothes shops, hairdresser? All that normal kind of thing."

"I can try, but he'll have to be damned careful," Ivan said. "If she hears about him nosing around he could join us on that ruddy list."

"That'll have to wait, boss," Geordie said, pointing at the door. "Delaney is on his way in and he looks happy."

James Delaney walked straight across to them and sat down with a sigh. "You were right. The Ambassador does want to see you this time. Better than that, he has already placed a call to the White House, no questions asked."

"How long before they come back to him?" Jim asked.

"Impossible to say. Ours will be one of many calls that they will put in front of the President today and it could take a while to get to him. Then, if he agrees to see you, they will have to find a slot in his diary and that's not easy."

"So what do we do? Just wait?"

Delaney nodded. "I'm afraid so, but you'd be better waiting in the Embassy so we can put you straight into an official car and whip you round there when they summon you. On the upside, the chef is doing chili con carne for lunch today and he's really good at it."

Chapter 21

The official Embassy car was checked through the White House security gate with minimal fuss, then drove up to the door, where two Secret Service agents were waiting for them. With no difficulty or delay they were escorted through the building and up a flight of nondescript stairs.

Sir Peter looked around at the nearest agent with a puzzled expression on his face. "This isn't the way to the Oval Office. Where are we going?"

"The Oval Office is for official business." The agent shrugged. "And the President says this is personal, so he wants to meet you in his apartment."

"Is that unusual?" Sir Peter asked.

"It's the President's own choice, since you are not being put in the official diary of meetings for today. He didn't say why."

They carried on and were ushered into a comfortable sitting room to find Randolph Baines, the President of the United States, working at a surprisingly small desk. He stood up immediately and came to meet them, hand outstretched in greeting. He shook hands with all of them and waved them to the chairs scattered about the room.

"Welcome, Ambassador, and you three gentlemen. I am truly delighted to be able to have you here to thank you, once again, for the great service you did to this country. Now before we get down to business, I have a question. After our last meeting I had my people look you up in our files. You've had quite an interesting time, but tell me,

Geordie, are you the Sergeant Peters who pulled that stunt with the bulldozer in Afghanistan?"

Geordie smiled and nodded. "That was me. It got me in no end of trouble when we got back to the UK."

"Yes, I heard that. If you had been one of our soldiers it would have got you a medal. But now, gentlemen, how can I help you?"

Jim cleared his throat and leaned forward in his chair. "You'll be aware we have been used as a special task unit by our Prime Minister for a few classified tasks. The new PM also decided he would use us one last time and Ivan and I were called back into the Army to do it for him. I think it would be embarrassing for him if I was to tell you what it involved, but it was successful."

The President grinned and chuckled slightly. "I take it that was something to do with the remarkable events in Gibraltar? In these days of phones with video cameras you could not expect that one to go unnoticed."

"I'm afraid that was us, sir. And that was where our present difficulty began. In the course of that task we got involved with an arms dealer who, it turns out, is borderline mafia or something similar. He was killed and his daughter Calanthe has taken over the organisation. In revenge, and at least partly to stamp her control on the business, she has put out a contract on us and our families."

The President looked gravely at them. "Obviously that's unpleasant for you, so how can I help?"

"Sir, these people are dealing in weapons of mass destruction and they will sell to anyone, as we found out. We were wondering if we could ask for your people to see if they constitute a threat to the US and if so would you consider shutting them down, or helping other governments to do so? In addition, our families are in hiding in Canada, in British Columbia to be precise, and we were hoping you could help with security for them, while we three also look to stop the contract."

President Baines stood up and walked behind his small desk. "Thank you for coming to see me. I appreciate the opportunity to repay a debt, but first I'm going to have my people look into this, to see what we can and cannot do. I'll call you back and tell you what our way forward is going to be, whatever we decide. Fair enough?"

Jim nodded as he stood up to leave. "Very fair, sir, and thank you."

Ivan hesitated. "Sir, I notice you have a very small desk in here while you have a much larger one down in the Oval Office. Is there a reason for that?"

The President chuckled again. "Pure sentiment, I'm afraid. Back in the days when I was a District Attorney I never dreamed of holding this office and this was my desk. I bought it from the department and had it brought here to remind me of when my life was my own, back in Seattle."

Chapter 22

The jangling of the phone next to the bed dragged Jim from a deep sleep. Disorientated, he grabbed the handset and pulled it towards him, knocking his water glass and a handful of change to the floor in the process.

"What?"

"And good morning to you too Jim. James Delaney here. I'm at the reception desk downstairs. Get some clothes on and get down here. There is someone who wants to see all three of you right now. Don't bother about the other two, I'll wake them up."

Five minutes later Jim stepped out of the elevator to see Delaney sitting in one of the black sofas in the lobby. Ivan was already there and then Geordie stumbled, bleary-eyed, out of the other elevator. The Royal Navy officer did not look his normal smart urbane self either. He stood and gestured for Jim and the others to follow him, then led the way to the automatic glass doors that slid back to let them leave the warmth of the hotel.

"What's so important at this time of night?" Jim asked, once they were away from any possibility of being overheard.

Delaney shrugged. "Don't ask me. You knocked over this particular wasps' nest. You are wanted at the White House and I've been dragged out of bed to take you there. Too classified for one of the normal Embassy drivers, apparently."

They climbed into the nondescript windowed van, grateful that Delaney had left it running with the heater on. He drove them out onto Wisconsin Avenue and turned right, away from the city.

"I've been told to take a roundabout route to make sure we aren't being followed. It seems that strange vehicles entering the White House in the middle of the night tend to spark off the conspiracy nuts and the press. We'll be driving all over the place on the way out, to throw the press off."

"Any clue why we are being taken in so late?"

Delaney shook his head. "No idea, though we do know that President Baines sometimes has trouble sleeping, so he gets up and gets back to work. Drives his staff bananas, I imagine."

The security formalities at the White House gate were cursory; they were obviously expected. As they drove up to the main building the two Secret Service agents stepped forward and opened the van doors. They were led inside again and then Delaney was deposited in a waiting room, while the other three walked onwards. This time they were led into the Oval Office itself, to find the President sitting behind the famous Resolute Desk. He rose up to greet them and waved them to the two sofas sitting either side of the carpet bearing the great seal of the USA.

"Welcome back, gentlemen. I'm sorry about the hour, but tomorrow is blocked solid in my diary and then I need to go out to Seattle to christen Boeing's newest airliner. I thought you might enjoy a visit in here to make up for it."

"It's very good of you to make any time for us at all, sir," Jim said, stifling a yawn.

The door swung silently open and one of the Secret Service agents came in carrying a tray of coffee mugs.

"Thank you, Markus. Now I don't usually have the Secret Service carrying trays, but they feel it's better than dragging the staff out of bed every time I'm being 'difficult'. They're probably right. Help yourselves, guys. Now, Ivan, I recall you had a weakness for chocolate cookies, is that right?"

Ivan nodded. "I do, sir. Why do you ask?"

Baines smiled at him. "Because the White House head chef is an absolute wonder at cookies, among other things, and I had her whip up a batch for you. I'm sure you'll let the others try just one, though."

Ivan leaned forward and took one of the cookies, then tasted it. The President was right: his head chef was a genius and the cookies were outstanding. He looked up to see the President smiling at his obvious enjoyment.

"I'll let her know how much you enjoyed them. She'll be delighted. Now, though, we have some business to conduct before you can all get back to bed. I had my people trawl through our files to see what we know about Christophides and his activities. I also put a call in to the President of Cyprus. I think I got him out of bed as well."

Jim lowered his coffee mug to the side table. "And what did you find, sir?"

"Quite interestingly, the President knows, or rather knew, Christophides personally. He tells me he was an honest businessman and they were shocked when he was assassinated very recently. His daughter has taken over, as you told me. He tells me she is rather beautiful, is that correct?"

Geordie nodded. "She is, sir. A bit of a stunner, but bad to the bone."

"Not according to the government of Cyprus it seems. However the Director of the CIA has other ideas. The Christophides group has pinged off their intelligence radars a couple of times and, when he looked into it, he brought a few things together that are worrying. It seems the family were offering two nuclear devices for sale on the deep black market. Is that something you know anything about?"

Jim glanced at Ivan and Geordie while he considered how to answer the question. This was highly classified and would be a huge embarrassment to the British government if he admitted his knowledge. He turned back to the President to find he was smiling.

"It's OK, Major, I already know about it. I dragged your Prime Minister out of bed as well. He let me know it was you three who went out and retrieved those two devices. He seemed to hint there was more to that story, but I guess you don't want to tell me it?"

"Mr. President, I would love to be able to tell you, but I think it would be better if it came from our PM. I've no doubt he would tell you in confidence if you asked him directly."

President Baines nodded slowly. "No doubt at all. We are rebuilding our relationship with the UK, among others, after the damage my predecessor did. Anyway, let's cut to the chase. The CIA are now convinced that the Christophides organisation is deeply criminal and present a very real danger to the security interests of the western world. If one of the terror groups had got their hands on those weapons, the nightmare scenario inside the USA does not bear thinking about. We are going to use our resources to shut them down and I have spoken to the Canadian Premier as well. Him, I did not get out of bed, thankfully. He is going to allow four US servicemen to take a leave of absence in British Columbia. They will stay with your family while you do what you have to do to stop the contract on your lives. Is there anything else you need?"

Jim sat back and looked at the President for a moment. Here was a politician and a man who honoured his debts. He had to admit, he was impressed.

"Mr. President, you are doing more than we could have hoped for. Thank you."

"You forget, Major," the President said, standing up, "this whole country owes you and your men a debt of gratitude. This is a very small repayment. But now I think you need to get yourselves back to bed and I need to finish the pile of paperwork on my nice big desk."

President Baines shook hands with the three men and ushered them to the door where the two Secret Service agents stood waiting. He stopped at the door and took Ivan by the arm.

"Just a moment, Ivan, I have something for you." He reached to a side table and picked up a plain brown paper bag which he handed to the big Welshman. "You don't need to share those."

Ivan looked inside at the pile of chocolate cookies. He grinned.

"Now that really is repaying the debt, sir."

Chapter 23

Delaney dropped them back at the Holiday Inn and drove home to try and get at least some sleep. Jim and his two men slumped into the sofas in the lobby once more.

"Well, gents, what did you think of that?" Jim asked.

Geordie yawned, then said, "He seems to be being pretty damn decent, but I guess he has seen a danger to the US that coincides with our problem, so that can't hurt."

Ivan leaned back and stretched. "I get the feeling he would have helped us anyway. For a politician he seems to be straighter than most and he's paying back a debt."

"My guess is you're both right. I think the US is blessed with an honourable man in the White House this time and he certainly seems to put the work in. Not sure how popular that is going to make him with the overseas heads of state he drags out of bed, though."

Ivan chuckled at the thought of senior people scuttling to answer the phone in the middle of the night. "All good, but what's our next move?"

"Have you heard back from your friend in Cyprus yet?"

"No, but with the time difference he should be awake by now. Might be worth a call to see how far he's got with finding our little criminal princess. My cell phone won't work here, though."

"I guess the desk clerk will be dozing somewhere behind the reception desk. He should be able to get you an international line."

Ivan heaved himself out of the low sofa and walked across to the desk. As he did so, Geordie said, "So, if she is there, what can we do about it?"

"One step at a time, I think. First we find her, then we decide what the hell we do to get her to stop this. In the first instance I think we need to get up to British Columbia and retrieve those poor souls from that fishing camp. With these four military people coming up to look after them, it should be safe enough to move them back into the cabin, where they will be more comfortable once the weather turns."

"I wonder who they will send."

Jim looked across at Ivan standing, speaking into one of the hotel courtesy phones by the wall. "Looks like he's got through. As to the other question, I don't know who is available. The US military are pretty heavily committed at the moment."

Geordie pointed across at Ivan. "He doesn't look full of the joys of spring. Guess we'll find out why, any second."

Jim watched Ivan walk back across the lobby. He certainly didn't look happy, but that could be for any number of reasons. He waited until Ivan slumped back down on to the sofa.

"Any joy?"

"Yes and no. As far as Mike can tell, she's not on the island. The house hasn't been shuttered up, so he guesses she will be back relatively soon.

It seems they own houses in various countries as well as a fair-sized motor yacht. A real millionaire's gin palace, apparently."

Chapter 24

Jim relaxed for the first time in a while as the Beaver lifted off the water of Vancouver harbour. He put the old plane into a gentle turn to the north and started to follow the coastline towards their destination. Geordie was already asleep in the second row of seats and even Ivan's head was beginning to nod. Jim smiled; and looked forward again; it had been a tiring few days.

The jumble of islands and waterways came into view and he leaned forward to take hold of one of the levers on the control console, then throttled back and adjusted the pitch of the propeller for the approach. The steady beat of the nine cylinder radial engine slowed and the nose of the aircraft dipped gently. Jim began scanning the waterways for any boats that might get in the way of a landing.

He selected the waterway that would bring him in closest to the fishing camp on the outlying island and set the aircraft up for a gentle straight in approach. The Beaver was drifting downwards on a controlled glide slope towards his intended landing point when Jim saw the large leisure trawler appear around a headland, heading straight for his intended landing area. He swore under his breath and decided there was no need to rush the landing, so increased throttle to go around again until the boat was out of the way.

The increased engine noise brought Ivan out of his doze and he looked around quickly. "What's up?"

Jim looked across at him, admiring the speed with which the big man came back to full alertness. "No problem, just a boat has decided to run through our landing area. Don't know how I missed seeing him during my check."

Ivan looked through the forward windscreen. "What the hell kind of boat is that? It looks like a trawler, but with no fishing gear."

"Not sure what you would call it officially. They have quite a few of them around Vancouver and Seattle. A trawler-style hull, but very comfortable inside. Particularly suited to this area when the weather gets a bit chilly."

Ivan looked down through his door window as they started to pass over the boat. "Turn left! Now!"

Jim heard three, then four thumps from behind him and felt the old airframe tremble under his hands. He side-slipped left and pulled back on the control column to put them into a sharp turn to the left. He levelled the aircraft and took it low across the water.

"What the hell was that about?"

Ivan looked back at Geordie, who was now wide awake. "Geordie. Crawl into the back and take a look down inside the fuselage for damage." He turned back to Jim. "That was us being shot at by the people on that trawler. As we passed over I saw four or five of them run out on the back deck and point weapons at us. They looked like automatic rifles of some type."

"Well, I felt them hit us, but the controls still seem to be fine and there is no juddering I can feel, so we could be OK. Lucky they didn't hit the fuel tanks in the floor below us."

Ivan looked back over his shoulder and watched Geordie pull the bulkhead trim off the press studs at the back of the passenger cabin. He pushed it to one side and looked down the almost square fuselage. Then he gave Ivan a thumbs-up before climbing back into his seat and putting his headset back on.

Geordie's voice crackled through their earphones. "Looks like we were lucky. There is daylight coming in through holes in the skin where about four rounds have passed through. I couldn't see anything to worry about, apart from the puncture holes."

"Thanks, Geordie," Jim said. "That's one piece of good news, but it's a pretty safe bet those beggars on the boat have found out about the fishing camp. We need to get down there pretty damn quick. I'm going to land on the other side of the island and we'll need to get across there in double-time to arrive before they do."

Ivan looked around the cabin. "Do we have any weapons on board?"

"I've got my old Webley .38 revolver, that you picked up for me in Yorkshire, and we have a flare gun mounted on the bulkhead above you, but that's it."

Ivan unclipped the flare pistol and checked it, then pulled open the small bag which was also clipped to the bulkhead, and slipped the three flares into his pocket. Jim by now had brought the Beaver around its wide turn and had it lined up with the other side of the island at low level. They could no longer see the approaching trawler. The aircraft slid down into the water and the pure white spray blasted up either side of the floats.

Geordie looked down out of the big window in the passenger door, fascinated by the floatplane landing. He pressed the transmit key on his headset.

"We've got a problem, guys. At least one of those rounds has gone through a float. If we leave it too long it's going to fill up."

Jim gritted his teeth and looked ahead at the island's rocky shore. "I'm going to run her aground on the beach, then. We'll come back and patch the float later if we can."

Chapter 25

The Beaver shuddered and trembled as the floats ground up onto the rounded rocks of the small beach, between the stunted trees. Geordie had the passenger door open and was climbing out before the propeller stopped spinning and Ivan was levering himself through the small co-pilot's door with the flare pistol in his hand. Jim made sure that everything was properly closed down before he, too, climbed out of the aircraft and stumbled over the stones of the beach up to the small ridge where his men were now lying.

As he dropped to his stomach between the two men Ivan pointed to the left. "The fishing camp is over that way. You can see the roofs, but I can't see anyone moving around."

"Probably a good thing," Geordie said, pointing off to the right. "That damned trawler has stopped in that small bay over there. I can just see their antenna between those two big rocks. It looks like they have anchored and, if you look between those trees a bit further right, I think you can see them getting into a small rubber dinghy to come ashore."

Jim looked where Geordie was pointing just as the rubber boat pushed away from the trawler. It was too far to see clearly how many men the dinghy held, but he did spot the man on the flying bridge of the trawler, with a rifle in his hands. Jim's eyes swept across the island as he took in the landscape he would have to use to defend the fishing camp. Then he made his decision and raised himself to his knees.

"Right, you two, the safest place for us is in the buildings of the camp. Simon should have his precious rifle with him and if David is doing his part there may be some of the Heiltsuk hunters there as well."

The three men pushed back from the ridge and dropped back down to the beach before cutting left to approach the fishing camp, out of sight of the attackers. They moved as fast as they could over the rough terrain and swung round the edge of a small copse of trees to approach the huts. Ivan, in the lead, stopped short and very slowly moved his hands out to each side of his body. Jim came up behind him and stopped quickly as he saw the dark-skinned man with the almond eyes looking at them steadily over the shining black barrel of a pump action shotgun.

"We're friends of David Red Cloud," Jim said, in the calmest voice he could manage.

"Where's the third one?"

Jim looked around, expecting to see Geordie close behind him, but the beach was clear. He turned back to the man with the shotgun just in time to see Geordie appear behind him and tap him on the shoulder. The dark-skinned man started to spin round, but stopped as Geordie took hold of the barrel of the weapon.

Geordie's signature smile lit up his dark face as he patted the shotgun owner on the shoulder. "Good job we're all friends here then, isn't it, mate?"

The man lowered his weapon and looked the three of them over. "I am Silas. David told me to guard these people. He said you would be coming back soon, but now these others have arrived we are outnumbered."

Jim nodded. "And outgunned – unless you have some more weapons?"

Silas shook his head. "Another shotgun like this that my friend Henry has with him and the boy has the Winchester. Megan has her double-barrelled shotgun, but that's all."

"Our attackers have automatic rifles at the least, so we need to be ruddy careful. Do you have cell phone coverage here?"

"No, too far out from the mainland and there aren't many towers in the forests anyway."

"And my satellite phone is back in the main cabin." Jim could have kicked himself for such a rookie mistake. "OK, Silas, you keep covering this side and we'll see what we can do to help. Keep your head down, eh?"

Silas returned to the bush he had been hiding behind without another word. Jim and the others turned away and headed towards the fishing camp, keeping as much foliage as possible between them and where they thought the attackers might be. As they came round the side of the first cabin Ivan spotted Simon lying on the roof of one of the other huts, peering around the chimney stack.

"I'll go and teach Simon some basic fieldcraft before he gets his damned head blown off." The big man set off at a run to the back of the cabin and climbed up onto the roof.

"Geordie, you're with me," Jim said, heading towards another of the huts.

They ran across the open space and into the largest of the huts that served as the camp kitchen and communal room. Geordie got there first and opened the door to find Megan standing inside cradling the double-barrelled shotgun with Sandra and Janet behind her.

"Hello, bonny lass, the cavalry's here."

Megan looked behind Geordie and smiled a little as Jim came into view. "I didn't hear the bugles and you seem to be a little light on weapons for now."

Jim came into the hut and gave Megan a quick hug as he looked around. "We are, but I'm not sure this is the best place for you three to shelter. The walls don't look like they would stop a modern bullet."

"Maybe not," Megan said. "We looked at the other options and this was the best of them. It's a fishing camp, not a fort."

Jim nodded thoughtfully as he looked around. "Geordie, can you turn some of these heavy tables over and make some kind of redoubt in the middle of the room? With the walls and the tables it should make a safer shelter when the metal starts flying around."

"What are you going to be doing, boss?"

"I'm going to scout around and see what these damned thugs are doing and then see what we can do about it."

Megan stood forward. "I'll come with you."

Jim smiled and shook his head. "No, I need you here. I want you to look after Janet and Sandra and keep that baby safe. With that shotgun you should be able to discourage anyone who comes through that door."

Chapter 26

Ivan crawled up the slope of the roof until he was alongside Simon, then he reached up, grabbed the young man's jacket and pulled him down from the apex of the roof. As he did so a round struck the stonework of the chimney and whined off into the distance.

"Lesson one, son, this isn't a video game. You get one life and no saves; keep your bloody head down. Your head sticking over the rooftop is a perfect target."

Simon looked across at the scar gouged out of the stonework next to him and swallowed hard. "Do you want to take the rifle, Ivan?"

Ivan looked the shaken young man in the eye. "No, Simon, that's your weapon, but what I will do is find you a safer location. Now slide off the roof with me."

They both slid down the slope of the roof and dropped the short distance to the ground. Ivan motioned the boy to follow him and stay low. Together they moved around the corner of the low shack and into some scrubby bushes on a low bank just beyond.

"Now then, keep low and look through the bush. That way you don't give them an identifiable shape to register. Keep movement to a minimum. Anything that moves attracts attention. Don't let the sun reflect off your scope, that's a hell of a giveaway. And keep quiet. If you see something, don't shout across to anyone. Much as I love John Wayne movies, we don't do it his way."

Simon nodded and slid forward on his stomach to peer through the leaves and branches. He kept the Winchester low at his side and scanned across the island in front of him. The view was not as good as it had been up on the roof, but the bullet hitting the chimney had been scary.

"Ivan!" Simon hissed. "There's something moving over to the right, towards where you left the Beaver."

Ivan moved slowly forward into a nearby bush. "Can you still see him and have you got a clear shot?"

"I can just see him now and then, as he moves. Shall I fire at him?"

"No, lad. If you fire you give away your position and we want him feeling good. With a bit of luck he'll be overconfident. He'll run into Silas over there. Keep watching for the others."

Simon turned reluctantly back to do as Ivan told him. As he did he saw a black ball fly through the air towards the clump of bushes they lay in. He felt Ivan's hand grab the back of his neck and force his head down into the dirt. He was about to protest when the grenade exploded and he heard the jagged, white-hot shrapnel fly over him and slam into the wooden wall of the shack behind them.

"That was way too close to be an accident. We've been spotted. Now slide back from the bank and round the hut. We'll find another position."

Simon did as Ivan told him and the two of them slid backwards and crawled across the dusty ground. As they reached the corner of the shed a burst of automatic rifle fire tore up the bushes where they had been seconds before. Simon stopped, but Ivan pulled his shoulder and they continued their dusty slide out of trouble.

"Where to now, Ivan?"

"Away from here, that's for sure. Whoever spotted us will be watching this area, so we need to move a bit further. With a bit of luck he will stay focussed around here and we can try and spot him."

Staying low, they moved left, using the bank at the edge of the fishing camp for cover. Once Ivan was satisfied they had moved far enough, he signalled to Simon and the two of them slid slowly up the bank to peer carefully through the patch of long scraggly grass. Ivan was the first to spot the enemy who had fired on them as he raised his weapon and scanned the area where they had been.

"OK, Simon, time for you to earn that rifle. See the two tall trees? Go left twenty meters and look at the base of the single fir tree. Target is kneeling at the left of that. Aim centre body mass and drop him."

Simon brought the rifle up to the aim then looked at Ivan. "Shouldn't I try and just wound him?"

"No, son, we need him out of the picture. Aim for the thickest part of him you can see and fire. Unless you want me to?"

Simon looked at Ivan for one second then returned to the aim. He found the man through the telescopic sight and placed the red dot on the man's chest. As he had been taught by the Heiltsuk hunters, he squeezed the trigger gently until the rifle bucked in his hands. As the rifle came back down he looked through the scope and could no longer see the enemy.

Ivan patted his shoulder. "Nice shot, Simon. Now let's move before his mates find us. Come on."

Chapter 27

Jim moved fast and low to the left of the banking that ran along the edge of the camp between him and the intruders. He saw Ivan mentoring Simon and smiled; the boy could not have a better teacher. If anyone could keep him safe it was Ivan.

He reached the edge of the banking and found a position from which he could get a good look across the island. The trawler sat on its own reflection in the still waters of the shallow bay. He could see one man had been left behind to guard the boat. That man had taken up a position on the flying bridge above the main cabin and was scanning the island, through the telescopic sight on his assault rifle.

The rubber dinghy the attackers had come ashore in was pulled up onto the rocky beach with the paddles leaning over the bow. He started to scan slowly to the right to try and spot any of the riflemen and was startled when a voice spoke beside him.

"There's one behind that shattered tree trunk. A lightning strike got that last winter. The leader seems to be staying back by that small jumble of boulders; he's the one with the binoculars. Two more are further over. One is walking into Silas and your boy dropped one."

Jim turned around and found he was looking into the dark, almond-shaped eyes of the second Heiltsuk hunter. The pump action shotgun across his arms looked well cared for, but had nowhere near the range of the weapons carried by the attackers.

"Hi there, Henry. So do we have a plan?" Jim asked.

"We did and then you landed your plane and everybody on the boat got overexcited and started shooting. Now we stay in cover and wait for them to get close enough."

"Then what?"

"Then we blast them before they do it to us. Simple really."

Jim looked back out across the island. It was a simple plan, just as long as the assassins cooperated. If they knew their business it was the recipe for a bloodbath.

"Did you bring any weapons with you?"

"A revolver and a flare pistol."

The man shook his head sadly. "So that's a no then? Still, the sound of firing should have carried by now, so we should expect help."

"Help from where?"

"From my people. Megan is one of our own and we have started to like you, so they will come."

"How are they going to get here without being seen and shot out of the water?"

"Major, I know you are a military man, but my people have been hunting and fishing these lands and waters for ten thousand years. Since before your people painted themselves blue to frighten the Romans. In all that time we learned a thing or two."

Jim looked at the man with the calm eyes, who turned back to watching across the island in front of them. He had seen men pretending to be calm in combat when their guts were really turning to water, but this man seemed truly calm. Maybe they really had learned something in those ten thousand years.

Jim watched carefully, but could see nothing moving. He felt the tap on his arm and turned to see his companion pointing off to the left before he wriggled down and moved along behind the low bank. Jim looked again where the hunter had pointed; there was nothing there, at least nothing he could see. He waited and then the hunter rose up and fired into a bush in front of them. The shot was answered with a howl of pain and then Jim saw one of the attackers stumble away to get out of range.

Confident that nobody was going to make it around this side of the narrow island, Jim dropped back and moved towards the main hut where he had left Megan and the others.

Chapter 28

Ivan lay close to Simon watching for the next chance to take a shot at one of their attackers. Everything was still and silent after the shotgun blast over to their left. Ivan was glad to see that Simon was a fast learner and had taken the teaching of the Heiltsuk hunters to heart as well as listening to his advice. They waited.

The low noise of an engine came from behind them. Ivan slid down the bank a little and turned over to look towards the noise. He scanned across the water until he spotted the low silhouette of a boat coming towards them. They were about to be caught between two fires. This could get difficult.

"Simon, let me have the rifle for a moment."

The boy turned over and handed the Winchester across to the Welshman. Ivan raised the weapon and scanned through the telescopic sight until he found the approaching boat. He could see there were four men in the boat, including the driver, and he saw that at least the two at the front were holding rifles. He was working out what course of action to take for the best when the driver stood up and looked straight towards him. The tension went out of Ivan's shoulders and he rolled over to hand the rifle back to Simon.

"What do we do, Ivan? With them behind us we're going to be in trouble, aren't we?"

Ivan patted the boy's back. "Never you fuss, son. That's the cavalry. The one standing up is

Raoul Martinez. He's a US Navy SEAL and probably the best soldier you are ever going to meet. He's worked with us before on classified missions and we know him well. I'm guessing the other three are from his SEAL team. Looks like the President keeps his promises."

Simon glanced behind him at the approaching boat and then turned back to watch for their enemies. "Shouldn't you go down to the beach and show him what to do?"

"Simon, the SEALs are the equivalent of our Special Boat Service lads and I'm just an engineer. Soldiers that good don't need advice from me. Anyway, we need to make sure these beggars in front of us don't cause them any difficulty coming ashore."

Across the fishing camp, in the main hut, Geordie had just heaved the last of the heavy wooden tables into place to form the safety redoubt in case of stray rounds. He stood up and eased his back while surveying his handiwork.

"Ladies, if you would like to hunker down inside my little fort I'll go and make us a brew of tea."

Janet looked across at Geordie's smiling face. "Do we really need to? Won't those walls stop anything coming this way?"

"No, bonny lass, the rifles those guys have got send out bullets that will punch through that wall without a problem. Those heavy-duty tables, though, should stop them. Now you get inside and I'll bring the brew so you can admire my tea-making skills."

As he turned towards the kitchen area the front door crashed back on its hinges as one of the attackers struck it with his boot. Geordie spun round to see the assassin's rifle coming up and swinging towards him. Then the man was gone, lifted off his feet and thrown back out of the cabin by the two-barrel blast from Megan's shotgun.

Geordie turned back towards his improvised redoubt to see Megan standing there holding the smoking gun, the tears just starting from her eyes. "Oh God, I killed a man."

"No, lass, you just saved your baby and everyone else in here."

"Geordie, your arm, you're bleeding."

Geordie looked down to the rips in the sleeve of his jacket. He pulled the rents open and looked at his arm. It wasn't hurting yet, but that wouldn't last. The four or five pellets from the shotgun blast had spread wide and caught him in the upper arm.

Janet dragged a table out of the way and walked quickly across to him. "Sit down, you. At least I can be some use now instead of sitting behind a table hiding. Sandra, help me get his jacket off."

"You sure you know what you're doing?" Geordie asked.

Janet grinned at him. "Good job you're wounded. A comment like that could get you a slap. I didn't always write children's books. I was a nurse for a long time and aren't you glad?"

With his jacket off Janet could see that five pellets had struck him in the shoulder and chest. None were life threatening, but they needed to come out to prevent infection. Geordie had been lucky.

"Look, I've got no anaesthetic, so this is probably going to hurt, but I have to get those bits of metal and dirty bits of your jacket out of you."

Geordie had been wounded before and he knew what to expect. "Go ahead, bonny lass, but someone else is going to have to make the tea."

Chapter 29

While Simon watched for their attackers, Ivan watched the SEALs bring their boat in to the rocky beach. There was no slowing down as the boat slid onto the stones and the outboard engine flipped up with the propeller spinning down to a stop. The four men were over the sides of the assault boat before it had come to a full stop and they moved up the beach at an impressive speed. Raoul was checking around him as they moved and, spotting Ivan, he swerved to the left and came towards him, keeping low as he ran.

Ivan turned over onto his belly and checked the area Simon was covering as the US Navy Lieutenant Commander dropped down beside him. "Nice of you to drop in, Raoul."

The newcomer's face split into a smile as he looked across at the big Welshman. "Hi there. I see your talent for getting into trouble hasn't deserted you guys. What do we have to deal with here and who's that with the Winchester?"

Simon glanced over his shoulder, nodded to the SEAL commander and returned to watching the area Ivan had allocated to him. Ivan smiled to himself at how quickly the boy was learning.

"That young man is Simon. He's Major Wilson's nephew and he's turning out to be a decent shot with that rifle. His dad was the first one these bastards attacked, so I guess we could say he's looking for a little payback."

Raoul nodded as he, too, scanned the ground ahead of them. "I can relate to that. We need to see if we can give him a helping hand along the way. What do you think we are facing here?"

"As far as we can see so far we have seven of them." Ivan shifted position so he could see past Simon's shoulder. "One stayed on their boat and six came ashore. One of them is at least wounded, maybe down, we don't know for sure. Simon hit him. There have been a couple of shotgun blasts, but I don't know the results of those. We know they have assault rifles, but we haven't seen anything heavier yet."

Raoul nodded slowly, never taking his eyes from the ground in front of him. "Assets?"

"Our side? Not enough, at least not until you four rocked up. We have two of the local First Nation people here, one out to each side. Good guys for sure, but only armed with shotguns. Jim has his old Webley .38 revolver and Megan has a shotgun as well. Plus I have a brass-barrelled flare pistol which I might hit them over the head with."

Raoul looked at Ivan. "I thought the Webley was bigger than that? Something like a .45, isn't it?"

Ivan was surprised that a modern SEAL would know about an old British revolver. "You're right, the service-issued ones were .455 calibre, but Jim's was a police-issued variant and they used the smaller round. We picked it up from a body we found during one of the odd jobs we have been sent on over the last couple of years."

"Nice souvenir, but not a lot of use here, I guess."

"Sadly true. Jim uses it mostly on the beach when he's fishing. There's an old bear that comes down to the waterside looking for fish. Jim scares it off if it gets too close. He usually chucks it a fish as well, though."

"Sounds like they have a working arrangement."

Ivan chuckled. "I think Jim quite likes the bear to …."

"Look!" Ivan stopped as Raoul gripped his arm then pointed. "Off to the right there, between those trees, there's something moving on the water."

Simon looked over his shoulder at the two soldiers laying by him. "Canoes. Two of them. I think it's David Red Cloud coming to help."

"Red Cloud? What is this, a John Wayne movie?"

"He explained it to me last week," said Simon. "His proper name is difficult for Europeans, as he calls us, so he uses the name David Red Cloud for his business. He thinks it makes him sound more exotic, too."

"I don't like civilians blundering about in the middle of this. Too much paperwork if they get hurt," Raoul said to Ivan.

"Don't assume these are civilians. These guys have been living here and hunting this area for ten thousand years or more. They move like ghosts and they don't waste ammunition. You might want to keep your three men back until the locals know who you are," Simon said.

"Seriously?"

Ivan nodded. "Simon's right, they are on our side and they know us, but they might make a mistake with you."

The three remaining SEALs slammed down onto the ground behind the low bank that spread across the area alongside the fishing camp. Each of them slithered forward to take up a firing position where they could dominate the land in front of them.

Raoul thumbed the transmit button of the small radio clipped to his jacket. "Eagle team maintain present position. Do not advance beyond the banking. Targets in front, be aware of friendlies moving in from the right. Watch and shoot." He turned to Ivan. "Now we see if your attackers know their business."

Chapter 30

"Ivan, David and his men from the canoes are moving forward," Simon said as he watched through the scope of his rifle.

"Good lads, those," Ivan replied. "Keeping low, but keeping moving. Doesn't let the scum find an ambush point. Look, you can see they are backing off."

"Should I fire at them?"

"Yes, son, put a few rounds across them to hurry them along, but be careful of the Heiltsuk. The last thing we need is an own goal."

Raoul handed the small set of binoculars to Ivan. "They've picked up their injured man. I think they are going to make a run for it." He looked to his right as Jim dropped down beside him. "I was wondering when you would turn up. How do you want to play this?"

"Hello, Raoul, good to see you. I think we need to make a statement to these bloody people. With David and his people coming in from our right if we advance now, angling left, we can push these creeps back rapidly and chase them off the island with their tails between their legs."

"You want them to get away?"

Jim nodded. "I do. If we kill them here there will just be another lot and then another. If we chase them off, the word will spread among others of their kind that we are not a soft target. Maybe, just maybe, that will make them think twice about another attack. You agree?"

Raoul looked at Jim for a moment or two. "Not the way I would do it, but I see the logic. I just hope you don't live to regret it."

Jim looked past the SEAL commander to Ivan. "What about you, Ivan?"

Ivan took the binoculars away from his eyes and looked at the two men to his right. "It's your call, boss. I think I'd prefer to avoid the slaughter as well. The last thing we need is to set up another bunch of blood feuds with these people."

"Good point," Jim said. "Right then, let's join the party. Simon, will you stay back here, please, and watch our backs?"

Simon lowered his rifle and looked over his shoulder at his uncle. "No, thank you. I'm coming forward with all of you. I don't want to hide here while you get all the fun."

Jim sighed. "Your mother is going to give me a hard time about this, but OK, let's go. Spread out, keep low and keep moving. Ready? Now."

Raoul spoke into his small radio and his three men rose out of cover and began to move forward with their weapons at the ready. Jim and his party did the same with Jim holding his Webley in his hand and Ivan carrying the brass-barrelled flare gun.

They moved across the open space towards the enemy, keeping a close watch to ensure the attackers did not stop and open fire. To their right the short line of the Heiltsuk men came into sight with Silas among them. From their left, Henry, the other Heiltsuk hunter, rose up and joined them, with his pump action shotgun held across his chest.

They kept moving forward carefully until Henry pointed into the low trees. "They're running for the bay where they left the dinghy. Looks like they are half carrying the one Simon dropped."

Jim looked where Henry was pointing. He was right: the tactic of moving forward, although risky, had worked. He resisted the urge to run forward and kept the group moving steadily. As they reached the edge of the small bay they could see the small overcrowded dinghy just reaching the swimming platform of the leisure trawler. The man they had left behind on the flying bridge of the boat started to raise his weapon then reconsidered when he saw the line of rifles from the shoreline swinging his way. He dropped the weapon to a side bench and held his arms out to the side of his body, then shrugged and moved carefully to the helm before starting the two heavy diesel engines.

As the men in the dinghy scrambled onto their boat, Jim could hear the power windlass in the bow winching in the anchor line. He watched as they helped the wounded man aboard and then turned to look back at the shore. None of them offered to raise a weapon as the boat started to move forward and turn away.

Ivan grunted. "Oh to hell with this. I've carried this useless piece of crap around the island, I might as well see if it works."

The brass barrel of the flare pistol caught the afternoon sunlight as he raised it and fired. The bright red flare arched across the water, dragging a trail of white smoke behind it, before plunging through the aft doors of the main cabin.

"Nice goodbye gesture there, Ivan" Geordie said as he walked up behind them. "Not a lot of use, though."

"I think you might be wrong there, Geordie." Simon pointed at the retreating boat. "There's smoke coming out of the cabin and the gunmen look a bit agitated."

Ivan raised the binoculars he was still carrying. "Looks like I've set the furnishings on fire. Oh dear, what a pity, never mind." He turned to look at Geordie and took in the sling supporting his arm. "Surely you didn't let one of them get you?"

Geordie grinned happily. "No, it was Megan who shot me and don't call me Shirley."

Chapter 31

Frank Eastman enjoyed driving the big RV. With the cruise control set for a comfortable fifty-five miles an hour and the radio playing country songs, he was in his element. The call from Ivan telling him to get the kids out of sight had been cryptic, but, despite his feelings about the Welshman, he knew he was not one to get over excited about a threat. He had taken the kids out of school within the hour and now they were heading north on the I-95.

He had decided that since they were missing school he would make the trip educational and also visit some of the places he had wanted to see for years. The first stop had been Cape Canaveral, before they left Florida. That one had gone down well, especially with Geoff. The boy was fascinated with space and, despite having seen the exhibitions before, he was over the moon to see them again. His wife, Emma, and his granddaughter, Marian, had tolerated the visit. Geoff's sister was really not interested in anything to do with space, unless it was tall, dark and handsome. He was going to have to watch out for that from now on.

He looked across at Emma in the passenger seat. She looked relaxed and happy, the way she usually was with her family around her like this. It was a shame they had only had the one daughter, but having the grandkids live with them was compensation for her loss. He looked over his right shoulder at the twins who were sitting at the small dining table behind him. As usual, Marian was fixated on her smartphone, while Geoff seemed to be playing another of his computer games on the laptop computer.

Emma checked her watch. "We should be in good time for the RV Park in Jacksonville. All the way from Melbourne with a stop in the Cape, the kids should sleep well tonight."

Frank nodded as he checked his wing mirror. "Yeah, it's going to have been a long day for them. Have you decided where we are stopping tomorrow night yet?"

"I have. There's a nice campground about six hours up the road, according to my guidebook."

He looked across at her. "Don't say the name."

"I know, I know, but are you sure we need to be this secretive?"

"That's what Ivan said. As long as the kids don't know where we are going they can't mention it to any kids they hang out with online."

Emma grunted and looked out of her window. "It seems all a bit cloak and dagger to me. I still don't know why we had to leave so quickly. Kika had just settled down for a snooze when you dragged us out of the house."

She looked down at the scruffy black dog sleeping between their seats. The dog looked up at the mention of her name. She managed two desultory wags of the tail before drifting back into dreamland.

Frank looked down at the wing mirror again. The black Ford was still there despite having had plenty of chances to overtake on this almost empty highway. The instincts developed during his career told him something was wrong, but he couldn't work out why he felt that way. The red BMW flew past him at well over the speed limit and disappeared over the low hill in front of them. Still the Ford stayed behind them.

"Geoff! Come up here!"

The boy never moved, lost in his computer game with his headphones on and the volume turned up. Emma turned and threw a balled-up piece of paper at him to attract his attention. The boy looked up and removed his headphones.

"What?"

"Geoff," said Frank, "go to the back window and take a look at that black car behind us. Tell me what you see."

The boy grumbled under his breath, then slid off the bench seat and stood up. He walked back down the RV and looked through the small rear window. The two men in the car stared back at him; neither of them smiled or waved. Geoff walked forward again and stood behind his grandfather's chair.

"OK, done that. Nothing special about it. Two men in the car and it's on New York plates. They must be tourists."

Frank looked in the mirror again. "Just keep an eye on it for me, will you? There's something about it I don't like."

Geoff shrugged and returned to his seat by the dining table. Marian looked up and raised an eyebrow in enquiry. Geoff shrugged again and put his headphones back on, then returned to destroying his enemies on the screen. Marian continued running her life on social media.

Chapter 32

The RV crested a low rise. As Frank looked forward and then in the mirror, he couldn't see another vehicle, just that damned Ford behind him. It couldn't be an unmarked police cruiser; if there had been a problem they would have been pulled over long before now. Without thinking, he reached down and touched the secure box mounted below his seat. He didn't open it yet; there was no point in alarming anyone, if his instincts were off the mark.

He looked forward again through the wide, bug-splattered windscreen, looking for a place to pull off and get the Ford to pass him. There was nothing visible for quite some way.

"Grandpa! That car's coming by us. The guy in the passenger seat has an MP5 in his hands."

Frank's eyes snapped to the mirror. "How do you know it's an MP5?"

"Duh! *Call of Duty*. My character has one all the time."

Geoff was right. The Ford was easing alongside them way too slowly. Frank's hand dropped beside his chair and flipped open the storage box. He drew out the Colt Python revolver with the six-inch barrel and laid it across his lap. If his instincts were right the .357 round from this highly accurate pistol would even the odds somewhat. He had always favoured revolvers over automatics. If there was misfire he just needed to pull the trigger once more to be back in action, rather than having to work the action of an automatic pistol.

He looked across at Emma. She looked puzzled, but she trusted him and followed his lead as she drew her own Armscor M200 .38 Special Revolver from her own security box.

Frank called to Geoff over his shoulder. "Watch him and tell me what he is doing, Geoff. Marian, put the damned phone down and get on the floor!"

The girl looked up, startled. Her Grandpa never spoke to her like that. She looked around at Emma, who just pointed to the floor. Marian slid off the bench seat and lay down, completely unaware of what was going on.

"Grandpa! He's cocking it and now he's opening the passenger window!"

"Hold on, everyone!" Frank yelled.

He watched in the mirror and judged his moment before he swung the wheel to the left, forcing the Ford to swerve. The RV kept swinging left and the Ford left the blacktop in a cloud of dust, then bounced into the median gap between the roadways. The pounding as the suspension flung the heavy car around did not allow the driver to regain control before the front right wing struck a boulder and ripped open the front tire with a loud explosion of escaping air. Frank stood on the brake pedal and brought the RV to a sliding stop. As soon as he dragged the parking brake on, he was through the door and striding towards the damaged Ford with the heavy Python held down by his side.

As the solidly built old man with the steel grey hair reached the wreck he took off his Miami Dolphins baseball cap and looked inside the car. Both men had smacked their heads hard against the dashboard and the car roof. They were both breathing, but unconscious. Frank straightened up and looked around. He walked to the left side of the car and raised the pistol. One round through the front tire, and another through the rear, ensured this car would not be troubling them for a good while.

He picked up the two magazines from the rear seat, then walked back up the tire tracks towards the blacktop and picked up the submachine gun that had fallen through the window before the thug could open fire on them. He removed the magazine and worked the action to clear the round out of the breech. It had been ready to fire, so he had no worries about having acted first. He walked back to the RV with a weapon in each hand and three magazines in the pockets of his cargo pants.

Emma was standing at the front of the RV ready to back him up with her revolver should it be necessary. He had trained her himself and now she was almost as good with her Armscor as he was with the Python. It gave him a warm feeling that she had backed his play without second-guessing him. That kind of trust was special.

"Are they dead?"

"No. We'll get going and then call 911. We should be a long way from here before the emergency services appear."

He climbed back into the RV and sat down, placing the Python back into its locker. The two kids were sitting wide-eyed on the bench seat at the table staring at him.

"Don't worry, kids, just a misunderstanding. We'll be at the campsite soon."

Chapter 33

In the following days they carried on heading generally north up the I-95, visiting sites of interest along the way. Most of them had been involved with the Civil War as both the children had to write a term paper about it by the end of the summer. This way, Frank hoped, they would have something out of the ordinary to write about and maybe get their grades up a bit.

In Charleston they saw Fort Sumter, where the first shots of the Civil War had been fired. Later they stopped in Richmond and visited some of the fine houses of the period that still stand. In Washington, they took the trolley bus tour around the city, with the funny and interesting commentary from each driver they rode with. In Baltimore they took the boat ride across the harbour to see Fort McHenry and to hear the story of the siege that had inspired the writing of the *Star-Spangled Banner*.

But then it was time for the part of the trip Frank had been looking forward to most of all. They took the I-83 north to York, then turned left off the interstate and headed across to Gettysburg, where he really wanted to visit the battlefield he had read so much about.

They found the heavily wooded RV campground and parked up under the trees. Frank hooked up the services to the vehicle while Emma started to cook and the kids took Kika for a walk through the trees and wandered around to see what they could find of interest. By the time they had finished exploring, Frank had the table set up next to the parking area and Emma had the meal ready. They sat around and ate in silence to start with.

"So what are we doing tomorrow, Grandpa?" Geoff asked.

Frank carried on chewing the very fine steak; he made it a rule never to speak with food in his mouth. He swallowed and took a sip of the icy-cold Sam Adams beer he had in front of him.

"I thought we might take the tour of the battlefield on the open-topped bus they have here. According to the people in the office, it goes to all the major points of interest and the ones it misses we can go back and see later."

Marian looked bored as usual. "So what deadly exciting things are there to see?"

"The cemetery where Lincoln gave the Gettysburg Address. The site of Pickett's Charge. They call that the 'high water mark of the Confederacy'. This would have been a very different country if that attack had gone another way. You should pick up all the brochures the National Park people have around for your term papers. It wouldn't hurt to raise your grades a piece."

Frank smiled to himself when he saw their faces drop as he mentioned their grades. He didn't want to come down on them hot and heavy, so he mentioned the problem quietly, but often. Maybe this trip would inspire them when they saw there was so much more to this country than just Florida.

He and Emma did the dishes in the RV sink, while the twins went across to the main campsite cabin to watch some second-rate reality show on the TV. Then, with Kika laying by his feet, Frank sat at the table outside in the evening air and cleaned his pistol and the MP5 sub machine gun. He hoped he would not need to use either again.

Chapter 34

The bus tour around the Gettysburg battlefield went well. The weather was kind and the guides remarkably well informed. Their patience was tested by both Geoff and Marian, but they answered every question with good grace.

Frank stood silently staring down the long, wide, grassy slope with his hat in his hands. Geoff slouched over and stood beside him. All he could see was a big field, he couldn't see what the problem was.

"So what's up, Grandpa?"

"I'm just standing here trying to imagine the raw courage it took to walk almost a mile up that slope with the Union army down behind that wall with rifles and artillery. Lines of men shoulder to shoulder, just walking as they got chewed to pieces. Almost beyond belief. And these were veterans. They knew what they were getting into before they left the cover of the trees. Yet still they came."

The boy looked at his grandfather's watery eyes and then turned to look back down that long open slope. Now he could almost see the ragged lines of men in grey and butternut with their proud but tattered flags above them. He reached out and took the older man's hand.

"When you write that report, son, you remember this place. Maybe those men were misguided, but never doubt their incredible courage."

Frank patted the boy's shoulder and they walked slowly back to where the bus waited for them. They walked past the silent cannon standing beneath the trees along the ridgeline and maybe for a moment they heard the final yell of those men from Virginia who made Pickett's Charge.

They were quiet as they made their way back into the campsite that evening. The sunlight through the trees dappled the top of their RV and gave them a cool evening after the warmth of the day. Frank sat outside in his folding chair as Emma cooked her signature chili. He watched the other campers pottering around doing whatever needed doing to prepare for the evening.

He watched the quiet industry all around him until he noticed the one man standing against a tree studiously not watching him. Frank's instincts kicked back in. There was something wrong with the picture he was seeing. How the hell had they been found again?

Frank settled himself in the chair and felt the reassuring bulk of the revolver against his back, under his denim jacket. He knew he had to do something, but it couldn't be in front of the kids. Marian in particular would probably freak out and he did not need either of them scared until he had them safe with their father.

Emma stepped down from the RV carrying bowls and forks along with an icy bottle of beer to help Frank wash down his meal. He waited until she was close before he spoke quietly.

"Don't react." She stiffened slightly, but did not look round. "We're being watched from over your right shoulder. Take a quick look as you go back in."

"Are you sure? We've been careful. How would they find us again?"

"Pretty sure, and I think I may ask our friend just how they are doing it. Keep the kids inside for a while."

"That won't be difficult. They are both glued to the laptop. Some reality TV garbage again."

Frank nodded and kept an eye on their watcher as she turned and left him. He waited until she was back inside, then he cocked his head as though she had spoken to him from the vehicle. He shook his head sadly, then took a pull at his beer before standing up slowly and walking towards the RV. As soon as the tall-sided vehicle was between him and the watcher he cut left into the trees at the rear of their parking bay. Moving quickly and quietly, the way the Marines had taught him before they sent him out to Vietnam, he circled around towards the site store and then walked back alongside the road on the bed of soft pine needles.

He came up behind the man, having checked that he was alone. As he reached him he produced the heavy revolver from under his jacket and rested it against the back of the man's skull. The watcher stiffened and was about to turn when Frank pushed harder with the barrel of the pistol.

"Don't do anything clever that you might regret, son. At this range I reckon this gun would lift the head right off your neck. Might be interesting to speculate how far it would fly."

"My wallet's in my back pocket and I ..."

"Nice try, son, but you've been watching me and my family for just too long for that to work. You know this isn't a mugging and I want to know why and how you tracked us down."

"I don't know what you mean."

Frank lifted the pistol away from the man's neck and swung it back against his ear, just hard enough to be painful, but not do any damage. The man recoiled in surprise, but stopped when the pistol returned to his neck.

"Now when I was working," Frank said, conversationally, "I was bound by all sorts of rules and regulations, but now I'm retired and you are threatening my family, those rules don't bother me anymore. Now it's personal and you should really understand that."

The man nodded just slightly. "OK, I get that. It's just business."

"Business to you, maybe; to me it's very personal. Now you and I are going to walk up the roadway here and then when we find a nice quiet spot we are going to have a talk. You better get used to the idea that you are going to tell me what I need to know. Now move."

The man pushed himself carefully away from the tree and started walking slowly up the track carved through the trees. Frank could see his head moving slightly from side to side. He had seen that before.

"Now, son, at this moment you are looking left and right judging when to make your run for it and deciding which way to go. You should know that I've been carrying this revolver for the best part of forty years and it's a hell of a long time since I missed a target as big as you. Calm down and you'll make it out of this with a whole skin."

Frank saw the man's shoulders slump fractionally as they continued walking. As they passed one of the wooden tables set under the trees Frank grabbed the plastic bottle that was standing there and slipped it into his pocket.

Once clear of the RV campground, Frank pushed his unwilling companion off the track and into the trees. They walked on until they came to a small open space with a lone tree standing in the middle of it.

"Now, son, you walk over to that tree and put your nose up against it. Then put your arms around it and take hold of your own wrist."

Frank stood back and watched as the younger man did as he was told. Then keeping the pistol pointing at his captive, he walked to the other side of the tree. From inside his jacket he produced a pair of handcuffs and snapped one loop over the man's left wrist, then the other over his right.

"There, now we can have a nice talk without anyone waving guns about, can't we?"

He stepped around the tree and ran his experienced hands over the man's body. Almost immediately he felt the firearm against the man's back. Lifting the jacket tail, he found an M10 submachine gun. Very small, but still deadly at short range. Under the man's armpit he found a Browning Hi Power automatic pistol and at his belt, a wicked-looking knife.

"I think we can dispense with the story you were going to spin me about just passing through, can't we? You wouldn't want to make me angry now, would you?"

The man eased his head around and looked at Frank. He swallowed. "OK, look, it's not personal, I told you that. There's a contract been put out on eleven people. Two of them are the kids you have with you."

"My grandchildren."

"I didn't know that. They were just marks. I needed the money and the pay for this job is big. That's why there's so many people trying to collect."

"Who's paying you, who gave you the job and how were you going to do it?"

The quiet tone of Frank's voice made the would-be assassin look around again. He looked into the older man's eyes and saw a depth of coldness there that struck him deep inside. He rested his head against the trunk of the tree.

"I don't know. You're all over the dark net. Pictures of the kids and some others and then details of where to start looking for you. Whoever it is wants those kids dead badly. It's good money for the contract. The hit would have been whatever way presented itself when the time came, I guess."

"What the hell is the dark net?"

"It's a hidden part of the Internet that most people don't know about. You need passwords and all that stuff to get there."

Frank looked hard at the man for a moment. "OK, no matter. Now how were you able to track me so easily?"

"The girl. She's on her phone all the time. We had someone tracking the signal and I was directed here to wait for the others."

"So there are others coming?"

The man nodded. "Yeah. I was just supposed to watch you and make sure you didn't leave until the others got here."

"How many?"

"Two. One's coming in from Buffalo and the other from Philly."

"When do you expect them?"

"Any time now. We were supposed to meet at the campsite store and then come for you after dark."

Frank gave a small cold smile as he looked down at the floor of the forest. He watched the creatures that crawled and made their lives in the leaf litter. Then he looked back at the man who had come to kill his grandchildren. He stepped forward, pulling the plastic bottle from his pocket. He upended it over the man's head and watched the sticky mess of maple syrup trickle down his face and neck.

"If it's any comfort, you won't lack for companionship for a while. I'll call the campground people soon and tell them where to find you."

"You can't leave me here!"

"Really?" said Frank as he turned and walked away.

Chapter 35

Frank walked briskly back to the RV. Emma was just serving the evening meal at the table and the two youngsters were sitting waiting. Geoff and Emma looked startled when they saw his face as he walked towards them. Marian noticed nothing as she stared at her smartphone as usual.

"Pack up. We're leaving."

"What about dinner? It's just …"

"Throw it in the trash. We need to go now – and turn that damned phone off."

Emma looked at her husband's face. He was not a man given to rash decisions or foolish actions. What she saw there worried her. She said not a word, but took the meal across to the nearest trash bin and scraped it in.

Geoff was puzzled but stood up and started to collect the plates and other dinner things as quickly as he could. Marian stayed where she was, glued to her phone. She looked up when she registered her grandfather's face a few inches from hers.

"I said, turn off that damned phone. Do it now and don't turn it back on until I tell you to. Have you got that?"

Marian nodded nervously and fumbled for the button to shut the device down. She stood up, confused as to what was happening until her grandmother took her by the arm and pushed her to the RV doorway. As soon as they were inside and the utilities were disconnected, Frank started the big vehicle and pulled out of their parking spot. He drove past the campground office and out onto the road that ran past the site.

They drove in silence until they were on the I-76 heading towards Pittsburg. Then Emma turned around and spoke to the two children, who were now sitting at the table side by side watching their grandparents.

"OK, you two, go back and make up the beds for tonight. I want to talk to your Grandpa." She waited until they had moved away from the table and gone down to the rear of the RV before she turned to Frank. "What happened?"

"They're still after us. There are two more of them heading towards the campground right now. That's why we needed to get the hell out of there. Sorry about dinner."

"But how did they find us? We haven't been followed. I know you've been checking and so have I."

Frank looked across at his wife. "Seems they have been tracking that phone of Marian's. She has the thing on all the time, so once they had found the signal it was easy for them to follow us. The one who was watching us was just to keep us from leaving, until the other two arrived to finish the job."

Emma turned and looked through the windscreen. She paused for a moment, then asked the question she was dreading to hear the answer to. "What happened to the watcher? I saw you walk him off into the woods."

Frank smiled a little. "I didn't kill him, though by now he might wish I had. All the bugs of the forest should have found him by now. They just love maple syrup."

Emma looked at him with her mouth open, then noticed the kids returning. "Explain that to me later. Now, more importantly, what are we going to do about dinner for these two?"

"Once we get north of Pittsburg, just after the I-279 joins the I-79 there's an Eat'n Park just off the highway. We'll stop there and then you three can bed down while I take us on to our next stop."

"Where's that going to be, grandpa?" Geoff asked.

"Niagara Falls. Somewhere every kid in America should see at least once."

"Then where?"

Frank glanced at the boy over his shoulder. "Canada."

Chapter 36

Frank drove through the night with Emma fortifying him with coffee at intervals. The rest of the time she dozed in the seat beside him. He pulled into the parking area at Goat Island just as dawn was breaking and found a spot at the back, away from the roads that passed by. Completely exhausted, he collapsed into his bed with instructions for Emma to wake him for lunch and until then to keep the kids close by.

Four hours later, when she woke him, he was still bleary-eyed, but struggled out of the bed to wash his face and comb his short silver beard. He stepped down out of the RV into the brilliant sunlight of a perfect northern day and looked around for the kids. He found them bent over the same laptop computer updating their Facebook pages and giggling at their friends' posts. Hungry by now, Frank rounded them up and they walked across the Goat Island Road to the 'Top of the Falls' restaurant.

They found a table with remarkable views across the Horse Shoe Falls and Frank promised they would walk down to Terrapin Point to have a closer look before they moved on. The waitress turned out to be friendly and very helpful, recommending the coconut shrimp starter and the fish and chips main course, although naturally Marian had to be different and took the fruit and cheese platter.

Lunch over, they walked down the pathway to the falls with the scruffy black dog bounding ahead of them. Frank stood with the two children by the railing, overlooking the water rushing past them to the long drop to their right. Emma wandered back up the hill to find the perfect spot to photograph the falls and her family with Canada in the background. Frank leaned on the railing and gazed into the water, he was starting to relax after the dash across the country to keep his grandchildren safe.

"Turn round slowly, old man, and keep your hands where I can see them. You two kids, stay right where you are."

Frank turned his head to the man standing behind him. The ugly black automatic pistol in his hand was sufficient declaration of his intent. Frank looked at the man's reddened and blotchy face.

"I suppose you thought this was funny?" the gunman said, indicating his face and neck. "Two hours I was stuck by that tree with every insect in the forest crawling over me biting and stinging."

Frank shook his head again. "How the hell did you find us this time?"

The gunman pointed to Frank's right and when he turned he saw that Marian had her phone in her hand. He swore under his breath and turned back to his assailant. The man had moved and was now leaning on the railing with the gun trained steadily on Frank's navel.

"So what now?"

"So now I kill those two brats and collect a nice chunk of change. You, I'm going to do for fun. I owe you that much. Now where's that wife of yours?"

"Right behind you, scumbag," Emma said in a quiet voice.

As the man spun round to face the new threat, Emma swung the pistol in her hand in a wide, rapid arc. It cracked against the gunman's face, right on the bridge of his nose. He rocked backwards and fell across the safety railing. Frank took two steps forward and grabbed the man's ankles and heaved upwards. The man flipped over the railing and with a small cry fell into the roaring water. He surfaced once and was then dragged down by the powerful swirling current as he raced unwillingly to the falls.

Frank and Emma stood looking across the water to where they had seen the man surface. There was nothing they could do. Frank reached out and took Emma's hand and gave it a squeeze.

"Nice swing there, old lady. Lucky there's nobody about that we have to explain to."

He bent down and picked up the automatic pistol that had fallen to the ground. As he straightened, he slipped it into his jacket pocket and turned towards the two children. The twins were standing shoulder to shoulder, wide-eyed and trembling. Frank walked forwards and took the mobile phone from Marian's unresisting fingers. He turned and threw the device as far as he could out into the river, then turned back to look into her bereft face.

"I wonder if that made it into Canadian waters." He put his hands on their shoulders and turned them around towards the area where the RV was parked. "Go and find that damned dog and then I think it's time I told you why we are really here and why I told you to keep that damned phone switched off."

Chapter 37

As they pulled into the bay at the Canadian Immigration checkpoint Frank looked back at the two youngsters sitting behind him. They were still pale-faced with shock at being told they were being hunted by people who actually wanted to kill them for money. To them it seemed like a bad dream and it had taken Frank and Emma a while to calm them when they had heard what was really going on.

Frank climbed down out of the RV and went into the building to speak with the Canadian immigration officers. He was greeted in a friendly way until he explained that he was carrying a range of hand guns and a submachine gun in his vehicle. The atmosphere turned distinctly colder and two of the officers went out to the RV to examine the weapons while the third started to call up Frank's details on the computer.

"Have you been to Canada before, sir?"

"I have, three times, when I was working as a Federal Marshal and was sent to escort prisoners back to the States."

"So you are aware that our firearms laws are considerably different to those in the US?"

"I am, and that's why I'm here telling you what I have on board."

The officer behind the desk didn't reply. He stared at his computer screen and glanced up at Frank before he looked down again and slowly shook his head. He whistled under his breath and picked up the handheld radio by his side.

"Harry, Paula, come back in here. Leave the weapons in the vehicle."

He waited until the two officers returned from the RV and beckoned them over to look at the screen. All three of them raised their heads and looked at Frank.

"Is there a problem, officers?" Frank asked.

"It seems not. There is an instruction on here to all immigration points that you are not to be hindered in any way and you are to be allowed full and free passage into Canada with anyone you have with you. The instruction comes from Ottawa."

"Really? I wonder why they put that on there."

"I have no idea. I've never seen an instruction like it. Welcome to Canada, Mr. Eastman. I hope you have a pleasant stay."

Frank retrieved his documents, thanked the officers and left the building. He started up and drove forward into Canada. Emma had selected an RV park just off Lundy's Lane and they pulled in there shortly after leaving the border crossing. Frank turned around and looked at Geoff.

"Geoff, when you are on that Facebook thing what information do you put in?"

"I just update my status, tell them where I am and what I'm doing. Things like that."

"That's what I thought. Open up the computer. I want you to update our location."

"But what if someone bad sees it?"

"That's what I'm counting on. Emma, can you get out your book of RV campgrounds and pick one near Buffalo. Geoff, you take a look and put that as your location on Facebook. Find some details from the book and tell them you are using the facilities. Something like that."

Emma pulled the book across and thumbed through it. Selecting one of the sites, she passed the book to Geoff.

Marian watched all this wide-eyed. "Then what, Grandpa?"

"Then we go somewhere else, but we keep telling all your friends on Facebook that we are heading back down to Florida. If the people who are after us do see it we should be able to keep them running in circles, at least, I hope so."

Chapter 38

Sarah Mansfield rose up on her knees from pulling out the last of the weeds growing on her late husband's grave. She looked at the gravestone and gave it a fond pat.

"There you are, Martin, all nice and tidy again. You always did like to see the graveyard looking neat."

She looked to the left where her son's military gravestone stood, the cap badge of the Royal Engineers neatly displayed with his name, rank and number above. It was a simple stone, but all the more welcome for that. The space the other side of him she had reserved for herself when the time came. She would have to think about where to put Ivan as well so they could all be together.

She heard the gravel crunch on the path behind her and turned to find a stranger standing there. She shaded her eyes with the trowel to get a look at him. Dark-haired with a well-pressed suit and shined shoes, he had a nice smile as he looked down at her.

"Hello, can I help you?"

"You can if you're the Reverend Sarah Mansfield. I'm looking for someone and I think you may know where he is."

Sarah stood up and put her trowel back into her small basket before wiping her hands on her gardening apron. "What's the name? I know where most people are in the cemetery."

"Oh, he's not buried here." The man smiled. "At least not yet. I'm looking for Ivan Thomas."

Sarah's heart sank and she felt an emptiness in her stomach. "What makes you think I know where he is?"

"Well, maybe you don't know exactly at the moment. Him and his friends have been covering their tracks, but you could find out for me." He smiled pleasantly again. If Sarah had not been there when the first attempt had been made on Ivan's life, she might have fallen for the charm.

"I haven't heard from him in some time," she said, thrusting her hands into the pocket of her apron.

The smile faded from the man's face. "I really don't have time for all this chit-chat. We're going to go into the house and you're going to phone him and find out where he is."

"And why would I do that?"

The stranger heaved a sigh and showed Sarah the folded knife in his hand. He pressed a silver button in the side and a blade flicked out. He gestured with the knife and Sarah shrugged and started walking to the front door of the rectory. Her mind raced as she tried to think of a way to get away from this killer and warn Ivan.

As she reached the heavy wooden door in the entrance archway to her home, she braced herself to swing it hard into the man behind her and make a run for her study, where she had left the pistol from the first attack. As she reached the door the man stepped up close behind her and put his hand on the door to hold it open. She sighed to herself and walked on towards the study, up the passageway with the creaking floorboards that Ivan had promised to fix.

"Where are you taking me?"

"To my study, to where the phone is and my phonebook," she answered.

"Don't you have your boyfriend on speed dial?"

"Usually, yes, but when he is out of the country he uses a different phone."

Sarah walked into the study with the stranger close behind her. The old Labrador looked up as she entered, wagged his tail once, then settled back down on his blanket. She walked across the room and stood for a second looking out through the bay window where her family lay.

She turned and pointed to the desk. "The phone book's in there," she said.

"Then get it and start calling."

Sarah opened the left hand drawer in the old walnut desk and looked down. The phone book was there, with the large black automatic pistol resting on it. She steeled herself to what she had to do and grabbed the pistol. She raised it with both hands and pointed it at the stranger's face. He looked startled for a moment, then put his head to one side and smiled at her.

"Nice try, Reverend. You don't use guns much, do you? The safety catch is on and the hammer is forward, so you haven't cocked it. Please feel free to pull the trigger. Nothing's going to happen."

He moved forward and reached up to take the weapon from her trembling fingers and then put it on the table beside him. He looked at her for a moment and then, having made his mind up, he drew the knife back ready to thrust it into her. The thrust never came as the large black Labrador lurched forward and sank its teeth into his arm. The man screamed in pain and tried to beat the dog off with his left arm, but Corby was having none of it and hung on.

Sarah did not want to see her late son's dog injured and so picked up the pistol again and swung it at the man's head. He grunted, fell to the floor and lay still. Corby released his arm and sat down with his tail wagging and his mouth panting open. She pressed the panic button Ivan had had installed for her before he left. She steadied herself against the table and then called the dog across to her. She ruffled his ears and told him what a good dog he was, again and again, as she listened to the police cars sliding to a stop outside the gates.

Chapter 39

The old bear sitting beside the waterway on the rocky beach in front of the cabin swung his scarred and grizzled head around to watch the canoes land and the people get out. He could see the rubber boat with its smelly engine landing on the slipway beyond. He didn't move; he couldn't see the one who gave him fish when they met in the mornings.

The people from the canoes walked across the beach and through the thin screen of trees, then into the cabin. The ones at the slipway had gone to the metal shed set into the tree line and he watched them carry a box and sheets of metal back down to the boat. They had pushed back into the water and started to go back the way they had come before he recognized the one who gave him fish. If he was leaving there was no more reason to stay here. He turned and ambled slowly back into the forest, being careful where he put the sore paw that was making him so short-tempered.

Out on the waterway the SEALs' boat was taking Jim and Ivan back to the Beaver with tools and equipment to repair the bullet damage to the float and to check that nothing else vital had been hit. Simple skin damage to an aircraft like this should not take long to repair and waterproof. But if any of the controls or electronic equipment had been harmed it could be problematic, with their limited equipment.

Ivan and Jim sat silently watching the edges of the forest as the boat slid across the glassy calm waters of the inlet. Raoul stood at the boat's wheel scanning around them as well. They could not afford to be careless and each man had a rifle close at hand. They saw no other boats and nothing to concern them before they swung into the bay where the yellow and white Beaver sat on its floats waiting for them. Raoul ran the boat gently onto the rocky beach and the three men unloaded the equipment they needed for a rapid repair.

They walked across to the aircraft and started their examination. It seemed they had been lucky. The bullet that had punctured the starboard float had made a clean entry hole below the waterline. The exit hole was considerably messier, as the bullet had been tumbling as it ripped out through the top of the float, but that could wait until they were back in the workshop. The damage through the fuselage was much the same, with clean entry holes and ripped exit wounds.

Using the mobile jack they had carried with them they lifted the float just far enough to allow them to fit a light alloy patch over the hole with rubber sealant around it to stop leaks on a temporary basis. That done, they lowered the aircraft down and carried out a detailed check of the whole plane before they pushed it gently back out onto the water. Jim climbed into the pilot's seat and started the engine, while Ivan stood up to his thighs in the cold clear water, holding onto the undercarriage to stop the aircraft drifting ashore with the gentle breeze.

With the engine started and running smoothly, Jim started the slow taxi back to the slipway by the cabin. Ivan climbed into the inflatable boat and Raoul drove slowly behind the taxiing aircraft to provide any protection that might be needed. Raoul's three men were waiting, scattered around the concrete slipway, keeping watch, and allowing Ivan and Raoul to receive the aircraft as it arrived and hook up the winch rope to tow it up the slope and into the shed set amongst the trees.

Once the aircraft was inside, Jim and Ivan set to work to do proper repairs to all the bullet damage while Raoul and his men carried out a further reconnaissance of the area around the cabin. As he finished putting away his tools at the end of the repair Jim heard Megan's pickup truck pull in around the back of the workshop. Wiping his hands on a rag, he walked out of the door see Geordie and Janet climbing out of the big red vehicle.

"What did the doctor say about your ventilation holes then, Geordie?"

"Oh, hi boss. He was quite impressed with the job Janet had done on me. It seems she really was a nurse back in the day. He's given me some painkillers to help with sleeping, but he was pretty unimpressed with the injuries."

Megan smiled at them both as she closed the driver's door. "You'll have to do way better than that to impress a doctor around here. They're used to logging and mining injuries. A few shotgun pellets are small beer to them."

"So nothing to worry about then? Did he say when you will be able to work the arm normally?" Jim asked.

"Didn't seem to think it would take long, though it's going to ache for a while."

Janet came around the front of the pickup carrying a bag of groceries. "We did get one useful piece of gossip for you, Jim. They found that trawler beached in a small bay just down the coast towards Vancouver. The cabin is pretty well burned out apparently, so Ivan's flare gun did the job."

Jim smiled. "He'll be glad to hear that. We've just finished patching the Beaver up, so let me take those groceries and you can get our wounded warrior here to help with making dinner."

Chapter 40

Geordie sat in the big chair by the window looking out across the beach to the inlet beyond. The moonlight had turned the water to a polished sheet of silver and the trees were clearly silhouetted against it. He knew one of Raoul's men was out there somewhere keeping watch, but he had seen no sign of the SEAL. He heard a slight scuff on the wooden floor behind him and turned to see Janet walking towards him.

"Can't sleep, Geordie?"

"No, bonny lass, the arm is aching and I've had my ration of painkillers for today. Besides, I wanted to do some thinking."

She sat down on the arm of the chair next to him. "Thinking about what?"

He moved to give her a bit more room. "Lots of things. How I caused all this problem for everybody. What I might do to stop it all. Whether I could have saved Sam if I'd gone to her and made her believe me. All that kind of stuff."

"Sam was your wife?" Janet said, looking down at him.

"Not for much longer. She left me and filed for divorce. I had the papers from her lawyer so it was over, but I still wouldn't have wished her any harm."

"Jim told me the man she was with ran away and left her."

Geordie nodded sadly. "He's an actor, plays all those tough guy action hero parts. I guess he won't get many of those once the word gets round about him. I'd like to look him in the eye just once to watch him explain it to me."

"Would you hurt him?"

She watched Geordie's head shake in the moonlight through the window. "No. He can't help being weak, but I want to make sure he feels it to his dying day. She was a lovely person and I'm sorry she's gone."

She stood up and looked down at the big capable man in the chair. The silver light from outside glistened on the single tear that slipped slowly down the dark skin of his cheek.

"Are you going to go back to bed or should I make us some coffee? It won't be as strong as Megan's, I'm afraid."

Geordie smiled up at her. "A coffee would go down well right now. The rest of them will be up soon anyhow and a change from Megan's patented paint stripper would be welcome."

"I think I'd better take a look at those dressings while it's quiet. Take your shirt off and come and sit near the light."

Geordie unbuttoned his shirt and dropped it on the table, then sat on one of the benches while Janet checked the dressings. He noticed her fingers straying from the site of the injuries and stroking his well-muscled chest and arms. He turned his head and looked her in the eye. They didn't speak as the moment hung in the air between them, then she leaned in and gave him a kiss, before standing up and walking across to the kitchen to make the promised coffee.

Chapter 41

Jim stood down at the waterside watching his fishing line snaking back from his favourite spot. He saw the bear from the corner of his eye as the old beast ambled towards him. He eased the Webley revolver in its holster just in case he needed to scare the animal off. There had been no problems before, but Megan had told him that an animal of this age could be unpredictable when it became more difficult for them to find food. The bear sat down at the edge of the rocky beach and watched him. It made no sound, but he could hear the low whistle of its breath as it waited.

He heard Geordie's voice from behind him. "Is it OK to come down there, boss? Only I don't want to upset your hairy friend."

Jim grinned over his shoulder. "Walk slow and don't make any sudden noises and we should be fine. He's never been aggressive yet. I think he's a bit past all that stuff."

Geordie walked carefully forward with one eye on the large animal that swung its massive head to watch him. He reached Jim's side and sighed.

"What's the matter, Geordie? Don't you think you could outrun an old bear?"

Geordie grinned broadly. "I don't need to outrun him just as long as I outrun you, boss."

Jim chuckled at the old joke. "Cheeky beggar. What's on your mind, or did you come down to help me fish?"

"Never been one for the fishing, you know that, boss. No, I needed a quiet word before I cause any more problems for you."

"For me? Sounds intriguing. So what's this word then?"

Geordie paused as Jim suddenly snatched the rod backwards and started to reel in. "Grab the landing net. I think we've got a nice one."

Geordie picked up the long-handled net and watched as the fish thrashed the surface of the water while Jim hauled it in. He noticed that the bear had stood up and was watching the struggle intently. As the fish came in range Geordie scooped it into the net and swung it gently ashore. Jim reached in and took hold of the silver and green fish before easing the hook out of its mouth. Rather than let it suffer Jim dispatched it with a sharp blow to the back of the head and then turned and tossed it to the waiting bear.

The bear grunted deep in its throat and picked the fish, almost gently, off the stones. It turned and walked slowly back into the trees, favoring its injured paw as it did so. The two men watched the big beast disappear and then Jim turned back and started to bait his hook again.

"That's one satisfied customer this morning. Let me get this cast out there and then you can tell me what you need."

Geordie waited as the rod flashed backwards and then forwards, sending the slender line out in a wide arc across the water. "Come on then, Geordie, what's bugging you?"

"Not bugging me. It's just that something has happened, or might be about to happen, and I don't want to make it happen if it's going to cause some difficulty to happen between us."

"That's a lot of happens. Just tell me what this is all about."

Geordie took a breath. "It's like this. I was up last night because the arm was aching and so I was sitting looking out through the window when Janet came to join me."

"She always was light sleeper; she'll have heard you moving about. Don't worry about it."

"It's not that, boss. We talked for a while and then she made some coffee and we talked for another couple of hours, before the rest of you started moving about. The thing is, I'm starting to have feelings for her and I don't want you to be pissed about it, what with her being your ex-wife and that."

Jim put the fishing rod down slowly and turned to face the man next to him. "Does she feel the same way?"

Geordie shook his head. "I have no idea. Maybe. I'd like to find out, but not if it's a problem for you."

Jim looked at the big man and put a hand on his shoulder. "Geordie, Janet is a great person. I still like her a lot. It was my fault the marriage collapsed, despite all she did to keep it going. If you can make her happy I would be over the moon. Just don't hurt her. I've done enough of that for the both of us."

Chapter 42

Ivan finished chewing the piece of steak and put down his fork. Looking across the table at Jim, he raised an eyebrow.

"So then, boss, here we are wrapped up nice and cozy in this cabin, but where do we go from here? The SEALs can't stay forever and we all have lives away from here that I, for one, want to get back to."

Jim pushed the plate in front of him away and rested his elbows on the table. He paused for a moment, then raised his head and looked around at the group who, by now, were all looking at him. All except Simon, who was attacking his steak with the undisguised enthusiasm of a growing boy.

He picked up his coffee and sipped it before speaking. "Good question, Ivan, and I wish I had as good an answer. The problem is that the delightful Calanthe has vanished off the face of the earth and unless we can get her to withdraw the price on our heads, we are stuck."

"So how do we find her?" Geordie asked.

"We have to wait. The CIA are looking and so is MI6. Until they find her bolthole there is no way forward that I can see."

The silence around the long rough-cut table could almost have been cut with a knife until Simon spoke. "That's not quite true, Uncle Jim."

Jim looked along the table as the boy took another slice of steak and carried it to his mouth. He waited until the young man had finished chewing it and was about to cut some more.

"Hang on a second there, Simon. What did you mean by that? What's not true?"

"You said there was no way forward, right? Well, there is. If I can get onto her website in the Dark Net, I can see where she is when she accesses it."

"Surely the CIA could do that?"

Simon grinned at Geordie. "Can I have this one? Don't call me Shirley, Uncle Jim, and yes they should be able to do it if they have the right kind of hacker, but we have developed something new."

"And do we have the right kind of hacker?"

"We do, it's me. I have been going to extra computer science classes after school and a bunch of us started to experiment when the teacher got boring. We've developed our own hacking method and, if we work together, we can mount a cyber attack that will get us into the guts of her website and let us look around at the control protocols."

Jim looked at his sister. "You knew about this?" She shook her head. "So let me get this straight, this cyber attack needs you to work as a group?"

Simon speared another lump of the beef on his plate, then with it hovering in the air he looked along the table. "That's right. It's the multiple attack avenues operating together that make it effective. Normal protection works on the assumption that attacks happen in series. We attack in parallel and we can each see what the other is doing, so we can exploit any weakness that gets exposed."

Jim looked at his nephew in amazement. "And you developed this?"

"I helped, but it was mostly Ron and Kev who developed the core idea. If you want, I can get the group together and give it a go."

"How long does it take?"

Simon gave a look at the juicy piece of steak on his fork and sighed. "It depends on the level of protections they have in place. For an ordinary website where nobody is doing anything illegal, it can be as little as two hours. If there is a threat anticipated they can put protocols in place that take longer to get round."

Jim looked around the table at the now smiling faces while Simon took the opportunity to get another mouthful of beef. There were nods from everyone except Janet and Sandra, who seemed a little bemused.

"OK, Simon, what do you need from us to make this happen?"

Simon swallowed and took a mouthful of his drink. "Fast broadband and a fast laptop. The connection here is way too slow and Megan's laptop is getting a bit old to keep up with this kind of system."

"Fine. Get your pals on board and tomorrow you and I are going down to Vancouver to get you the fastest laptop available and then you can use the web connections in the university. Unless you want to use their machines as well?"

Simon shook his head. "No, we need to stay out of their system. Their firewalls will get in the way and we don't want anyone to see it going on. It's pretty illegal, after all."

Chapter 43

Jim sat to one side of his nephew and watched as the young man's fingers blurred across the keyboard. With his headset on he was keeping up a running stream of chatter to the rest of his team back in East Anglia. Every now and then he would glance across at Jim and give him an encouraging nod, before returning to the attempt to crack open the offending website.

Then he paused. His hands rested on either side of the keyboard as he gazed at the screen.

"What's happening, Simon? Has it worked?"

Simon shook his head slowly. "Not yet, but Rashid has come online and he's getting himself up to speed with what we have done so far."

"Rashid?"

Simon glanced at Jim and nodded. "That's right. He's really brilliant at this stuff. Ron and Kev designed it with help from me, but Rashid is something different. It's like he can feel the code. He does things instinctively and they work. We reckon he's some kind of android like Mr. Data." Seeing Jim's puzzled expression, he explained. "Mr. Data is in *Star Trek*. He's an advanced robot."

"I'll take your word for it. The only one I remember is Mr. Spock, but I take it that's old stuff."

"Spock is original series. Data is TNG. Wait. Yes, here we go. Rashid is on top of it and now we crack them open."

Simon's fingers started flying around the keyboard again as he rattled off technical terminology into his microphone. Jim waited a few moments and then got up to walk among the bookshelves of the university library. It was a good job that he had made friends with the librarian to be allowed in to use the building before normal opening time. He had settled himself into a chair with a book that supported his doctoral studies when Simon came around the corner.

"We've got the IP address for the computer the website owner last logged in from. That gives us a location. They are in southern England in a place called Thames Ditton. It's right on the side of the River Thames. You can see it on Google Maps if you like."

"Are you serious?" Jim asked. "How certain are you?"

Simon looked a little offended. "Absolutely certain. I don't know who is there, but I know that is where the site was accessed from about ..." he looked at his watch "'... ten hours ago."

"Brilliant. Show me the house."

They walked back to where Simon's new laptop lay and Jim stared at the image on the screen. It was a large house with gardens that reached down to the bank of the Thames at a point where the river split to flow either side of a heavily wooded island.

"Simon, that's remarkable. Would you thank your friends for me? I've got to make a few phone calls and then we can work out a plan for our next move. That location has given me an idea."

Chapter 44

Carrying only hand luggage, the three men cleared the immigration procedure at London City Airport quickly. Jim checked his watch and pointed across to the small coffee bar in the arrivals area.

"We might as well grab a quick breakfast here before we go. Our contacts are not due to meet us for another half hour or so."

"How far to where we meet them?" Ivan asked.

"Not far at all. They should be waiting for us in the southern end of the Royal Docks."

A snatched breakfast later they were walking down to the dock where two Rigid Inflatable Boats waited for them. The first was orange with two silver Honda motors on the back. The second was almost entirely black and powered by two Mariner outboard engines. The two crews were equally different. In the first boat sat a young couple dressed in bright boating waterproofs, while in the second the two men wore black dry suits with dull green life jackets.

As they neared the boats Geordie turned to Jim. "So what's RAFSA when it's at home? They've got it marked up on the back of the black boat."

"That's the Royal Air Force Sailing Association; they have a small number of these RIBs for supporting sporting events. The other boat is from a charity called Northern Exposure Rescue and both groups often work together to provide safety cover."

"So why do we need the RAF again?"

"With the gun laws in this country we need someone from the armed forces to supply us with the weapon we want. Major Irwin has managed to get us the rifle we need and these guys should have it with them, all zeroed and ready to go."

"OK then, Geordie," Ivan said, moving forward. "That's us with the air force and the boss in the jolly orange one. Come on."

Jim watched as his two companions climbed down off the dock into the RAF boat and shook hands with the two men crewing it. He turned to climb down into the other RIB.

"Hello, Moira, Chris. Long time no see."

As Moira busied herself untying the mooring line Chris said, "So where was it we saw you last?"

Jim sat down on one of the inflated side tanks and stowed his hand luggage behind the driver's seat. "It must have been up at Rutland Water for that big regatta. Not one of my best races. I got thoroughly beaten. Still, it was a pleasant weekend away from the stress."

Chris nodded and settled into the driving position. "You ready to go? On to Thames Ditton it is then. This early in the morning there shouldn't be much traffic on the river and the lock keeper at the Gallions Point Marina is waiting for us. We should make good time, until we get upriver to where the speed restriction starts."

Once out into the river, the two RIBs accelerated and cruised alongside each other up the middle of the broad waterway through the capital.

They passed through the massive rotating gates of the Thames Barrier, designed to protect London from flooding, and carried on around the wide bend with the massive white dome of the O2 Centre, standing on what is effectively a headland.

As they passed the banking district of Canary Wharf, the unmistakable profile of Tower Bridge came into sight. Chris adjusted the boat's course to take them directly beneath the center of the two lifting spans of the bridge. As they passed beneath it they could see the forbidding grey stone walls of the Tower of London to their right and HMS Belfast to their left. As with much of this part of the river, they were driving through history.

The boats carried on under London Bridge, then Southwark, Blackfriars and Waterloo bridges passed behind them. As they swung around the bend after Waterloo Bridge, the tower of Big Ben came in view alongside the Houses of Parliament.

Chris turned round to Jim. "Fancy calling in for a subsidized beer in that den of iniquity?"

Jim grinned at the old joke. "No thanks, I'd need to change my shoes on the way out after wading through all the bullshit."

Chris chuckled and turned forwards again. Jim looked at the great gothic building and wondered whether the Prime Minister was keeping his word and actually trying to help. He turned forward in time to see the headquarters of MI6 appear on the other side of the river, alongside the Vauxhall Bridge. And now he wondered if the agents of MI6 and their counterparts in MI5 were doing their part to stop this massacre. His thoughts were answered as his phone rang. The screen did not display the calling number and he smiled to himself as he pressed the call button.

"Jim Wilson. Do you have an answer for me?"

The voice at the other end did not identify itself. "We do. Your friend is in residence, as you suspected. What do you need now?"

"We should be there in the very near future. Hang back and watch for developments, but please don't interfere yet. I'll let you know when it's your turn."

The phone connection was broken without a response. Jim put the phone back in his pocket and then looked across to Ivan and Geordie in the black boat that was running alongside them. He gave them the thumbs up sign and pointed forwards. Ivan tapped the RAF driver on the arm and the big Ribcraft accelerated away up the river.

Chris watched it go and then turned back to Jim. "Do you want me to keep pace with him?" he asked.

"No thanks, just hang back, please. I need my two lads to get into their place before we arrive."

"And you're sure you don't want us to hang around where we drop you?"

Jim shook his head. "No. It's better if you push off upriver a way and come back when I call for you. Safer that way."

The big man at the wheel shrugged and reached down into a storage box in the side of the console. He passed Jim a handheld VHF radio.

"It's quicker than dialing me on the mobile phone and we'll be well within range."

"Frequency?"

"Already set. Just press the button and talk when you need us."

Jim nodded his thanks and slipped the small radio into an inside pocket, before returning to watching the riverbank slide by. Moira walked back from the bow seat she had been occupying and opened a coolbox behind the driver's seat. She pulled out a thermos flask and passed around the plastic cups that were also in there.

Jim took the cup. "How long till we get there?"

Moira looked around with a practiced eye. "From here about thirty minutes, give or take. Does that give your two people time to do whatever they are doing?"

"Plenty of time," said Jim, taking a sip of the coffee.

Chapter 45

Having left the city, the banks of the river became greener with lawns reaching down to the banks from increasingly smart houses. Jim was startled as a large flock of screeching birds flew low over the boat.

"What the hell were those?"

Moira grinned. "Parakeets."

Jim looked to see if she was joking. "Parakeets? In England?"

"That's right. It seems a few escaped from captivity and they have been successful in breeding and, as you can see, they have quite a colony now. Maybe global warming is helping them."

"Well, I'm damned. You learn something new every day."

They paused at Teddington Lock and then moved through it behind a large pleasure boat that seemed to have had a party on board, judging by the empty beer cans scattered around the deck and articles of clothing hanging from the safety rails. They overtook the boat and its bleary-eyed skipper before Chris started to slow.

"According to the GPS, we are almost at the house you want."

"Thanks, Chris. As soon as I am ashore take yourself out of sight up the river. I'd appreciate it if you could be on standby in case I need to get the hell out of there quickly."

"Is that likely?"

"Anything is possible, with the young lady I am going to see."

Chris turned the boat in towards the well-manicured lawn of a large house and nosed into the reeds at the edge of the river. Jim stood and walked to the bow of the boat and stepped onto the inflatable bow tank, then onto the shore. He stood for a moment and watched as the orange RIB reversed out into the river, then drove away in the direction they had been traveling.

He turned and walked calmly towards the big house, careful to keep his hands in view as he did so. He saw movement in the wide glass conservatory and a man in a white jacket and black trousers came out to meet him. From the corner of his eye Jim saw movement in the bushes to his right and there was the armed guard he had been expecting.

White Jacket stopped and waited as Jim came closer to him. "This is private property. Turn around and go back the way you came."

Jim smiled. "Sorry, I can't do that. I need to speak to Miss Christophides about something of mutual interest."

"There is nobody here of that name. Go away."

"Son, don't waste my time. I know she's here and unless I miss my guess, her bedroom is that one with the large picture window on the left. The one with the very lovely Calanthe standing in it watching us."

"It does not matter. You are not invited here. Go away."

Jim smiled and tried to look relaxed despite the bodyguard, who was obviously watching him. "I tell you what. I will just stand here and you go and ask Miss Christophides if I can join her for breakfast at that table I can see on the terrace over there. I promise she will want to hear what I have to say."

The man stayed where he was and removed a phone from the pocket of his white jacket. As he did so the jacket swung open, giving Jim a glimpse of the shoulder holster under his left arm. The man dialed a number and waited, then spoke in rapid Greek. Through the wide upstairs window Jim could see that Calanthe was on the other end of the call and was nodding as she spoke.

The man finished the call and put the phone away, never taking his eyes off Jim. "You come to the table. Miss Calanthe will be here in a moment. First I search you."

Jim stood quietly as the man patted him down looking for weapons "Satisfied? What's for breakfast?"

The two men walked to the table that was covered in a crisp white tablecloth and Jim was pointed to a chair at the end with his back to the river. He had counted on that, as Calanthe would want to enjoy the view. White Jacket brought an extra place setting and laid it in front of him. Jim sipped at the excellent coffee that was poured for him and waited.

He was halfway down his coffee cup when Calanthe appeared through the conservatory door. Dressed in a simple yellow dress that highlighted her Mediterranean complexion, she really was as beautiful as he remembered. She sat at the far end of the table and contemplated him for a moment or two.

"Well, Major. I did not expect to see you again. In fact I was hoping that, by now, there would be no way of seeing you."

Jim gave her his most charming smile. "Sorry to disappoint you, but that's what I wanted to talk to you about."

They both paused as White Jacket came to the table carrying a wide silver tray with their breakfast on it. He laid the tray down and served a full English breakfast to Jim and a fruit platter to Calanthe.

"I assumed that the condemned man would want a hearty meal for his last one," Calanthe said sweetly. "Please enjoy it."

"Very considerate of you, but I came to discuss you removing the contract you've put out on us."

"And why would I do that? I don't think you understand what your situation is, Major."

Jim chewed a mouthful of excellent sausage, swallowed, then said, "So why don't you enlighten me?"

Calanthe put down her coffee cup carefully. "Very well. You, or one of your men, assassinated my father. If it was one of your men, it must have been on your orders. With his death I took over the business as his only heir. In my business it is important to appear strong from the start, so his death could not go unavenged. When you met him, he told you about dealing with a rival by sinking his boat, with him on it. He did not tell you the whole story. Before he sank the boat he had the crew taken off and made to watch. They could then tell the story and spread the word that my father was to be taken seriously. This is the same thing. I take my vengeance and your deaths send the message I need."

Jim nodded. "I see your point. You need to understand that your father was killed because his orders caused the death of a special person. An eye for an eye, so to speak. So maybe we can stop, having declared that we are even?"

Calanthe gave him a brilliant smile. "How sweet and how simple your view of the world is. We are Greeks and we take family honor very seriously. Plus, in this case it is a matter of business, so I will not withdraw the contract."

Jim put down his fork and looked along the table. "Very well, if humanity does not work for you, let's make this about business. I will make you the same offer I made your father when we dealt with him. Withdraw the contract and I will let you continue in business. If not, I will let it be known that you supply arms to terrorists and the various governments that have been victims of terror will shut you down."

Calanthe folded her napkin and put it down slowly next to her plate. She sat back in her chair with her hands resting on the table to either side of her chair. Jim watched her eyes roam over his face as she thought about the proposition. He returned to his breakfast as she considered her options.

"An interesting offer, Major, but I decline. In fact, if I raise my hand from the table the bodyguard behind you will drop you where you sit and your body will float in the Thames. However, it would be unkind of me not to let you finish your breakfast."

Chapter 46

Geordie wafted the small spider away from the lens of the scoped rifle and returned to watching Jim, sitting at breakfast across the river. He and Ivan lay in the long grass shaded by a copse of broad leaf trees, completely invisible to any security people around Calanthe's house.

The RAF boat had delivered them to far side of the small island and then traveled on upriver to await their call. Geordie and Ivan had moved slowly into position and set themselves up in a sniper's nest by the time Jim arrived. The bodyguard in the garden would be unaware that any threatening move towards Jim would be his last. So far the plan was working out as they had envisaged.

Ivan shifted position slightly as he stared through the powerful binoculars. "Get ready. The boss has just scratched his right ear."

Geordie flipped off the safety catch in answer to the agreed signal. He started to breathe slowly and evenly, waiting for his moment.

Across the river Jim looked around at the bodyguard behind him and the white-jacketed valet to his right. "Miss Christophides, I thank you for breakfast. It really was excellent, but I'm afraid it's time I left you now. Don't get up."

Calanthe looked surprised for a second and started to raise her hand. "Don't do that just yet, Calanthe, I need to show you something." Jim said. "Are these plates anything very special? No matter. Just sit still and watch."

Jim took the cutlery off his plate and laid it down on his snow-white napkin. Then he picked up the plate and held it out at arm's length to his left. He turned it so the porcelain was vertical and waited, then raised his right hand.

The plate shattered and pieces flew across the table and across the terrace. The sound of the shot rolled across the lawn a heartbeat later. Calanthe brushed the fragments from her dress and looked up at Jim.

"And now what?"

"And now, as I said, I am leaving. I tried to be civilized about this, but you turned me down. This was a small demonstration that we are willing and able to 'reach out and touch you', as the snipers say. If your two thugs try anything, they will die where they stand and if you try to leave this table before I am off your property I'm afraid it will be the last thing you do."

Calanthe nodded as she scanned across the river, trying to identify where the shot had come from. She could see nothing. The river ran calmly by and the birds sang in the trees. She looked back to Jim.

"Very well, you have made your point. Now what?"

"Now you reconsider your contract and if you are reasonable this all goes away. If not, I'm afraid I will have to have you put out of business."

She looked at him steadily from her lovely brown eyes. "Major, you may leave. You win this round, but I will be increasing the bounty on your head and on the heads of your two men. This isn't over."

Jim bowed slightly as he stood up. "I thought that might be your response, but I tried, so now my conscience is clear."

He turned and started walking down the lawn towards the river, speaking into the small VHF handset as he did so. The orange RIB appeared from his right and nosed into the bank. He stepped aboard and stood by the steering console as they reversed into the river. He waved briefly to Calanthe, who still sat, stony-faced, at her breakfast table.

Chapter 47

Once clear of Calanthe's house, the black RIB came alongside the orange one and the two men transferred across, having first thanked their RAF helpers. The RAF boat peeled away and drove off to where its trailer was waiting to take the boat back to its storage shed.

Chris drove his boat back into central London and pulled alongside the Millbank Pier where Jim and his men disembarked, after thanking Chris and Moira profusely for their help. They walked up the gangway of the pier to the riverside path which runs beside the main road known as Millbank, and then walked along it towards Lambeth Bridge. As they came opposite an unmarked, nondescript grey office block, Jim indicated a bench set by the side of the broad path and they sat down.

"So what's the story here, boss?" Geordie asked.

Jim gave a backward nod of his head. "That building behind us is where MI5 live. Far less flashy than the wedding cake building that MI6 have, but just as important to us. I called them before you transferred between boats, so we are expected."

"I take it we're not going to knock on the door then?"

"Not really. Getting into either the MI5 or MI6 building is a pain in the backside. It's simpler if one of them goes for a walk and meets us over here."

Geordie nodded and looked out over the river. "Well, it's turning out to be a nice day for it. Might have been even better if you'd let me drop the hammer on the lovely Calanthe, though. Might have saved a lot of trouble."

Ivan's phone rang and he stood as he pulled it from the inside pocket of his jacket. "Back in a minute," he said as he walked to the wall of the embankment to take the call.

"Tempting as it might have been to deal with Calanthe your way, I don't think it would have stopped anything. Somebody else would have taken over her organization and the wheel of vengeance would have started to roll again, for the same reasons."

Geordie rested his elbows on his knees as he leaned forward and nodded. "You could be right, but did you expect her to give up because you asked nicely?"

"No, but there's a young man in a leather jacket walking this way, paying no attention to us at all. I think our contact is here and I think you may hear the next part of the plan, if it's worked."

Geordie leaned back. "Well, I hope it's a bloody cunning plan. I'm getting tired of being the target."

The young man in the brown leather jacket and blue jeans sat down and drew a guidebook out of his pocket. He pointed to a page and showed it to Jim.

"Hello, Major. Glad to see you made it away from Calanthe's house safely."

Jim tapped the page with his forefinger. "That went just as planned, luckily, and thanks to Geordie's excellent shooting."

The young man turned the page and showed that to Jim. "So you're Geordie Peters? Are you the one who pulled that stunt with the bulldozer in Afghanistan?"

"Yep, that was me."

The man chuckled. "Nice to meet you. I'd love to have seen that. Now, about Calanthe, our people moved in after thirty minutes as you asked and she was gone. We found a couple of puzzled cleaners and a cook. Apparently, as soon as you were out of sight, all hell broke loose and they got out of there as if their arses were on fire."

Jim smiled as he pointed at the guide book again. "Any idea where she went?"

"Not yet, but the airports and seaports are being watched. We'll let you know once we spot her."

Geordie leaned over and pointed at the page as well. "Are you certain you actually will spot her?"

The young man stood up and nodded as if thanking them. "Absolutely certain. We've had the 'witch's warning' from Downing Street that this has to be done right."

Jim and Geordie leaned back as the man walked away, consulting his guide book as he went. "So how does that help, boss?"

"We've got her running. Your shot scared her, despite her not showing it. She will have heard by now about the MI5 raid from her house staff.

We need her off balance and that's just what we've started."

Geordie smiled as Ivan came back and sat down. "Important call, Ivan? You just missed the meeting with a spy."

Ivan looked after the man in the leather jacket, but he was nowhere to be seen. "Shame, I'd have enjoyed that. Anyway, that was Frank on the phone giving me an update. They are into Canada and heading for the cabin. They were crossing the prairie as he was speaking to me. He reckons they will cross into Alberta tomorrow and be at the cabin in two or three days. They've had three attempts made on them, but he's pretty sure they are in the clear now."

Chapter 48

Simon watched Raoul walk out through the cabin door to take his turn on watch. One moment he could see him and then nothing. The SEAL commander melted into the forest as though he had never been there. No matter how many times he watched them do it he was still fascinated by the skill of these tough, quiet men.

He returned to cleaning the Winchester rifle that had become his pride and joy. Megan had decided that, since he used it so well, it should be his and had said that she would use her shotgun for scaring bears from now on. He worked the mechanism smoothly a couple of times to work the light oil around the working parts and then loaded the weapon again ready to be used if the attackers were foolish enough to come back.

The SEAL that Raoul had relieved came up the steps to the balcony of the cabin. He nodded to Simon as he went inside and dropped his equipment behind the door, ready for use. Simon marveled at how little these capable men seemed to speak. There was no bravado or bragging about their exploits, just a quiet confidence that was all the more impressive.

Checking his watch, Simon realized it was breakfast time and there was no way he was going to miss the pile of pancakes and maple syrup he had been promised. He was getting quite a taste for the traditional Canadian breakfast and, when there was bacon available to go with it, he made sure he was there to get his share.

Megan was walking from the kitchen with the large platter of breakfast pancakes as he entered and put his rifle back in its rack over the door. He turned just as the first high-speed round shattered the glass in the window and ripped the platter out of Megan's hands. The pancakes flew across the room and the smashed jug of syrup carved a glistening golden arc through the air, before the syrup and glass splattered across the cabin floor.

Simon spun back around and slammed the heavy wooden door before grabbing his rifle from the rack. When he turned back to check on Megan, he was relieved to see she was unhurt and moving quickly towards where her pump action shotgun was kept. More rounds struck the cabin walls and rattled the door as the three SEALs boiled out of their room, grabbed their weapons and equipment and ran to the hatch leading down into the void below the cabin.

Simon had been down there with them a couple of days before and knew they had dug foxholes connected by sheltered crawlways under the building. They could move to wherever the threat was coming from without being seen. Once in position, he knew they could produce very effective fire on any enemy and had practiced for just this event.

Megan came back into the main room with her shotgun and a bandolier of shells. She handed Simon two boxes of extra cartridges for the Winchester and settled down in the position she had been allocated by Raoul, next to where her collie dog was happily licking up the maple syrup. Her job was to keep in cover and blast any attacker who made it into the cabin. Through the kitchen door Simon could see Janet and his mother filling buckets with water in case the enemy used incendiary rounds against the wooden building. He could see that Janet's first aid equipment was already set up on the kitchen table in case of injuries. He was amazed at how calm his mother looked. The nervousness she'd always had around his father was gone, to be replaced by someone he hardly knew.

Keeping low, he crawled across to his position by the window that looked out over the waterway. He picked up the small green telescopic periscope that Raoul had left there for this and peeped over the lower window sill. He tracked the device backwards and forwards; there was nothing moving out there, just the quiet water reflecting the clear morning sky. He moved the shattered glass to one side so he could kneel to fire when a target presented itself and then, as he had been taught, he waited.

Chapter 49

Across the waterway the man who had fired the premature shots had finished cursing himself for his clumsiness. It seemed there was no major harm done. The woman he was aiming at had disappeared from view and the boy had made it inside the cabin, that was true, but there had been no return fire and no other activity he could see. The others would be in position in minutes and then the attack could begin in earnest. He was already planning what to do with the bonus he would get for taking these people out.

Through the telescopic sight on his rifle, he scanned across the front of the cabin that was screened by a thin line of trees. He could see nothing moving around the cabin and through the shattered window he could see nothing moving inside either. Every now and then he caught a slight reflected shine as the sun glistened on a glass fragment at the bottom edge of the window.

He shifted his position slightly to get a clearer view of the rest of the team arriving from the left. They should be coming through the trees any second now. His job was to cover the front of the cabin and drop anybody trying to come out to mount a defense. Too easy with a weapon like his, at this range.

Beneath the cabin one of the SEALs spotted the movement of the gunman and focused on the low bushes he was hiding in. He waited until the shooter moved to return to his original position and fired a single round. Although he never saw the man, he had guessed where his head must be and taken the shot. The gout of blood and brain matter that looped out of the bush and fell back confirmed his guess.

Inside the cabin Simon saw the gout of blood from across the waterway through his mini periscope. He knew what it meant and he felt a little sick, knowing that another human being had just died. Geordie had been right: killing a man was serious. Even if he hadn't done it himself, he was sorry it had happened. He was no longer sure he would be able to pull the trigger if the time came.

In the dark crawlspace below the cabin there was no celebration, no high fives. The three men down there stayed quiet and waited, alert and ready for whatever came next. Each was scanning his own sector and worrying about where Raoul, their team commander, had got to.

The SEALs waited, watching for movement. In the dense forest that surrounded the cabin on three sides they could not see far. Listening intently, they could hear the movement all around them. Obviously these were city-bred thugs and not used to moving silently in woodland. If they managed to get too close, there could be a problem if they decided to set the cabin alight or plant explosives.

A five-round burst of automatic fire peppered the stout tree trunks that made up the outer wall of the cabin. That had come from the left side. Seconds later another burst came from the right and then another from the back of the cabin where Megan had her pickup parked up. The SEALs smiled at each other from their foxholes. Civilians might have been rattled by the initial attack and they guessed that had been the intention. These SEALs were all combat veterans and knew that indiscriminate fire was not the thing to worry about. Once the aimed shots started to land, then it would become serious.

There was a pause and then weapons opened fire from all three sides, away from the waterway. The men beneath the cabin ducked down and counted. They were obviously outnumbered. As the burst of firing ended, each man held up his fingers to the others to indicate how many attackers he had estimated. From what they had heard, it was somewhere between fifteen and twenty assassins out in the woods and coming closer. To collect that many killers, Calanthe's people must have trawled every low-life bar and den of iniquity for hundreds of miles.

The SEALs gave each other grim smiles. This could be difficult, but they were the best and it gave them their favourite gift. A target-rich environment.

Chapter 50

Raoul sat perfectly still in his hide. The only thing moving was his eyes behind the camouflage net he wore over his head as he watched the clumsy movement of the attackers as they closed on the cabin. One came within five feet without seeing him. They were all too focused on the target ahead of them, all too blinded by the large payout they would receive after the killing. The SEAL waited patiently for his time to act.

He watched, still unmoving, as the first blast of fire announced that this group was in place. The second and third bursts showed him where the rest were approaching from. Then the noise and distraction as they all fired allowed him to move rapidly into a better position to start doing damage.

The silenced MP5 he was carrying was not the ideal weapon for this job. He had not anticipated so many attackers at one time. A sniper rifle would have suited his plan much better, but he had to use what he had available. Maybe he could change weapons later as the fight developed. He slipped silently between the trees, making sure he did not stand on anything that would make a noise and give away his position.

From behind a tall broken stump, he could see across the fallen trunk of the tree that he was now twenty feet from his first target. He raised the submachine gun and selected single fire. Taking careful aim, he double tapped two rounds into the back of the man in front of him. Not very sporting, but highly effective. The man slumped into the leaf mold of the forest floor and lay still. Raoul scanned left and right to ensure the man going down had not alerted his companions. There was no sign of any reaction and none of the other attackers were visible from here. He ducked under the fallen trunk and moved forward to his victim. The rifle clasped in the dead hands was far more suited to Raoul's needs and he pried it loose before checking the man's pockets for spare ammunition.

With the rifle in his hands and the MP5 now slung across his back, Raoul moved back into cover to identify his next target. He moved carefully and silently from tree to boulder to tree, scanning around him every second. A movement to his front left alerted him to the position of the next gunman. The red woolen hat pulled low on the man's head gave him a perfect aiming mark and the rifle, swinging backwards and forwards as the man looked for a target, showed where his target was focused.

He raised the rifle he had just picked up and aimed through the optical sight. The slight magnification made the target even clearer and he waited for a clear shot through the branches. The gunman must have sensed something, as his head spun round to look directly at Raoul. Through the sight, his startled blue eyes were clear as day as Raoul squeezed the trigger and extinguished another worthless life. The man flew backwards into the forest debris, his finger clamped down on the trigger of his weapon, and a long burst of fire erupted from his assault rifle. The rounds cracked through the woodland in a sweeping arc, sending the other assailants diving for cover.

With the enemy on this side of the cabin now alerted, Raoul withdrew into the gloom of the forest. He listened as the surprised men shouted to one another to find out who had fired. Once well clear of these attackers, he moved left and swung round to work his way behind the group advancing on the rear of the cabin.

Through a gap in the trees he could see that they had taken cover and were ready to slaughter anyone who came through the back door or who showed themselves at either of the two ground-floor windows. He considered his options, then smiled to himself.

Chapter 51

Raoul moved closer to the end of the line of men working their way towards the rear of the cabin. He could still hear the confused shouts from the group on the right who had been strafed by their dying comrade's last action. He checked over his shoulder to ensure he could not be seen by the rear group, then raised the rifle and fired five rapid rounds into the right- hand group before ducking back into cover and withdrawing rapidly.

As he slipped through the trees into the dark shadows he could hear the alarm from the right-hand group. They had found the body of one of their fallen number and now they were being fired on from their left. The lack of discipline from these thugs took over and three of them opened fire towards where the last five rounds had come from. The bullets cracked through the forest, bringing down pine needles and splintering bark from the trees. The group to the rear of the cabin threw themselves to the ground, yelling in protest, and two of them returned fire.

The SEAL commander was well clear by now, moving quickly and silently through the trees to position himself behind the last group, over at the left of the cabin. By the time he was in the position he wanted, the fire between the two groups had died down as they realized a mistake had been made. Two of the men, in the left-hand group, had raised themselves up and were peering through the undergrowth trying to determine what was going on. Their pale city faces showed up clearly against the dark green of the forest and Raoul smiled again. This was a gift.

Hidden in the dark of the trees, he raised his captured rifle and fired quickly before swinging the weapon twenty degrees to the right and firing again. The first man went down quietly with just the gurgling of blood in his throat. Raoul had aimed higher, but was satisfied with his first snap shot. The second rapid shot was rewarded with a blood-curdling scream from the man he had hit. The whimpering and loud moaning continued, so Raoul assumed he would live and be a burden to his comrades if they went to look after him.

The ball that flew across the gap to the cabin looked black against the sun. It struck the ground and rolled into the crawl space before exploding. The shrapnel from the grenade pounded against the solid wooden floor of the cabin, but did not penetrate. The blast wave from the explosion flung the floor hatch open and stinking, dark smoke boiled into the room above.

One white-hot piece of jagged metal struck a steel fixing bracket holding two support beams in place and ricocheted downwards into the nearest foxhole. It ripped into the right shoulder of the soldier sheltering there and he clenched his teeth together to keep from screaming and giving away his position. Hissing softly to himself, he assessed the wound as best he could, then ripped a field dressing from his kit and shoved it into the ugly gash to stem the bleeding. He knew the real pain would hit him soon and make him useless to the fight. To avoid that, he took the small ampoule of morphine from his belt first aid kit and injected through his clothing into the fleshy part of his left buttock. He hoped it would mask the pain long enough to allow him to keep returning fire when that time came.

He could feel the fire in his shoulder building as he waited for the morphine to kick in. He transferred the automatic rifle to his left side where he could still use it without tearing the wound any further. He reached across himself and withdrew the M1911 automatic pistol from his belt holster. He cocked that with some difficulty and laid that to his left-hand side as well. Maybe all that training from his drill sergeant in offhand shooting was about to pay off.

Chapter 52

Inside the cabin, the floor hatch exploded upwards and then clattered to the floor. Simon sat where he was, but swung the rifle round to cover the hatchway in case the enemy were about to come through. After a second or two he realized that could only happen if the three SEALs below him had been taken out of the fight and he was confident that would not happen easily.

He saw that Megan was sitting calmly in her allocated position with the pump action shotgun across her lap. Uncle Jim had called her "Mama Bear" before he left and he knew she would protect the child she carried. There was nothing for him to worry about there. He swung his head to look into the kitchen where Janet and his mother were laying on the floor to keep out of harm's way. He was just in time to see his mother start to get up to look out of the window.

"Mum! Stay down, they are all around us. Stay low until it's over."

She turned her head and looked at him, amazed at the confidence in the young man who was the son she hardly recognized. The quiet boy who kept out of his father's way was rapidly becoming a man. Being treated with respect by Jim and his two men had worked wonders on Simon. She lowered herself to the floor and, despite the fear, she smiled.

Simon nodded to reassure his mother. Then the front door smashed open as one of the attackers booted it. He had managed to get onto the veranda while the wounded SEAL was down in his hole, staunching his bleeding. The man grinned as he swung the automatic rifle around the room searching for his target. His smile broadened as he saw Sandra laying on the kitchen floor and raised his weapon to the aim. The smile vanished as Megan moved from behind the wooden bench she had been using for shelter. His weapon swung rapidly back towards her. Not rapidly enough. Her shotgun roared in the enclosed space and the man staggered backwards to come to rest against the doorpost. Firing from the hip, most of her blast had missed him, but before he could react and fire, she jacked the slide of the pump action shotgun.

Simon saw the horror on her face as the slide jammed halfway to inserting the shell. The gunman in the doorway chuckled and raised his weapon. The 30-30 round from the Winchester struck him high in the chest and spun him sideways. The second round hit him in the arm and pushed him through the door. The third round came close behind with Simon jacking the weapon's action as fast as he could. He took a heartbeat to aim and the round slammed into the man's chest and ripped out his heart. He was dead before he tumbled down the short staircase at the front of the veranda.

Simon swallowed hard and then walked to the door. He pushed it shut and then dragged a bench across to jam it closed. He turned to see a tear trickle down Megan's cheek as she placed a hand on her stomach.

"He was aiming at my baby."

Simon walked across the room and guided her back to the relative safety of the position she had been given behind one of the turned-over benches. He put an arm around her shoulder and gave her a quick hug.

"He's not going to hurt anybody anymore. You hold the Winchester and let me clear the jam in the shotgun."

She smiled a little as she took the rifle and held it pointing at the door. Simon smiled back to encourage her and then busied himself getting the shotgun back into action. She had been near death and her only thought had been for her baby. That was real courage. With the jam cleared, he handed the shotgun back and took possession of his Winchester again. He sat on the floor and fed four rounds into the tube magazine to make sure he had a full load again before moving back to his position.

Chapter 53

Raoul was getting worried. With his three men effectively pinned down beneath the cabin and only him mobile, the advantage was with the attackers. Sooner or later they would realize that all they had to do was to set the cabin on fire and wait for their targets to try and escape. He could take more of them down, but the odds were stacked against him and, once he was down, the people in and under the cabin would be in deep trouble.

He started to move silently back and around to the right to attempt to sow more confusion. The quiet voice from behind startled him and he dropped to the ground, swinging his weapon as he did so. He found himself looking into the dark almond eyes of David Red Cloud.

The unsmiling man spoke again. "I said, are you having enough fun, or would you like some help?"

Raoul let out a breath. "I'll take any help I can get right now. What did you have in mind?"

David said nothing, just raised his fingers to his mouth and let out a bird call. He looked down at Raoul.

"Are you staying down there or do you want to join in?"

Raoul stood and looked at the calm face. "What happens next?"

"Look around you."

Raoul looked left and right into the dark shade of the forest. At first he could see nothing and then he spotted slow movement. Then more. He realized he was looking at a line of people moving forward absolutely silently. Some had rifles, others had knives and then he spotted at least one of the men carried an oddly shaped club. He looked at David.

"We are on all three sides. Any minute now this will all be over. Some of them may even survive if they are not too stupid."

Raoul became aware that movement had stopped. Try as he might, he could not see the men any longer. They moved in these woods like ghosts. David raised his fingers again and issued the bird call once more. There was a flurry of movement.

Slim Jackson was famous in Vancouver for being a cold, hard killer. Anybody with any sense knew better than to mess with Jackson. He raised his rifle and aimed the underslung grenade launcher at the kitchen window. He had loaded an incendiary round, so this should be fun.

His finger froze as he began to squeeze the trigger. The cold steel across his throat had all his attention and the quiet voice hissed in his ear.

"If your finger twitches just the tiniest bit your guts will be on the forest floor before the round leaves the tube."

Slim started to turn his head and thought better of it as the knife moved closer and he felt his own blood trickle down his neck.

"You don't know who you're messing with. You take that knife away before I shove it up your ass."

The slight chuckle behind him chilled his heart. "Very good. A Clint Eastwood reference. I didn't expect that one. Now, lower the weapon very carefully, city boy, before you find out what trophies the First Nations take."

"What do you mean trophies?"

"The plains Indians take scalps; up here in the North-West we take heads. You going to lower that weapon now?"

Jackson didn't dare to nod. He lowered the weapon and let it fall to the leaf debris beneath him. He stood very still, hardly breathing, just waiting for his chance to turn the tables.

"On your knees, shithead."

The Vancouver thug dropped to his knees and waited his time.

"Right now, you are wondering how you can spin round like they do in the movies and kill me with some tricky move. Not a good idea, son. You've been trying to kill one of our own and some friends of ours, so any excuse would suit me fine. Lean forward slowly and clasp your hands around that tree."

Jackson did as he was ordered and became aware that there was another shadowy figure right there. His hands were grabbed and pulled forward before being tied tightly together.

"You done, Silas?"

"I'm done. He's going nowhere."

"Show him."

The one called Silas moved to where Jackson could see him. He was carrying one of the strange clubs.

"See this? This is a weapon my people have used in war for ten thousand years or more. Its name translated into English is 'Face Splitter'. You make one sound and I'll come back here and show you why. You got that?"

Jackson couldn't speak. The quiet voices scared him so much more than screaming enemies had in the past. He nodded and tried in vain to control his bladder.

Chapter 54

All around the cabin silent capable men moved forward, each one behind an enemy. The legacy of thousands of years in this environment ran in their blood and they knew every inch of their lands. The city-bred thugs never knew what hit them.

Some found themselves with a knife at the throat like Jackson. Others spun round with their weapons raised and were shot down where they stood. Two or three realized what was happening and tried to run forward, away from the silent vengeance slipping through the forest. The weapons of the SEALs beneath the cabin chopped them down before they could turn and fire. One attacked Silas and proved the Face Splitter was well named.

The survivors were herded, none too gently, onto the rocky beach in front of the cabin and made to sit cross-legged in a line while their hands were tied behind them. Janet came out of the cabin and gave the wounded ones some rudimentary first aid. She had taken some morphine from the first aid kits carried by the SEALs. She decided against wasting it on the people who had tried to slaughter them.

The Heiltsuk brought the dead down to the waterside and laid them out in a row as well. The weapons were collected and placed on the veranda of the cabin, along with all the spare ammunition they took from the attackers.

Raoul stood on the veranda with David, looking down at the backs of the sorry bunch on the beach. "So how did you know what to do?"

David looked at him with a steady eye. "Napoleon Bonaparte always told his Marshals to march to the sound of the guns. We heard the firing and came. We had been waiting for something like this, ever since the attack on the fishing camp."

Raoul looked at David in surprise. "You know your military history."

David nodded. "Europeans don't have a lot of history, at least not compared to us, so we read their stories. Just because we live out here in the forests doesn't mean we are ignorant of the rest of the world."

"I didn't mean it that way. Whatever. I'm damned glad you came when you did. It could have gotten difficult. So what do we do with these now?"

David looked at the sun slowly dropping in the sky. "I've called the RCMP. They should be here fairly soon. Probably not before nightfall, though, and this cabin can be difficult to find in the dark. I will send one of our young men up to where the track joins the highway. He can guide them in."

"Sounds good. I'm going to see what's happening to my man. He took a nasty piece of metal in the shoulder."

Raoul turned and walked back into the cabin. One of his men was helping Simon repair the floor hatch and another was brewing the coffee for all the Heiltsuk. The dog, Bracken, sat behind the man in the kitchen hoping for scraps. The injured man sat on one of the rugged benches with his arm resting on the wide table. Janet was carefully removing the field dressing to examine the wound. Raoul stood and watched, trying not to distract her.

Janet peeled the dressing away and dropped it in the bucket by her side. "You've made a fair mess of the flesh and there's dirt and clothing in the wound. Looks like you missed smashing any of the bones. Quite lucky really."

The man relaxed his gritted teeth as she finished peeling the bloody field dressing off. He looked down at the mess his shoulder had become and then smiled at her.

"You think that's lucky?"

"It looks worse than it is. We need to get it cleaned up before that morphine wears off or it's going to hurt like hell. And then we need to get you to a surgical unit as quickly as we can to start putting it back together properly."

"OK, start when you're ready."

Janet nodded. "Sandra, can you sit across the table, please?" She waited until Sandra was settled in the spot she had indicated. "I need to do this carefully, so I don't want our patient here flinching and moving. If you hold his hand, that'll keep him nice and still."

Sandra looked doubtful. "He's a big man. I'm not sure I'll be able to hold him if he moves."

Janet smiled and looked at her patient. "Sandra, I was a soldier's wife for quite a few years, you may remember. If he's holding the hand of an attractive woman he won't want to show the pain and he'll stay still even when he wants to scream. At least, that's the way it would work with a British soldier, in my experience."

Raoul chuckled behind her. "It's the same for ours, I promise you."

"Good. Sandra, take his hand and gently bring it towards you till I say stop."

Sandra reached across the table and took the wounded man's hand. She gently and slowly brought it towards her. He carried on smiling at her, though she could see his left hand clenching with the pain.

"That's far enough, just hold it there." She turned to the soldier, who still hadn't given his name. "Are you ready? I'm sorry, this is going to hurt, but we need to get the dirt out of there as soon as we can and it's quite a way to the hospital."

He nodded, never taking his eyes off Sandra's. "Before you start. Will I be able to play the violin after this?"

"Once the healing's done, no problem."

The man grinned. "That's good to know. I couldn't play it before."

Chapter 55

David Red Cloud came through the cabin door as Janet finished cleaning the wound. The injured man had not flinched, although his face was drenched with sweat. She applied a clean field dressing and tied it off before fitting a sling to immobilize the arm.

"And now I've got some good news for you."

"What's that?"

"Now it's time to give you a second shot of morphine. It should hold you until we get you to the hospital and into surgery."

"How am I getting there?"

"That'll be me and my pickup truck," said Megan.

David grunted. "Unless you want to use the Beaver? That's what I came to tell you. We've spotted Jim's aircraft on approach."

Megan shook her head and wiped a stray strand of hair from her face. "Too late. It'll be dark before we could get him loaded and the plane refueled. Plus, Jim doesn't have clearance for night flying yet. So you're stuck with me."

"And me," said Janet. "I'd better come with you and talk to the doctors about what I've done so far. Our friend here is going to be too fuzzy to make sense very shortly."

The wounded man looked up at Janet. "And is my friend Sandra coming too? I need someone to hold my hand."

Janet smiled at him. "You're going to be just fine, aren't you? Sandra, do you want to come? We'll go and have a drink somewhere civilized, after we drop this reprobate off."

Sandra gave a small smile. "If I can have my hand back I'll go and get my jacket."

Megan looked at Raoul and David. "And you two had better go and tell Jim what's been going on here while he's been swanning around, having a good time."

The three women were ready to climb into the pickup by the time Jim and his two companions reached the cabin. They looked around at all the spent brass cartridges lying around in the forest edge and at the bullet holes peppering the stout wooden trunks of the walls.

Geordie and Ivan wandered across to inspect the row of men sitting cross-legged under the watchful eyes of the Heiltsuk. Ivan recognized the bad-tempered old man, Silas, from one of their previous visits to this area.

"Nice stick, Silas. What's that for? They need a spanking?" Geordie asked with a broad grin.

Silas grunted and pointed with his ornately carved weapon. "Ask the one with the wet pants. He's just had a lesson in First Nation history."

Ivan tapped Geordie on the arm and pointed down to the rocky beach. There, a Heiltsuk Qatuwa was nosing in to the shore. Four men stowed their painted paddles, climbed out, then lifted the body of the first sniper out of the canoe and carried it up the beach. They laid it down gently next to the other dead attackers and walked across to see David. As they reached him the first of the four held out the sniper rifle with its large telescopic sight. David shook his head and pointed up the short staircase to where the other weapons had been stacked.

Inside, Jim crossed the room to Megan. He took her in his arms and held her close before kissing her forehead.

"Looks like it was bit exciting while I was away?"

She looked up at him with serious eyes. "More than you know. I think Santa's sledge is going to be heavily loaded with stuff for Simon this year. He saved your life and now he's saved your baby's life."

"What happened?"

Megan smiled. "I'll let him tell you about it. I have to take our wounded soldier to the hospital and then we are having a short girls' night out."

"Take someone with you as an escort."

"Jim, I don't need an escort. I'll take the shotgun."

"I think a pump action shotgun in a hospital is going to be a bit obvious. Take this." He pulled out his Webley revolver from the back of his belt and handed it to her. "The sight of that hand cannon should be enough to frighten off any would-be problems."

She looked down at the heavy pistol. Jim was right, it was an ugly-looking weapon, but convincing. She took it from him, cracked it open and checked the load. It slipped comfortably into the deep pocket of her winter jacket.

Janet walked up to them. "If you've finished canoodling with my ex-husband we need to go. The sooner we get our boy here into a nice clean bed with pretty nurses the sooner he'll stop mooning over Sandra."

Megan smiled. "Be right there. We can compare notes about Jim all the way to town. Jim, go talk to Simon. He's just killed a man and the reaction hasn't set in yet. He needs to know it was justified. Let him talk it out."

Jim nodded. "I know the drill. Once I've talked to him I'll let Ivan have a word. He's the best I know at this kind of thing."

"Good idea. I think he hero-worships Ivan just a bit. Almost as much as he does you."

Jim looked into Megan's eyes. "How are you doing, though?"

"I'll be fine. I've got the girls to talk to once we get to the hospital."

Chapter 56

Aristide Papadakis sat in the back of the borrowed Land Rover watching the controlled confusion as the Cypriot Police assembled their strike force and loaded them into a convoy of seven other Land Rovers. Matt, his team leader, leaned against the vehicle side, idly watching and chewing a long-expired piece of gum.

"So Ari, how does it feel to be back in the old country?"

"My old country is Brooklyn, Matt. My family came from Athens anyway. I've never been to Cyprus before."

His team leader turned and looked at him. "No? I thought that's why they sent you over from Langley for this job."

Ari chuckled. "Last minute replacement. The guy who should have come fell down the damned stairs on his way to a briefing. Broke his leg in three places."

"So why'd they pick you?"

"It says on my file I speak fluent Greek. You see the local LEOs laughing behind their hands when I speak to them? Seems I speak it with a Brooklyn accent."

"That where you learned it?"

"Had to. My granddad never learned English even after being in the States for twenty years or more. And I lived over the Greek restaurant my folks run, so I was hearing Greek all day long."

Matt looked over at the third team member who was sitting in the shade of the police barracks wall and waved him over. "So how come the CIA haven't deployed you to Greece before now?"

Ari watched the lanky figure of Ralph uncurl itself from the rock he sat on and amble across towards them. "I'm not field operative. Signals Intercept Analyst, that's me. I sit all day in a cubicle listening to people talking about Greek food and soccer. Every night I go home at the same time to my wife. I don't do excitement."

"What's up?" Ralph asked as he slumped against the vehicle.

"It looks like we're nearly ready to go."

"How the hell can you tell?"

Matt grinned. "The chaos is slowing down and the Chief Inspector just came out on the steps over there and is looking around."

Ari shielded his eyes against the morning sun that was just peeping over the barracks wall. "Are we sure he's the only guy who knows this is going down?"

Matt shrugged. "That's what they told me. He was called into the Minister's office and briefed on the raid. None of these men know where we are going and he has had every one of them hand in their cell phones. He will lead and control the raid once we get there."

Ralph stood up and stretched. "So it should be a complete surprise, you think?"

"I guess we'll find out. Here we go. He's signaling start engines. Ralph, you drive. Ari, hang on back there. These roads can be a bit rough."

The Chief Inspector stalked to the vehicle by the gate and climbed in. The gate swung open and the trucks left, one after the other in rapid succession, with the CIA observer team following on behind. The lead vehicle set a fast pace and the convoy was out of the city in minutes, with the roads quiet this early in the morning. They barreled through the countryside, kicking up clouds of gritty dust as they rammed through a couple of small villages on the way to the villa on the slopes of Troodos mountain.

The convoy raced down the narrow lanes until the lead car swung in to the wide open gate of the villa. They drove beneath the shady trees and slid to a halt on the stones of the driveway in front of the imposing house. The police officers swarmed out of the Land Rovers with their weapons at the ready. The Chief Inspector stood in the middle of it all detailing groups of men to take positions around the house. Satisfied, he strode towards the wide marble steps that led to the tall, wide front door, with two files of men trotting behind him. As he passed the CIA team he beckoned them to follow him.

Matt swung his legs out of the Land Rover and gave his men a sideways nod towards the house. "If this was a movie this would be the part where I say 'Showtime!', don't you think?"

The three men walked calmly up the white stairs and into the cool interior. They looked around at the imposing paintings hanging on the walls of the wide hallway. A bowl of white flowers had been knocked over on the highly polished mahogany table in the middle of the hall and water dripped to the floor.

From all around them they could hear the clumping of police boots and excited shouts as the officers ran from room to room, attempting to secure the house. The crashing and commotion slowed as it became clear that the villa was empty. The Chief Inspector came across the hall to them, red-faced and irritated.

"They are gone. The computers are gone or destroyed and the filing cabinets are empty. We have nothing."

He looked towards the door as two of his men came in dragging an older man between them. They stopped in front of their commander and let the old man find his feet.

"And who are you?"

"I am Dimitri. I look after the gardens for Miss Calanthe. She likes the gardens to be neat. Oh, somebody has knocked over her vase. She will be displeased."

"Never mind that, what happened here?"

"Today?"

"Yes, today. What happened?"

The old man scratched his ear and looked at the police commander. "Same as every day. I came to the foot of the stairs to get my instructions from Miss Calanthe. She is very proud of her garden, she tells me exactly what she wants me to do each day."

"And then?"

"Then? Oh yes, the manservant ran down the steps with the phone for Miss Calanthe and gave it to her. She listened for a minute, then she turned away from me and ran into the villa shouting for all her people. There was a lot of shouting and noise and the cars were all brought round to the front very quickly. I had just finished raking the gravel back in place when you came and ruined it again."

"Keep going. What did they do next?"

"They all ran out of the house carrying papers and those small computers. They loaded them into the cars and they drove away in a big cloud of dust. No, that's not right, one car stayed behind and two of the men went back into the villa with big hammers and I heard them smashing things. Then they left as well."

The police commander's ears were glowing red with irritation and embarrassment by now. "You two take him to the station and take his statement. Get it all down." He turned to the CIA team who were standing quietly by. "It seems we have been betrayed. Probably by somebody in the minister's office." He held his hands out and shrugged in a helpless gesture. "It is ever the way."

Chapter 57

The three-man CIA team stood at the top of the marble stairway and watched the Cypriot police drive away in a cloud of dust and spinning tires. The search of the villa had become desultory as soon as they realized Calanthe had been warned and everything they needed had been taken. As quiet descended the three Americans walked back inside the cool hallway.

Matt looked around speculatively. "Either of you two hungry? I missed my breakfast for this foul-up."

Ralph brightened up at the mention of food. "Hey, Ari, didn't you say your old man ran a restaurant? Any of his skills rub off on you?"

Ari looked around. "If you know where the kitchen is, I can knock something up."

Matt pointed at a discreet corridor that led off the main hall. "Down that way. I found it during the first look round."

They walked down the corridor and into a large, well-equipped kitchen. Ari took a look through the food stores while Matt and Ralph found plates and cutlery. Ari carried a mound of food items across to the cooker and turned to the other two.

"This should take me about twenty minutes. Then you find out what real Greek cooking is about."

Matt grinned at Ralph. "Sounds good to me. We can take a look round while we're waiting, to see how the other half live. Ralph, you take upstairs, I'll take down."

Ari carried on happily chopping slicing and crashing about with pans until breakfast took shape. He was about to put it in a warm box on the oven when the other two walked back into the room.

"Good timing. Take a chair and I'll bring it over."

Ari dished the food onto the plates and walked to the table. As he did so he saw the other two members of the team smiling at him strangely. He paused and looked at them; then he saw the laptop computer resting on the table between them.

"Where the hell was that?"

"The lovely Calanthe had it hidden under the pillow of her bed. Ralph found it. I'm guessing she was using it last night and forgot about it in all the excitement."

"Do we know what's on it?" Ari asked as he sat down.

"Not yet. We thought we'd get an analyst on the job after breakfast."

"Me? Yeah, OK. Maybe we should take it back to the office before the bad guys come back?"

Matt nodded as he chewed his food. "Good thinking. Hey, this tastes good. You know what it needs? A nice bottle of celebratory wine."

Ari stood up wiping his fingers on a paper napkin. "I saw the wine cellar over there, down those steps. I'll see if they have a good Greek wine for you."

He left the table, crossed the room and trotted down the cellar steps. At the bottom he found himself in a cool, concrete-lined cellar with a vaulted ceiling. The racks of wine bottles were impressive in quantity. Now to see about the quality. He wandered slowly along a rack, lifting bottles out and examining the labels. He stumbled slightly as the toe of his shoe caught on something on the floor.

Looking down, he found a semi-circular groove worn in the concrete floor. Not deep, in fact he was surprised his toe had caught on it. Just bad luck. He returned to the search for a good bottle. As he found one he smiled and turned back towards the stairs.

His smile faded and he turned back to look at the groove. He looked at the rack and then back to the groove. Putting the bottle down, he walked across to the left-hand end of the wine rack and pulled. It was heavy with the wine bottles, but swung smoothly towards him. He stood staring at the wide metal door that had been exposed.

Recovering himself, Ari walked to the bottom of the staircase to the kitchen. "Matt! Ralph! Get down here!"

He heard the chairs scrape upstairs as the two men stood. He waited and watched as they came down the stairs. Matt looked at him enquiringly and he pointed to the pulled-out wine rack. The three of them walked to the end of the wine rack with Ari holding his bottle to avoid it getting kicked over. Ralph tried the door to find it was locked. He grinned.

"Ari, you may be the wine specialist on this team, but now it's time for my party trick."

He withdrew a small leather wallet from his pocket and flipped it open to expose a range of small bent metal tools in elastic loops. He dropped to his knees in front of the metal door and selected two of the tools. Ari realized he was looking at lock picks. The tools slipped into the keyhole and Ralph began to manipulate them, with his head tilted to one side, listening for the sound of the levers moving.

The lock clicked and Ralph smiled up at them as he tried the door handle and pulled the door slightly towards them. He checked through the slightly open door for any booby traps and then got to his feet.

"Looks OK," he said as he swung the door open.

Matt stepped into the room that had been exposed and fumbled beside the door for a light switch. Finding it, he flipped it on and neon strip lights flickered into life. Ralph gave a low whistle as he gazed around the room. Along the left-hand wall was a long wooden rack half full of Russian-made AK74 automatic rifles, standing vertically. At the end of the room he could see rows of American 66mm anti-tank rockets laid out, side by side, on three large tables.

Ari walked forwards to the stack of heavy-duty green plastic crates that ran down the middle of the room. He ran his finger along the smooth surface and looked at it. No sign of dust, so these boxes had not been here long. He read the yellow painted printing on the side of the top crate and turned to Matt.

"So what's a Javelin?"

"Javelin?"

"That's what it says here."

Matt moved to stand next to Ari and looked at the crate closely. "A Javelin, my analyst friend, is an Anti-Tank Guided Missile, and one hell of a weapon to be sitting in a cellar in Cyprus. Get that one open, will you?"

Turning away, the team leader walked towards Ralph, who was standing by another wall of crates. These, too, were made of smooth green plastic with yellow writing down the side.

"And what have you got there?" Matt asked.

Ralph looked up. "Stingers. Ten of them, with control units. You don't think these could be …?"

Matt nodded. "They could be. We'll need to check serial numbers. Get one of them open."

Ari flipped open the sliver metal catches at each end of the Javelin crate and lifted the lid clear. Inside, cushioned by precisely cut high-density foam, the missile lay in all its deadly menace. He watched as Matt came back to him and read the serial number, then compared it to whatever he was reading from the screen of his smartphone.

"What were you and Ralph talking about just now?"

Matt looked up from his screen. "What? Oh yes. About six months ago there was a raid on a National Guard armory in Montana. Two of the people on security detail were murdered and weapons were stolen, including Stingers and Javelins. We thought it was the work of one of those separatist or survivalist groups that seem to proliferate up there and it was kept quiet so we didn't cause a panic."

"Why would there be a panic?"

"Ari, you really need to get some training about weapons when you get back to Langley. A Stinger would be ideal for bringing down a civilian airliner on approach to any airport in the country. If there was a scare like that, then transport across the US could be disrupted."

"And you have the serial numbers of the weapons that were taken?"

"Every CIA field operative around the world has them. Things like that come out on intelligence bulletins for us to look out for. It's opening up now. Read the number on that plate to me."

Ari read the number and Matt scrolled down through the short list. He nodded and turned to Ralph.

"OK, Ralph, read me the number on that one."

Ralph turned back to the box he had opened and read the number from the silver and black plate on the side of the missile. Matt scrolled again through the list on his smartphone, then grinned.

"We hit pay dirt. These are the weapons that came out of that armory. These people are even more serious players than the Brits thought. Take a look round for any small arms ammunition. There were some specialist rounds taken at the same time that we need to find."

"Not to appear dumb, but what were they?"

"Armor-piercing rounds. Designed to penetrate a bulletproof vest. If that stuff gets out in the world it could pose a massive threat to all law enforcement officers. If they are more nervous they could end up shooting first and asking questions later. A terrorist's dream as trust in the police vanishes."

The search of the cellar did not find the armor-piercing bullets, despite rummaging through many boxes of conventional rounds. Matt eventually called a halt.

"Ralph, stay here and lock that up again. I need to call this in to Langley and I'll get those cops back again before Calanthe and her people return."

Chapter 58

Matt conveniently forgot to mention the laptop computer they had found when the Cypriot police reappeared. They waited until the Chief Inspector had placed his men to his own satisfaction before they waved and drove away to their discreet office overlooking the seafront in Larnaca.

Ari seated himself at the desk by the window and opened up the laptop. He watched as it went through its startup routine and was surprised that it did not call for a password. It seemed that Calanthe had been over-confident in her physical security. No doubt one of her staff was catching hell for forgetting this machine.

The file list that came up when he selected it was extensive. This was going to take some time. He settled in and started to work through the folders. There were at least three email accounts with messages stored in sub files and then he found files of women's fashion items. Obviously Calanthe wanted to look her best when dealing with customers.

He found a file labeled *Amphitrite* and recalled that this was the name of Poseidon's wife, the legendary goddess of the sea. Opening it up, he found photographs of a remarkably beautiful white motor yacht. Searching further, he found documents referring to maintenance and upgrades to the boat. The invoice for the Larnaca marina caught his eye. He found it was the bill for services to the boat called *Amphitrite* owned by the

Christophides family. He spun round in his chair and called Matt across to look at the screen.

"Look at this. According to the police, Calanthe has not gone out through the airport or caught any of the ferries. This says she has her own boat and, looking at it, I think that it's perfectly capable of traveling long distances. It has a berth in the marina here, so we should be able to see if it's still in port."

"I'll take Ralph and see if we can find it. You keep going through that computer."

Ari went across to the fridge and took a can of local cola back to his table. It was far too sugary and nowhere near as good as the colas he was used to. It was cold, though, and he was thirsty. He sipped at it as he carried on searching the file system. He nearly choked on the drink when he opened up the next file.

Before his unbelieving eyes he found he was looking at a letter from a group calling themselves *Harakat-e-Inqilab-e-Islami* who were planning to attack the USA and had particular needs in weapons. They used a Russian name for the devices that he was not familiar with, but as he read on and they discussed yield and damage areas it became clear that the weapons were nuclear. He swallowed hard. A potential nuclear attack on the US and he was the only one who knew about it. The next file was the response from Calanthe stating that they had four of the weapons that were needed. Next was discussion about price, delivery dates and locations. He checked his watch; only four days away. The targets were given:

Washington, Boston, New York and Philadelphia. With that spread up the east coast the area would be devastated.

He looked in vain for any information about where the weapons were stored and how they would be moved. Eventually, he did find a list of all the places where the organization stored weapons ready for sale. The contact details of the person in charge of each was given, with further details of the people working for them. He sat back and stared out of the window.

He was still staring when the door opened and Matt came back into the apartment followed by Ralph. "Slacking? You were right about the boat, but it's gone. They left port this morning, according to the harbour master. No idea where it's heading. Did you find anything else useful?"

Ari turned slowly from the laptop and looked at Matt. "You could say that. We need to talk to someone a long way up the food chain in Langley and they need to get Homeland Security in the room while we do it."

"That sounds serious."

"It doesn't get any more serious. We are going to owe the Brits big time after this."

Chapter 59

Frank steered the RV out of the gas station and back on to the Trans-Canada highway. He was tired and looking forward to taking a break once they found the campground outside Calgary. That was going to be another two or three hours despite the excellent wide road. Emma brought him a coffee in a travel mug and set it in the cup holder by his side.

"You want me to take it for a while?"

He smiled at her. "I'm OK and you're as tired as I am. How about we stay two nights in Calgary and get some rest, before we start the last two days through the Rockies?"

She nodded and turned to look forward at the wide road stretching away in front of them. "I think that's a fine idea. It would be a shame if we ended this trip in a roadside ditch through you being too tired to drive."

"That was my thinking as well. Maybe we'll have time for you to make your pot roast, too. I haven't had that in way too long."

She smiled at him. "If you see a grocery store, pull over and I'll get the things I need for your pot roast. We need a few other things as well."

He nodded forward. "Looks like you get your wish right away. There's a mall coming up. Might be an idea to get the kids some bigger jackets. Winter's coming and we are heading for the mountains."

Emma looked across at him. "Do they need them already? It's a lovely warm day."

"That it is, but winter comes suddenly up here and I've seen a few of the wild animals by the roadside are starting to turn white. That's a sure sign winter is not far away."

"All right. Well, we better get you one as well. You know how you hate the cold, old man."

"And you, too, old lady. Living down in Florida all these years thins the blood. At least, that's my theory."

He pulled the RV over into the right-hand lane and indicated that he was going to turn. Slowing down, he made the turn into the mall car park and found a place to stop near to the buildings.

He turned his driving seat around and looked at the two kids sitting at the dining table. "OK, kids, we are going shopping. You two need a warm jacket and a winter hat with ear flaps. You better find yourself some decent boots and gloves as well, while we're at it."

Geoff groaned, but Marian cheered up at the thought of trawling round a mall buying clothes. All four of them left the RV and Frank locked it carefully before they walked through the glass sliding doors into the shopping mall.

He put an arm around the boy's shoulder. "Never mind, once we've got our stuff we'll go sit in the food court, while these two girls touch everything in the stores. You can choose anything you like to eat."

"Anything?"

"Sure, why not? It's been a long time since we had a chance to eat where somebody else did the cooking."

As expected, finding clothes for Geoff and Frank took no time at all. Emma and Marian were a different story. True to his word, Frank took his grandson to the food court, after a visit to the computer game store and a new game for the laptop. The boy wandered around the various stalls trying the free samples before deciding on Orange Chicken and rice. Frank took a cheeseburger and they settled down to wait.

Frank was just becoming anxious about finding the campsite before nightfall when Emma and Marian appeared round the corner with shopping bags and broad smiles. They flopped down at the table and both sighed.

"You want to eat before we leave?" Franks asked. "Only we're burning daylight here and there's a ways to go yet."

Emma took the hint. "We'll grab something to go and eat it on the road."

Geoff liked that idea. "Me, too. I like eating on the move:"

Frank shook his head in wonder. That boy must have hollow legs. He eats like a horse and never puts any weight on. Collecting the food in flip top Styrofoam boxes didn't take long and Geoff carried all three, while Frank helped with the bags.

With the bags dropped on the big bed at the rear of the RV they were back onto the main highway in minutes. Frank drove and listened to the excited chatter about the things Marian and Emma had bought, while Geoff just ate his burger and checked his Facebook account.

"Oh no!"

Frank picked up on the distress in the boy's voice. "What is it, Geoff?"

"It's Facebook. I must have got the settings wrong. It has been automatically telling my friends where we are. I just had a message asking why I am talking about Georgia when Facebook says we are in Alberta."

Frank sucked his teeth. "Who can see that?"

"Anybody who looks at my page. I'm sorry, Grandpa. I made a mistake."

Frank checked in the big wing mirrors; he could see nothing there to worry about. "Never mind, son, people who never make mistakes never make anything. It'll be all right."

He hoped he was telling the boy the truth.

Chapter 60

Geoff came forward and sat in the co-driver's seat while his Grandma finished her lunch. His shoulders were down and his head sagged forward. He looked at his Grandpa with watery eyes.

"I'm sorry about this, I really am, Grandpa. Are you sure we're going to be OK?"

Frank looked across at the boy and made sure his worry didn't show. "We'll be fine. Have you changed the settings on your laptop now?"

Geoff nodded. "I have, but what if they know where we are?" He looked out at the wide open flat prairie that stretched for miles all around them. "There's nowhere to hide out here if they come looking for us."

"That's true, but it also makes it more difficult for them to sneak up on us, doesn't it?"

He hoped he sounded confident. In truth, Frank was a worried man, though there was no point in letting the kids get upset. There'd be time enough for that if the killers found them. He checked his wing mirrors again and then scanned the road ahead for anything that looked out of place.

Emma came forward and sat next to him as they approached Redcliff. "Geoff is very upset. Can you say something to him?"

"I already have. He'll get over it and I'll sit him down for a talk this evening when we get to Calgary. It's an easy mistake to make."

He paused and stared into the wing mirror. In it he could see two pickup trucks neck and neck following him up the road. He knew he was just above the speed limit and they were closing fast. He put his foot down on the accelerator pedal a little harder and kept watching them approach.

"We've got company. Emma, can you get ready to take the wheel? Don't slow down and when I tell you, move into the middle of the road so they can't get by."

Emma leaned forward and looked into the mirror on her side of the RV. "Are you sure they're after us?"

Frank looked again, he was in time to see a man in each truck rise up and lean over the cab roof. Even at this distance he could see they were holding rifles.

"I'm sure. Move over here and take the wheel."

He stood and let Emma slide into the seat below him. She took the wheel and he moved out of her way and back into the living area of the RV. He opened the cabinet beneath the sink and pulled out the MP5 submachine gun he had stowed in there as well as the two extra magazines.

He turned round to find the two children staring at him, their faces anxious. "Right, you two, lie down on the floor and stay there till I tell you different."

He opened the locker next to him and dragged out two heavy suitcases. He laid them on the floor behind the children. Full of clothes, they might just stop a bullet. It wasn't much, but it was all he had.

He walked quickly to the rear of the RV and knelt down by the bed. He moved the curtaining to one side slightly and peered out. The thin metal walls of the vehicle would not stop any flying bullets, so concealment was his only choice at this point.

He waited until he could be absolutely sure this was an attack and then yelled loudly to Emma. "Now, Emma! Move to the middle!"

She had been waiting for his instruction and watching the pickups get closer, so swung the wheel immediately. The big RV rolled on its soft suspension as she weaved it out to block both traffic lanes. Both pickups slowed for a second, then the left-hand one of the pair drifted left on to the median strip and accelerated to get past them. Frank saw the gunman in the back swing his weapon across and grin as he prepared to fire.

The first two rounds struck the back window and shattered the glass; the next three went into the small bathroom. Two shattered the small washbasin and the third punched a hole in the toilet bowl, spilling water all over the floor.

Frank had no more time and took his chance. Rising up, he pushed the MP5 through the shattered window and let loose with a full magazine at the pickup that was trying to overtake them. It was a long time since he had fired an automatic weapon, not since Vietnam in fact. His training from those years came back to him from somewhere in the back of his mind that he usually kept closed off and locked. The rounds flew. Two struck the gunman in the chest and flung him to the bed of the truck. Another smashed the windscreen glass and others punched through the bodywork, along the side of the truck. The round that sealed the deal was the one that ripped into the front tire, slicing it open with an explosion of compressed air. The truck swerved as steering was lost and then flipped completely over, again and again, until it came to rest on its roof.

Frank had no time to look and see if there were survivors. In truth, he didn't care. He ripped the empty magazine off the weapon and inserted the next, before pulling the cocking lever and turning his attention to the second pickup.

Chapter 61

Joe Martello watched in horror as the first pickup spun in the air and bounced across the median strip of the highway. Then he smiled. The payoff for taking these kids out would only have to be shared two ways now. He raised his fist and banged on the cab roof.

"Shut this bastard down! Come on, man, open fire!"

Standing in the bed of the pickup and steadying himself across the cab roof, Brett Ogley had every intention of doing just that. Watching his friend get trashed in the first pickup had distracted him and now it was time for payback. He took a firmer grip on the assault rifle in his hands and raised it to aim at the speeding RV. At this distance he couldn't miss. His target looked like the side of a barn.

As he flipped the safety catch to automatic he saw the white hair of the man in the RV come into view through the rear window and smiled to himself. The smile vanished as the MP5 spat fire through the broken window. A round pinged off the cab roof next to him and he dropped to the cargo floor of the truck to avoid the next. Another two rounds came through the windscreen and exited through the window at the back of the cab, showering him in sparkling glass fragments.

The next burst was aimed at the engine compartment of the truck, in an attempt to slow it down or immobilize it. One round smacked into the brake cylinder and ripped the lower pipework away. The hydraulic fluid stared to leak out, but fell clear of the hot engine and had no effect on their speed. A second round tore a gouge through the windscreen washer bottle and the rest of the 9mm rounds bounced harmlessly off the engine block.

Another burst shredded the seats on the passenger side of the cab, missing the driver, who stamped harder on the accelerator to try and overtake the RV. The big clumsy vehicle weaved backwards and forwards across the lanes of the highway and the driver decided against trying to overtake on the median strip, after what had happened to his companion.

Emma could see the wide Trans-Canada highway stretching ahead of her and knew it was only a matter of time before the faster truck managed to get past them. She had to do something. As she chewed her bottom lip with worry, she saw the green and white road sign on her right pointing the way to CFB Suffield five kilometers away. If she could get there, surely the attackers would not follow them on to a military base? She saw the side road come up and heaved the wheel around, nearly toppling the heavy RV on its side. The wheels on the right lifted off the road then fell back down as she completed the turn.

Behind the RV the pickup made the turn, almost throwing the gunman out of the back. He raised himself back up to the cab roof and aimed his weapon. He started to fire in short controlled bursts, making sure to hit the RV every time.

Frank ran forward and threw himself down between the suitcases and the two crying children with the dog lying between them on the floor. Emma kept the RV wandering from side to side on the much narrower country road as she pressed the vehicle to its highest speed. The ditches either side stopped the pickup from passing them. She could do nothing about the bullets hitting them and tearing through the thin metal walls. Two of those bullets crashed through the windscreen causing the wind to whistle past her ear, though she could still see to drive.

She continually checked her mirrors to keep the pickup in view. Her swerving was making things difficult for the gunman, but it was only a matter of time before somebody was hit. She looked again in the mirrors, then looked forward. She could not believe her eyes. Rumbling down the road towards her was a massive tank. The armored vehicle took up more than its share of the road and she would have to slow to get past it.

Chapter 62

Emma was wrong, it wasn't a tank. It was a Challenger armored recovery vehicle, designed to pull tanks out of ditches or to drag them from a battlefield when damaged. It was trundling down the road from Camp Crowfoot, the British Army base at Suffield, to test out the engine that had just been replaced by the workshops.

Corporal Tanner, the vehicle commander, sat on top of the steel monster enjoying the sunshine and chatting though the intercom to his driver, Craftsman Hearn, who sat inside the body of the vehicle. Both men were Recovery Mechanics who belonged to the workshop of the Royal Electrical and Mechanical Engineers based at the base behind them. The rearing horse and lightning strike of their cap badges glistened in their greasy berets.

Tanner saw the RV driving erratically towards them and ordered Hearn to slow down and move to the right, as far as he could. At the next swerve of the camper van he saw the pickup behind it and saw the gunman firing at the vehicle in front of him. He realized he needed to do something and do it fast. He gave the driver his instructions and waited for his moment.

The RV squeezed past with nearside wheels spinning dust up from the road edge. Tanner saw the pale face of the woman gripping the steering wheel as she went by. He also saw the bullet holes in the windshield. He gave the order and the 61200 kilograms of metal jerked as the right-hand track spun forwards and the left-hand one went backwards. The massive vehicle spun on the spot, tearing up the road surface and forming an impenetrable barricade between the RV and the pickup.

In the speeding pickup, Martello slammed his foot down on the brake pedal and was alarmed as it sank to the floor of the cab with virtually no resistance. The pickup slowed hardly at all and he heard the screaming from Ogley as he, too, saw what was about to happen when an unstoppable object meets an immovable one.

Tanner and Hearn ducked down into the vehicle as the pickup plowed into the armored side of the recovery vehicle. The tail end of the pickup rose into the air and Ogley was catapulted out of the truck and over the top of the armor-plated side screen. His neck snapped as he hit the road surface beyond and he knew no more. Martello was not as lucky.

The pickup striking the armored vehicle at that speed stopped instantly and Martello was impaled on the steering column as the wheel collapsed. The engine tried to carry on moving forwards and ripped out all the pipe connections in the engine bay. Gasoline and the remaining hydraulic oil sprayed across the hot engine and across the sparking electrical connections that flailed around. There was a gap of almost two seconds before the fuel ignited in a fireball that enveloped the cabin of the pickup and rolled over the armored vehicle. Tanner could hear the pickup driver screaming as he rose up and looked down at the fire consuming the truck. He and Hearn fired their on board fire extinguishers at the wreck and then reversed the steel monster away from the mess that blocked the road.

The two soldiers climbed down off the vehicle and contemplated the fire raging in front of them. In the distance they could hear the sirens as the camp fire truck raced out of the barracks towards them.

"Those fire guys are pretty fast," Hearn said, looking up the road.

Tanner nodded. "They have to be, to get out onto the prairie when the training groups start a grass fire. The oil companies would sue the hell out of us if we burnt one of their wells down."

Hearn looked at the burnt and blistered paintwork up the side of their recovery vehicle. "You do know we are going to have to repaint the whole damn thing now, don't you? The ASM is going to have a screaming fit when he sees that mess."

Tanner shrugged. "We were already on his shit list for ruining the engine, so we'll just be a bit deeper in it this time."

Hearn nodded his agreement. "We'd better take this beast off the road and back to the workshops. You've got the crash report to fill out and I can't wait to see how you explain this one."

A kilometer further on Emma steered the damaged RV up to the gate of Camp Crowfoot. The Military Policeman manning the gate, in his scarlet beret and camouflaged uniform, held up his hand to stop her and then walked slowly around the vehicle looking at all the holes. He came back to the driver's side window and looked at the pale and shaking woman.

"Looks like you ran into some damned big insects on the way up here, ma'am."

She gave him a weak smile. "Something like that."

The policeman smiled back. "Pull your vehicle over to the side of the road there, please ma'am, and we'll see what's going on here."

They both turned around and watched the camp fire truck fly through the gate with its sirens screaming towards the pillar of black smoke down the road. "I take it that's something to do with you?"

Emma nodded tiredly. "I guess it is. Over there, you say?"

"That's right. I'm just going to call the security officer. He won't keep you waiting."

Chapter 63

Inside the RV Frank sat up painfully and tapped the kids on the shoulder. "Sounds like it's all over. You can get up now."

He looked down as the two tearstained faces lifted up and looked at him. This had been a close one and clearly the children had realized it. There would be nightmares tonight, for sure, and not just in the children's dreams.

Frank levered himself to his feet and walked to the front of the vehicle. He put a hand on Emma's shoulder and felt her shaking with the release of tension. He sat down in the co-driver's seat and held her hand.

"Oh god, Frank, I was so scared. I thought we were finished."

He patted her hand. "And we would have been, except for you. You just saved the kids' lives and a grateful old man."

She smiled at him and sniffed quietly as she wiped away the tears of relief. "Are the children all right?"

He nodded. "Scared out of their wits, but untouched and, so is Kika. They'll take a while to get over it. It was pretty frightening back there, but then it always is with your driving."

There was a knock on the door and Frank forced himself out of his chair and walked across to open it. Outside were two army officers both looking along the side of the damaged RV. The taller one looked up at Frank and nodded.

"Good morning, sir," the taller one said. "I'm Lieutenant Colonel Mike Durant, the base commander, and this is my security officer, Captain Radcliffe. Would you mind telling us what's been happening?"

"Hello, Colonel. I'm Frank Eastman and that's my wife Emma in the driving seat. My two grandchildren are in the back as well, a bit shaken up as you might imagine."

"I see, well, perhaps we should take them somewhere away from the RV to calm down while you tell me your story. We've got a nice coffee shop just over there and they do some good sugary cakes that might help."

"That's kind of you." Frank leaned back through the door behind him. "Emma, kids, come out now. We're going to have a drink and a cake with these nice people."

The three in the van collected their scattered wits and climbed down. The Colonel led them across the street to the coffee shop. Emma and the two children settled in one booth while Frank sat in another with the two officers.

Frank stirred his coffee and looked at the two men sitting quietly waiting for him to speak. "A little while ago I got a phone call from my son-in-law, Ivan Thomas. He used to be a Sergeant Major in your army. He's retired now."

"Wait a minute, I know a Sergeant Major Thomas. He works for Major Jim Wilson, is that the one?"

"Well yes, he does work for Wilson," Frank said, surprised.

The Colonel gave Captain Radcliffe a big smile. "This should be a good story. Jim Wilson is a complete trouble magnet. He was here not long ago with Thomas and a Sergeant. What was his name? Ah, Peters, that's right."

It was Radcliffe's turn to look surprised. "Geordie Peters? I met him in Afghanistan after he pulled that mad stunt with the bulldozer. Crazy man, but highly capable."

Colonel Durant turned back to Frank. "Sorry, Mr. Eastman, do go on with your story."

"As I was saying, Ivan phoned me and told me to get the kids and get the hell out. It seems these three had gotten themselves into trouble with some crooks and a contract had been put out on their lives. They must have done something special because the contract includes Ivan's two children. We've been on the run ever since and this was the fourth attempt that's been made to kill us."

The Colonel sat back in his seat and looked at Frank. "Would you like to meet the two young men who saved you? Dan, will you go and find them please? Bring them here if the ASM has finished shouting at them."

The Captain left and Frank turned to the Colonel. "ASM? What's that?" Frank asked.

"An ASM is the Artificer Sergeant Major. He runs my workshop, fixing the tanks and other trucks for the battle groups that come out here for training. This one is quite a fearsome character and very protective of his equipment. Stopping your attackers has damaged the recovery vehicle, so the two soldiers will almost certainly be getting a damn good shouting at by now. Don't worry, I'll smooth it over later."

"Getting shouted at for doing the right thing. It sounds like my time in the Marines in Vietnam."

The Colonel nodded and smiled. "The same in all armies, I guess. Now, we'll also need to find you a place to sleep while we repair your RV."

"Can you do that?"

"Oh yes. I have a full REME workshop here. We can get just about anything repaired or built from scratch. But tell me, where are you heading for after this?"

"We need to get to the coast of British Columbia. That's where the three guys are holed up trying to find a way to put a stop to all this while keeping the families safe. Ivan tells me they have some special people looking after them out there."

Durant smiled again. "I think I can help with that. I'll sort something out once your RV is ready for the road again."

Chapter 64

On the bridge of HMS Huntingdon, Lieutenant Commander Nick Evans surveyed the calm blue waters of the Mediterranean as his Type 23 frigate carved its way towards Malta. The goodwill visit to Valetta harbour would give his crew some well-earned shore leave. The last two months of patrolling off the Syrian coast with the Americans and other allied navies had been taxing and even a little bit dull.

Now they had been relieved and were on their way home with just a couple of flag-waving stops to be made. It would be good to be back and then he could see how much of a mess his football-mad sons had made of his garden. He turned away and spoke to the lieutenant who stood behind him.

"I'm going down for breakfast, John. You have the bridge."

"I have the bridge, sir."

Evans had made it almost all the way back to his cabin when he heard the tannoy call. "Captain to the bridge. Captain to the bridge."

He sighed and turned around making his way back up to the spot he had just vacated. He looked round and everything seemed normal.

"What is it, John?"

"Admiralty signal, sir. Came in encoded and marked urgent. It's being decoded now."

Evans grunted. "Huh, they probably want us to invite some buck-toothed female relative of the Admiral on board for the cocktail party in Malta."

He opened the flimsy signal that the yeoman handed him. He read it twice and then again. He folded it and handed it to the Officer of the Watch.

"Take a look at that, John. There might be some excitement in the offing. The Admiral's relative will have to wait."

Lieutenant John Charteris looked up from the message and grinned at his commander. "Stopping and boarding a motor yacht with terrorist sympathizers on board. I should say so. May I volunteer to lead the boarding party, sir?"

Evans nodded his agreement while scanning forward through his powerful binoculars. "Of course, John. I think you'd be ideal for the task. Select your crews and arm them. I think we'll send two boats across when we find her, and let's have the chopper ready to launch in, shall we say, thirty minutes. Your relief should be here in about five minutes anyway, so better get started."

As Charteris left the bridge Evans smiled to himself. That young man was going to go far if there was any justice. He read the signal again. His instructions were to stop and board the motor yacht *Amphitrite*, conduct a thorough search and arrest Calanthe Christophides if she was aboard. The yacht was being used to support terrorism, so he was permitted to use whatever force was necessary to carry out his task. Exactly the sort of free hand every frigate commander since the days of Nelson had dreamed about.

Sub Lieutenant Greenway appeared on the bridge to stand his watch; he seemed a little flustered to find his Captain there, but no watch officer to relieve. Evans nodded to him and returned to scanning forward. This exercise would be good for Greenway, he thought, give him something to get his teeth into.

"Right then, Paul," Evans said. "We have a task from the Admiralty. A boat owned by a group who are supporting and enabling terrorism has left Larnaca in the last few hours and it seems we are the nearest naval vessel. We are to stop and board her. All other allied units have the same orders, but I want her. What do you recommend?"

The young officer flushed slightly and stared out to sea. Evans waited to see if he was thinking clearly. He did like thinking officers.

"Well, sir, we are close to Cyprus, so she can't be too far away from us. We need to put our best operators on the radar and get the Lynx in the air in the direction we think she is moving. I don't recommend action stations until we are closer. No point in tiring the crew until we have to."

Evans nodded. "Go on."

"We don't know if the yacht is armed, but with terrorists that is a real possibility. I would have the Lynx armed with the waist-mounted machine gun, rather than just missiles. That way we have a stepped response. The boarding party should be armed and the 4.5 inch gun should be loaded and ready for a shot across the bows if that becomes necessary."

"Good. Anything else?"

"Yes, sir. I think I would be the ideal person to lead the boarding party, sir."

"Nice try, Paul. The first lieutenant has beaten you to it. If they are as close as we hope then you will stay as Officer of the Watch to support the action. Good enough?"

"Thank you, sir, that will be fine."

Evans hid a smile. It was clear the young man felt it was far from fine. His turn would come and it would be useful to observe him here on the bridge.

Chapter 65

"Radar reports multiple contacts ahead of us, sir."

"Noted. Direct the Lynx to carry out a fly by to identify our target."

The twin-engined Lynx helicopter lifted off from the aft deck and pulled rapidly ahead of the frigate. The boat crews were closed up and awaiting orders. The ship was as ready as she was going to be. They waited for the report from the Lynx pilot.

"Aircraft reports Motor Yacht *Amphitrite* dead ahead on our present course approximately eight miles."

"Thank you, Paul. Full ahead, if you please, and try not to run down any of these fishing boats."

The powerful turbines responded rapidly, driving the ship forward. Evans was pleased to see that Greenway was conning the ship effectively and safely.

The starboard lookout was the first to spot her. "Target ship in sight, sir, dead ahead. Lynx is circling."

"Thank you." Evans turned to Paul. 'Bring us in on his port quarter, if you please. I want to be able to see more of what he is doing. Yeoman, tell him to heave to."

The yeoman turned to his radio. "*Amphitrite, Amphitrite*, this is Royal Navy warship approaching you from astern. Heave to and prepare to be boarded."

They waited. There was no response. "Again please, Yeoman."

"*Amphitrite, Amphitrite*, this is Royal Navy warship approaching you from astern. Heave to and prepare to be boarded."

"Sir, radar reports target has increased speed."

Evans raised his binoculars. Radar was correct. He could see the bow wave of the yacht was increasing. He sucked his teeth, considering his options.

"Very well, Yeoman, give them the fire warning, then instruct the helicopter to move in ready to fire."

"*Amphitrite, Amphitrite*, this is Royal Navy warship approaching you from astern. Heave to and prepare to be boarded. If you do not comply, we will fire upon you."

No response again. Evans waited. He sighed and lowered his binoculars.

"Yeoman, instruct the helicopter to fire a burst across her bows. Paul, have the gun loaded with star shell."

Greenway looked puzzled. "Confirm star shell, sir."

"Confirmed. We will escalate this slowly."

Through the binoculars Evans watched the side door of the helicopter slide open and the heavy machine gun swivel out. He could not hear the firing, but saw the muzzle flashes as the weapon fired a five round burst. The line of white bullet splashes stood out against the bright blue sea, no more than twenty meters in front of the yacht.

"Nice shooting. Remind me to compliment the gunner. Any change in speed from the …?"

"Lynx reports target vessel is returning fire with small arms, sir."

"Very well. Tell them to withdraw to a safe distance. One star shell round from the 4.5 inch gun right above them, if you please."

Greenway passed the order and seconds later the gun mounted on the foredeck fired. The star shell burst directly above the yacht. Far less impressive than when it was used at night, it was still a very bright light and they could not fail to understand the message.

"One more time with the warning, Yeoman."

"*Amphitrite, Amphitrite*, this is Royal Navy warship. Heave to and prepare to be boarded. If you do not comply, we will fire upon you."

The tension was building on the bridge as they waited. "No response, sir."

"Thank you, Yeoman. Mr Greenway, two rounds across her bow. Let's see if that gets her attention."

The foredeck gun spat twice and the rounds flew across the narrowing gap before striking the water and sending up large plumes in front of the yacht.

"Royal Navy Warship. This is *Amphitrite*. We are in international waters and you have no right to stop me. I shall lodge a formal protest."

Evans strode to the radio. "*Amphitrite*, this is Royal Navy warship. Captain speaking. You are a terrorist vessel and under the rules of engagement in force in this area I have every right to stop you. You will heave to now and prepare to be boarded. If you do not comply, I will be obliged to fire into you."

"Radar reports vessel slowing, sir."

"About bloody time. Bring us to a halt off his port side and then launch the boarding party. Keep the helicopter on over watch."

Chapter 66

The first of the boarding party boats came alongside the yacht to where the boarding ladder had been lowered. Lieutenant Charteris was the first man up the ladder with his Chief Petty Officer close behind him and the rest of the party following them. As he came level with the deck there was a burst of automatic fire and a row of holes were stitched across the Lieutenant's chest. As he fell back against the safety rail, Chief Petty Officer Murray took rapid revenge by blasting the gunman backwards with the SA80 rifle he carried. The rest of the boarding party, enraged, spread out and hunted the crew down. By the time they were in control of the yacht three more of the crew were laying in pools of their own blood and the rest were on their knees on the after deck with their hands behind their necks.

The yacht's Captain, in his immaculate white uniform, strutted down the companionway from the bridge with his head held high and his cap at a jaunty angle. The cap went over the side as two able seamen grabbed him and slammed him to the deck. Winded by the impact, he struggled to breathe and his haughty demeanour vanished.

He was on his knees, with the rest of the crew, by the time Nick Evans came aboard to find out what the hell had happened. Evans paused at the top of the boarding ladder where the Lieutenant's body lay with a blanket over his face. The medic squatting by him looked up.

"Nothing I could do, sir. He was dead before he hit the deck."

"Fair enough, son. Which of the bastards did this?"

The medic pointed to where a pair of feet protruded from behind a deck winch. "That one, sir. The Chief took him out."

"I see, and are there any more casualties?"

"Three more dead, two wounded and a lot with bruises. None of them ours, sir."

Evans nodded slowly, then walked aft to where his crew were holding the yacht's crew. He looked along the line of his men and could see they were still furious. The yacht's crew looked battered and cowed. He walked across to the Captain in his torn white uniform.

"Right, Captain, first order of business. Where is Miss Christophides?"

The man looked up at him. "I know nothing about this person. You have the wrong ship."

Evans looked up and summoned the Chief Petty Officer. "Chief, select four men as a firing squad, then take this piece of shit to the aft rail. He gets one more chance to answer my questions, then you get to shoot him and we ask the next one."

The Greek captain paled. "You would not dare! You cannot do this."

Evans leaned down until his face was a few inches from the Greek's. He could smell the garlic on his breath and see the sweat on his forehead.

"Do you want to bet your life on that? A very fine Royal Navy officer lies dead on your deck. Killed by one of your crew. We already know you people are terrorists. Do you think, for one second, anyone is going to object if you and your crew die in a firefight?

The Greek swallowed. "She took the helicopter about an hour ago. She was going to land in Turkey and then take a commercial flight. That is all I know."

Evans stood up. "Have you searched the yacht, Chief?"

"Just finished, sir. Three crates of AK74 assault rifles. Two Browning .50 machine guns and five rocket-propelled grenades. Quite a leisure cruise they were planning."

"So it seems. Get these things handcuffed and transferred across to the ship and then get Mr Charteris taken over separately. You stay aboard with four men as a prize crew and I'll send Mr Greenway across to command. You'll be taking her on to Malta. I think you and your team deserve a little bit of a run ashore when we get there."

Chapter 67

Megan dropped her passengers by the Emergency Room entrance and drove off to find a place to park the pickup truck. She found the parking area around the corner and left the truck there. She contemplated leaving Jim's Webley revolver in the cab so there was no fuss as she went into the hospital, but she knew how much he enjoyed the pistol and would be upset if someone broke into the truck and stole it. Plus, of course, she would then have to explain why she wasn't carrying it when he had given it to her for her protection.

She tucked the big clumsy weapon in the belt of her jeans at the back where her jacket would cover it and walked to the ER. As she walked in she saw Sandra deep in conversation with the wounded SEAL in the waiting area and Janet describing the injury and her actions to a young doctor. They both looked round as Megan walked up.

"What the devil is going on in your neck of the woods?"

Megan raised an eyebrow. "How do you mean?"

The doctor pointed at the SEAL. "You bring me this one with a shrapnel wound from an explosion in a mine. Then we had that other one with a bullet in him from a hunting accident who was also burned from a camp fire. In fact, here he comes now. We are just letting him go home."

He pointed to a man being wheeled through the area in a wheelchair. He was heavily bandaged and looked very sorry for himself. The man pushing the chair was a different case altogether. He looked distinctly rough around the edges, with an unmistakeable threatening manner as he walked. He regarded them with a furrowed brow as he passed by, but said nothing.

"In any case, it seems you have done a good deal of our initial work for us, so I'll take your wounded friend off your hands. We'll get the surgeon in to take a look at him and I guess he'll be in surgery first thing in the morning. He'll have to stay with us for a couple of days to make sure there's no infection. You can call the desk to see when to come and pick him up."

The three women walked out of the hospital and stood together contemplating where to go next. Megan noticed the injured man from the wheelchair struggling into the passenger seat of a panel van, while his supposed helper stood by, talking on the phone. They spotted a bar across the street and decided that one drink wouldn't hurt before they drove back to the cabin.

Janet and Sandra settled down in a booth while Megan ordered at the bar. She came back to join them with the waiter following her, carrying the jug of beer and three glasses.

Sandra looked a little concerned. "I don't usually drink beer. In fact, I don't drink much at all."

Janet grinned at Megan. "I think she can make an exception tonight, don't you? Her new boyfriend won't mind."

Megan joined the teasing. "Yeah, how does it feel to have a boyfriend who never mentions his name? You don't know anything about him, do you?"

Sandra sipped her beer and put the glass back down on the table. "He explained that. It seems that people in these special military units keep their identities close to avoid reprisals. Anyway, his name is Robert Paradiso, he comes from Boston and he has nearly finished his twenty years in the Navy. After that he is going home to join his family electronics business."

"Is that it? No offers to whisk you away to a tropical island for a romantic weekend?"

Sandra blushed. "Nothing like that, but he has asked if he can buy me dinner when he is properly back on his feet."

"A date?" Janet giggled. "You are a fast worker, aren't you? I never knew that, when I was married to your brother."

Megan was quiet for a moment and then looked at Janet. "So why did that marriage fail? You seem to get on well with Jim."

Janet's smile dropped from her face. "I do and I did then as well. He's a good man. I just couldn't stand the separations any more. I was lonely and scared for him the whole time he was away. It just got too much for me."

Megan nodded slowly. "I can see that. No feelings left for him now?"

Janet gave Megan a very small smile. "Even if there were, it's too late. He's besotted with you, or hadn't you noticed?"

Megan returned the smile and looked down at her watch. "Time to go, I think. It's getting late and we don't want Jim sending out search parties."

They slid out of the booth, waved their thanks to the waiter and walked to the door. It was getting chilly outside and they could see their breath on the breeze as they walked towards the car park. Megan looked to where she had parked the pickup and saw that just behind it was a panel van that looked very similar to the one they had seen earlier. She must be imagining it.

They walked up to their truck and Megan was fishing in the pocket of her jeans for the keys when she became aware they were not alone. The rough-looking man was standing by the van and then she saw another one to the left and a third was coming towards them from behind. Megan paused and looked at each in turn. Then she saw the knives in their hands, held low and ready for an attack. She hesitated for just one second before she reached under her jacket, behind her, and pulled the old Webley out of her belt.

She recalled the lesson Jim had given her weeks before and held the heavy weapon in a two-handed grip to control it. The first round passed through the thigh of the man they had seen in the hospital and he went down to the ground like a sack of coal. She spun round towards the man behind her, who was running at her with the large ugly knife raised. Her first round skimmed across his arm and the second took him in the throat. He went down, choking and coughing blood.

She spun round to where she knew the third man stood and was horrified to see that he had grabbed Janet and held her in front of him, with the wicked-looking blade across her throat. The seconds slowed to a crawl as they stared at each other, both wondering what the next move could be.

Sandra brought the standoff to an abrupt close when she swung the tire iron from the back of the truck against the man's head. The knife fell from his nerveless fingers and clattered to the ground between Janet's feet. The assailant followed as he crumpled and lay still.

Megan moved forward and put an arm around Janet's shoulder. "All over, sweetie, no harm done." She looked over at Sandra. "Nice swing, girl. You play a lot of baseball?"

Sandra steadied herself on the truck's side. "In England we call it rounders."

"Whatever you call it, it seems to have worked on laughing boy here."

The three women turned as one when they heard movement from behind the pickup. The first attacker was struggling to get up and into the van. Janet walked across to him, still a little shaken, and kicked him hard on his wounded leg. The man screamed and fell back to the ground. Megan and Sandra applauded quietly.

"You stay right there, pal. The police are going to want to talk to you and here they come now," she said, as the three police cruisers pulled into the parking lot with their roof lights flashing and bathing the scene in surreal light.

Megan put the Webley down on the seat of the pickup and turned around with her hands held well clear of her body. The other two women walked slowly to stand beside her and as they held their arms out they took each other's hands and waited for the police.

Chapter 68

Now that the CIA were convinced that Calanthe's arms dealership was a clear and present danger to the USA, the President ordered the gloves to be taken off. The agency prepared to raid all the storehouses that had been found in the laptop and friendly governments were only too happy to cooperate, once they knew what was at stake.

Less friendly governments were not quite that simple and the President and the Vice President were busy on the phones to other heads of government all afternoon. The Russian president in particular was alarmed to find out that nuclear backpack weapons were missing from his arsenals. He ordered an immediate meeting of the national security committee. In an unusual move and to prove good faith, the second and third trade attachés from the US Embassy were invited to observe the operation from within the Kremlin.

The lights in the Kremlin burned late that night as the Russian security committee tried to work out how anybody had been able to walk out of a secure facility with four nuclear backpack devices. There had been rumours of arms being sold on the black market for years, but now there was proof and the committee worried about how to explain its failure to the President.

The tall double doors were flung open by two soldiers and the President walked in, followed by two men in grey suits, and stood at the foot of the table. He looked around the room; few of them could meet his gaze. When he spoke it was in a worryingly quiet tone.

"Chairman, in one week from this moment, I will stand here again and you will render to me a report on every weapon store in the country. You will account for every weapon from our ICBMs down to the last officer's pistol and the last soldier's bayonet. Do you understand?"

"Mr President, it cannot be done in such a short time. We have to assemble teams of inspectors and the number of arms to check is vast. I am sorry, but it cannot be done."

The President stayed very still and looked the committee chairman in the eye. "It can be done and it will be done. You will not assemble inspectors who will lie to me. Every officer in the armed forces will render a report on the weapons under his command. Every junior platoon commander will account for the weapons he controls, every company commander and every regimental commander will do the same. They will pass their reports up the chain of command. If any report is found to be false, the officer who made it will be arrested, as will every officer above him, up to the one who found the falsehood. Every warehouse will be checked by the storekeepers who run it and the same penalty applies to them. Now do you understand?"

The committee chairman spread his hands helplessly. "But Mr President, only a week it is not …"

"General, relations between us and the United States are improving rapidly, now that

President Baines is in office. He is a man we can deal with honestly. The economic benefits for this country are potentially enormous. Now, however, you have failed to maintain the security of our weapons and it seems that four Russian-made nuclear devices are on their way to decimate American cities. Can you conceive of how the American people will react?"

"I sympathise with the Americans, but it cannot be the fault of this committee and we cannot carry out the checks you want in such a short time. I am sorry, but ..."

"Enough! I accept your resignation. Deputy Chairman, you have been promoted. Get on with the task I have given you." He turned to the wide doors behind him and summoned the soldiers forward with a gesture. He pointed to the old chairman who stood pale-faced at the head of the long table. "Arrest that creature. Hand him over to the Provost Marshal."

He turned back to the table and very quietly said, "One week and all of you are responsible for the accuracy of this report. All of you."

Elsewhere in the world the raids continued all that day and the next day. South Africa, Guatemala, Japan and Australia all had secret weapon stores and all of them were raided. In only one of those, the one in the countryside outside Canberra in Australia, was there resistance. It was quickly and effectively quelled and the bodies of the three guards removed for secret disposal.

Chapter 69

Heinrich Oberhausen checked his watch for the fifth time in as many minutes. His three-man section lay along the shallow ditch beside him, as they waited for the appointed time to move. Two hundred meters to his left he knew another four-man team lay in wait, although he had seen no sign of them. The main assault would be formed up by now on the far side of the house and he and his team were ready to stop anyone trying to make a run for it this way.

He was still a little stunned that he was here. He had never imagined that when he joined GSG9 he would one day be operating just outside his home town of Detmold. He had passed the house he grew up in and the school he attended as he moved into this position. Hell, he had even seen his sister through the window of her house and now international terrorism had come to this quiet German town.

The dawning sun was just silhouetting the massive *Hermannsdenkmal* statue that overlooked the town when he checked his watch again. Thirty seconds to go. He tapped the stock of his Heckler and Koch G36 assault rifle to get his team's attention. Keyed up as they were, the slight sound was enough to get their attention. He held up his fingers in their prearranged signal to be ready. In the pre-dawn light he saw them stiffen as they prepared. None of them moved, not wanting to bring any attention to themselves.

He heard the main assault start as the larger part of the unit made their rapid entry to the front of the building. He could picture what was happening as he listened for any sound of the MP5 submachine guns they carried. With the distraction of the assault he and his men now slid forward into their firing positions and waited and watched the rear of the building. Since the two vans were parked on this side, under the trees, any attempt to escape would probably come this way. He and his men were ready to stop that if it happened. Where the driveway made a sharp turn and would slow any fleeing vehicles, Otto and his team were waiting as backup to ensure no terrorist left the scene.

There! A burst of fire from the house. And another! Much too loud for the MP5, so the enemy were fighting back, trying to kill his comrades. He heard the MP5s open fire and he heard the scream, but could not tell who had been hit. He prayed it had not been one of the GSG9 operators.

The back door of the house flew open and three men ran out, all armed. Heinrich smiled slightly within his face mask as the order to throw down their weapons came from Jürgen to his right. The three men raised their weapons and all three fired at where they thought the call had come from. That was enough. With no further orders needed, his section opened fire with carefully aimed shots. All three men were thrown back and lay still. Heinrich waited in case more of the terrorists appeared.

One of the main group of GSG9 operators appeared in the doorway and gave the all clear signal. They had taken possession of the house. Heinrich and his team stood and walked, in a well-spaced line, down the slight slope, still wary in case of ambush. As they reached the downed terrorists the two men who had been detailed for the task disarmed them and checked them for signs of life, while he and his fourth man kept watch. The fire had been too accurate and none of these would be in a position to harm any innocent person again.

Heinrich left his three men guarding the rear of the building and went inside to report to the assault commander. He found him sitting on the staircase having a wound in his leg dressed by the medic.

The commander looked up. "Typical, only one injury and it has to be me. Are your people all right?"

"No problem, sir. Three terrorists attempted to leave and opened fire on my position. They were dealt with in accordance with standing orders."

"All dead? Good. No messy court cases to grind through. I'll send the Crime Scene team round to deal with them. No telling what they might have in their pockets."

The commander patted the medic on the shoulder as he finished applying the dressing. He used the banister rail to support himself as he stood up. Heinrich could see the pain in his face.

"Do you need help?"

"No. I shall play the wounded hero. It hurts like hell for a small wound, though."

The medic smiled. "Not so small. It has torn some flesh away. You will have a fine scar for the beach when you sunbathe. Are you sure you do not want the morphine?"

"No, not yet. Maybe when the search is over. It clouds my mind too much."

There was a shout from the cellar doorway and the commander hobbled down the few stairs to the floor level. "Heinrich, I have changed my mind. Lend me your shoulder or I am liable to end up in a heap at the bottom of the cellar stairs."

Once in the cellar, the two men stared around at what the search team had found. Assault rifles in racks. Machine guns lying on transit boxes. Russian rocket-propelled grenades. And ammunition. So much ammunition.

The commander whistled softly. "The CIA agents have done well. This could have been the equipment for a huge attack or many, many smaller ones. Open the vans and see what is in there. The Americans are asking us to look for something very special and it isn't down here."

Heinrich trotted up the staircase and then out to the two vans where his team waited, watching the forensics team examine the bodies. He waved them towards the vans and they opened the rear doors. Inside were tripod stands and on those were mounted automatic grenade launchers, with racks of grenades ready for use next to them.

Heinrich reported his finding to his commander, who turned to wave over a man with a clipboard making notes of everything they had found. "Ulrich, leave that for the moment. Go and find the satellite phone and contact the American liaison officer in Berlin. Give her an idea of what we have found, but tell her we have not found the special weapons they were worried about. Then call Headquarters in Berlin and tell also them what we have found. It seems our enemies were planning something spectacular for us, before the Americans gave us this information."

Chapter 70

Just outside Nuevo Laredo in Northern Mexico, in the scrubland between the Boulevard Luis Donaldo Colosio and the Rio Grande, the weapon store was hidden within a tumbledown old farm building. The Federal Police threw a wide cordon around the building in the early hours of the morning. An hour before dawn the soldiers of the *Grupo Aeromóvil de Fuerzas Especiales del Alto Mando* made the final assault on the building.

The assault was fast, hard and professional. Even the two CIA operators, present as observers, were impressed. After a very few minutes the assault commander sent one of his men to bring the Americans forward. They entered a run-down farm building with no sign of the promised weapon store.

"So, *Commandante*, it seems the information we gave you was wrong. Your men have missed a night's sleep for nothing."

A broad smile broke through the camouflage paint across the Mexican officer's face. "Not quite, *señor*." He turned to the man standing behind him. "Show them what you found."

The soldier stepped forward and pulled a rusty sheet of corrugated iron to one side. Below it a set of concrete stairs led down into the earth. The Commander indicated that the two Americans should descend. At the bottom of the staircase they looked around in the gloom, until one of the soldiers threw a switch and the ceiling lights came on throughout the large modern space.

They looked around slowly as the Mexicans watched their reactions. "Holy shit, will you look at all these weapons!"

The rack after rack of weapons was impressive. Machine guns, assault rifles, sniper rifles and anti-tank weapons were all around them. Boxes of ammunition of all calibers were stacked along the left hand wall, in bays marked out with blue paint lines on the white concrete.

"That is not all. Come look around here."

The two Americans were led around the end of a rack of weapons to where the Mexican Commander was pointing. Set into the floor were steel rails that led to a metal door, built into the wall at the rear.

"What the hell?"

"It is a narrow gauge railway. My men have followed it for a short way; they stopped when they judged they were under the border between our countries. They found small flat cars that a man can push along these tracks to carry heavy loads. I think maybe your information was good, no?"

The CIA men looked at each other and then around the store room they stood in. "*Commandante*, did your people find anything strange? Maybe some large backpacks? Anything like that?"

"Backpacks? No, nothing like that, but they did find these." He pointed to manuals lying on a side bench near the rail lines. "They are in Russian, although none of the weapons we have seen in here so far come from that country."

The CIA operators picked up the manuals and flipped through them. They looked at each other and nodded. They had found what they feared.

"*Commandante*, my government will be grateful for your assistance and that of your soldiers, but we have to leave you to secure these weapons. We will go through that tunnel and see where it goes."

The commander nodded and watched as the two Americans turned and swung wide the metal door. They drew the automatic pistols from inside their jackets and set off along the tunnel beside the two shining steel tracks.

Half an hour of careful walking brought them to the end of the track where three of the flat handcarts stood empty. Beyond them was another set of wide stairs leading upwards. Moving silently and carefully, they mounted the stairs. At the top they found themselves inside what looked like a disused barn. The trapdoor to the stairs had been flung open and left.

Walking towards the wide doors, they found tire tracks in the soft sand and beer bottles lying around. As they reached the doors the first man peered through the gap.

"Where are we?"

"As far as I can see we are in the edges of Laredo. We are back in the USA. We've come right under the Rio Grande."

"Hell, that means the nukes could be anywhere by now."

"How so?"

"I'm guessing those tire tracks are from a small truck. With the nukes loaded on it they could head north up the I-35 to San Antonio. From there they could take any of the Interstate Highways that pass through there. We need to get Langley and Homeland on the case right now. It looks like the attack is really going down."

Chapter 71

Frank walked slowly round his RV. True to his word, the Colonel had asked the REME workshop to repair the bullet damage and they had done a terrific job. He couldn't see any sign of the holes that had been punched through the metal skin and when he went inside the woodwork was perfect. The washbasin and the toilet bowl had been replaced with new items from an RV supply store in Medicine Hat. The engine had been taken out and given a full service, after which she had been wheeled into a paint shop more used to spraying tanks. The result was an RV that looked better than the day he bought it.

He turned around to find a row of grinning soldiers in their oil-stained overalls waiting for his verdict. He walked across and shook every one of them by the hand and thanked them. At the end of the row he came to Tanner and Hearn. He felt a catch in his throat.

"Guys, I owe you my grandchildren's lives. There are no words for that. Thank you."

The two men smiled and Tanner spoke for both of them. "Not a problem, Frank. It'll make us as famous in the Army as that crazy man Peters and his bulldozer stunt."

Frank nodded to them, too emotional to speak, and walked back to his vehicle. He started it up and listened to the sweet note of the engine; she had never sounded that good. He drove slowly out of the workshop and across the road to the main camp where Emma and the two children were waiting with the base commander in the coffee shop.

"Like it, Frank?"

"Colonel, your people have done a perfect job on it. I don't know how to thank you."

The Colonel smiled. "That's an easy one. Jim Wilson is a good friend of mine and Ivan Thomas is a friend of his, so just keep those children safe."

"I'll do that. Your armorer gave me more ammunition for the MP5, so I'll still have a surprise for any more of them."

The Colonel looked at Emma with an eyebrow raised. "You didn't tell him?"

She shook her head. "No, I thought it would be better coming from you."

"Fair enough. Well, Frank, I've had a word with our hosts, the Canadian Army, and they in turn have spoken to people in Ottawa to get clearance for my idea."

"What idea would that be?" Frank asked.

"When you go outside you'll find there are two Land Rovers waiting to escort you to British Columbia. There are four men in each one and they are all armed. They'll take you all the way there and the RCMP will be checking on you as well. I think you can sleep easy at night now."

"That's very good of you, and I'll accept the help for the kids. I'm not sure our luck would have held out much longer."

Chapter 72

The Deputy Sheriff on duty listened to the complaint from the owner of the gas station on I-35. A panel van had been abandoned in the parking lot beside his store and was blocking access. He expected the police to move it. He paid his taxes after all, as he had reminded the deputy at least three times during the call. The deputy looked at the board behind his desk to see where the cars were patrolling that night. Marvin was closest, or he should be, if he wasn't asleep somewhere behind a billboard, again.

He reached across to pick up the microphone in front of him and put out the call. "Car four, car four. You awake, Marvin?"

The radio crackled. "I'm awake, Carson. Nothing happening out here. What do you want?"

"OK, Marvin, take a run out to the gas station on thirty-five. The owner say some fool has abandoned a panel van there and it's getting in the way. Check it out and see if you can move it for him."

The deputy could hear Marvin muttering as he keyed his microphone. "I'll try not to die of excitement."

Carson chuckled and returned to playing the solitaire game on his computer. As he reached for the mouse the screen changed and the alert screen came up. He clicked on the icon and read the urgent message. So somebody in Laredo had stolen a truck or a van and was probably driving north towards San Antonio. They were to look for anything suspicious. What the hell was that supposed to mean? No description, no number, nothing. He printed off the message and threw it in the tray for the Sheriff to deal with in the morning.

He had almost finished the next game of solitaire when the radio burst into life. "Despatch, Despatch, this is car four. You there, Carson?"

"I'm here, Marvin. What've you got?"

There was a pause. "I've got a dead man. Two shots to the chest and one to the forehead."

"What? Where?"

"In the back of the panel van you sent me to take a look at. I opened the back doors and there he is stretched out, dead as mutton. Worst thing is, I know him. I pulled him over about two months ago for a faulty tail light. Can't recall his name. It'll be in the log. He was heading down to Laredo after a delivery here in town."

Carson reached out and pulled the message back from the tray. He read it again, slowly this time. When he reached the bottom he checked the signature block and swallowed. Homeland Security. Oh shit, what had they landed this time?

"Marvin, stay there. Don't touch a damn thing. I got some calls to make. You wanted excitement, man, you've got it in spades tonight."

Chapter 73

President Baines sat in the war room beneath the White House and gazed at the blank white screen in front of him. Around him in the darkness sat senior military officers and officials from Homeland Security, the FBI and CIA. None spoke as they waited for the President to finish absorbing the detailed and horrifying briefing they had just listened to. Previous holders of his office had encouraged discussion after security briefings, but Baines was different; he insisted on time to absorb the material and to consider it. He encouraged his advisers to do the same.

Randolph Baines cleared his throat and leaned forward in his chair. He turned to the Directors of Homeland Security and the CIA, who sat together to his left. He then leaned back and looked at the young woman standing at the podium who had just delivered the briefing.

"Thank you, Kelly, that was a very clear briefing. Terrifying, but abundantly clear." He looked around the room. "Right now, people, I wish I had my three British friends here to describe this in their own colorful way, but now give me some options. Just what can we do to stop this?"

The room was silent until the FBI director spoke. "To be totally safe, we need to stop every vehicle on every road heading towards the target cities from Texas, but we can't do that because they could be coming from every direction or just one and the manpower requirement would be huge."

"Not to mention the legal problems of stopping and searching citizens going about their lawful business," Kelly said from the platform.

Randolph Baines put his fingers to his forehead and rubbed his temples. Sometimes that helped with the tension headaches, but not tonight.

"Are we dead sure about what was found in San Antonio, Kelly?"

"Yes, Mr. President. The security camera from the factory complex next door showed the packages being cross-loaded into four smaller vehicles. A van, a pickup and two cars. We have the make and model plus the plate numbers for all of them. No colours, though, since the pictures were taken at night using infrared."

"Did we see who killed the driver?"

"We did, at least we think we did. The camera picked up three flashes from inside the truck and then a man climbing out of the driver's door. Nothing from facial recognition yet."

"So if we stop every car, pickup and van of the right type we can check the numbers and we've got them?"

"No, sir, not really," the FBI Director said glumly. "Those number plates can have been changed anywhere and anytime. The vehicles are all common makes, so there are thousands of them and we have no idea which routes they took. Traffic cameras are being checked now."

"And we have the legal problem, too. We have no right to stop every citizen just because of the car he chose. The Supreme Court would tear us a new one."

The President held his hand up for a moment. "Maybe, maybe. Now instead of telling me all the things we can't do, give me some options about what we can do."

The Army General sitting away to the right side of the room stood up. "Give me the word, Mr. President, and I can put a ring of steel around all four cities. Nothing would get through without being searched."

The President nodded slowly. "While that is an attractive option in principle, the people carrying these weapons may well be wanting to be martyrs. In which case, as soon as they reach an Army roadblock they trigger the bomb. It may reduce the number of casualties to some extent, but still not an attractive option. Give me something that doesn't involve a nuclear explosion on US soil." He looked around the room. "Anyone?"

"Uh, there is one thing that might help."

"Who are you?"

"Mark Jennings, Mr. President, from the National Nuclear Security Administration."

"What have you got for us, Mr. Jennings?"

"In our inventory we have devices that can detect radiation even at low levels. Our inspectors use them all the time and they can be used to check a car or a truck to see if it is carrying anything suspect."

"Can they be used from a moving car to check the car alongside, for instance?"

"They can, sir, and if we use them in conjunction with standard Geiger counters we can spread the checking out quite a bit."

"Thank you, Mr. Jennings. That may be our first reasonable step. Anybody got anything else to offer that doesn't bring the road network to a standstill and or panic millions of our citizens?"

"Right, then we move on Mr. Jennings's idea. NNSA will collect every one of their detectors and ship them to the four threatened cities. Have the air force fly them in on fast jets if necessary. The military will have detectors for use with their weapon systems and nuclear engines on naval vessels. Universities will have Geiger counters for use in laboratories and there must be other places I haven't thought of. Get them all and then I want patrol cars, police and others cruising the roads looking for radiation."

"Uh, Mr. President, that's not quite how it works."

"Tell me then, Mr. Jennings."

"There are any number of things that emit radiation harmlessly that can trigger a detector. Granite worktops for kitchens, for instance. We need to know the specific radiation details so we don't chase down red herrings."

"I'll have that for you inside the hour. In the meantime, Homeland, you will coordinate and get this thing moving. Just one more thing: when you find these people take them down so they don't have chance to trigger the bomb."

"How do we do that Mr. President?"

"Every circumstance will be different. The people on the spot must make that decision, but I will issue an Executive Order here and now. Lethal Force is authorized. Now I have to speak to the

President of Russia to get you your information on backpack nukes."

Chapter 74

"Good morning, Mr. President. We have been expecting your call." The voice from Russia was completely without accent. "President Zhukov is coming to the phone now."

"Mr. President, a sad day for all of us and very worrying."

"Evgeny, this conversation will go much quicker if we stop calling each other Mr. President. We discussed that at the summit meeting if you recall?"

"Randolph, my apologies. I was not sure if this crisis might have soured our relationship."

President Baines smiled to himself as he sat in the Oval Office looking out at the garden. "Evgeny, I do not believe for one moment that this is an act by the Russian Government. We are both fighting terrorism, so personal animosity will only get in the way."

Evgeny Zhukov allowed himself to relax just a little, as he gazed through his own window across Red Square. "I should bring you up to date. Our arsenals are being examined across the country as we speak. With much regret, I have to tell you that the backpack nuclear devices did, in fact, come from our stockpile. The people who sold them are being rounded up now, but that does not help you."

To try and keep things as friendly as possible, President Baines forced a chuckle. "I am sure it was difficult for you to tell me that, Evgeny. However, it may give us a slight advantage."

"How can it?"

"My experts tell me each nuclear device leaks radiation to some extent and that radiation is unique to each type of device. It depends on the nuclear material used to build it. We have detectors that can find radiation, but we need to know precisely what we are looking for."

There was a pause as President Zhukov absorbed that. "So if my nuclear experts speak to yours we might be able to find these damned things?"

"That's about the size of it. Can we do that urgently?"

Zhukov reached out and pressed a button on his desk. "I have summoned my aide; he will be chasing the right people for you in a moment. There may be a problem, though. These devices were built during the Cold War and the people who made them may not be around anymore."

"Do you have any in your armories that have not been sold yet?"

Zhukov paused. "We do."

"Can you put one on a fast jet and send it to our Ramstein airbase in Germany? Our people there can examine it and identify the radiation signature. Whichever one gets the answer first may save us vital time. I will warn the NATO air defence people to expect it."

"It will be done." He waved to the aide who came through the door to tell him to sit down. "I have another offer for you to try and help that is a little more delicate."

"Delicate?"

Zhukov cleared his throat as he decided how to broach this. "Randolph, the USA has agents in this country who are here to keep an eye on what we are doing."

"Well, I ..."

"Please, Randolph, we are both adults. You know this and I know this. We also both know that I have agents in the USA. Some of those have particular skills and contacts who could help us."

"Go on."

"With your agreement, I will issue instructions for them to join the hunt. They will not be acting within your laws. If your law enforcement people get a phone call, or an email, using the code word 'Borscht', it is from one of my people and they should act upon it."

Randolph Baines leaned back in his chair. He had not expected this level of support from Russia. Maybe that fine bottle of Scotch whisky they had shared at the last meeting of the G20 had paid off.

"A generous offer, Evgeny, and gratefully accepted. Now let me give you something in return. If your people run foul of US law enforcement during this operation they should use the code word 'Canada'. Then we all know we are on the same side."

"I thank you for that. If any of my people are involved with your police or other agencies I hope we can discuss what happens to them next."

"We can and we'll give them time to pack their bags before we give them a first class ticket on the plane to Moscow."

Chapter 75

Ivan took the call on his mobile phone and stood up from where he was laying the log fire. The nights were getting colder and the big log burner warmed the room well, provided it was started early enough in the day. He brushed his hands down his dirty trousers and walked towards the door.

"Going somewhere, Ivan?" Geordie asked. "Need some company?"

"Emma called. They are just turning off the highway now. They spotted the marker I left at the end of the track. She says they've got some friends with them."

Geordie rose and walked to the door behind the big Welshman. As he passed the row of weapons standing against the wall he picked up a sub-machine gun and a spare magazine from those they had captured from the attackers.

"What do you need that for?"

"You said they had friends with them. I'm making sure that wasn't code telling us they are in trouble."

Ivan gave Geordie one of his rare smiles. "Good thinking, but not necessary. They really do have some friends with them."

The two men walked around to the back of the cabin where the track emerged from the dark tunnel of the forest and waited. They could hear the unmistakeable whine of a Land Rover in four-wheel drive, approaching with another engine singing along behind it. The camouflage-painted vehicle drove into the clearing and pulled over to the left to park. Half a minute later the big blue and white RV pulled up behind it, to be followed by yet another Land Rover.

The RV had hardly stopped when the side door crashed back on its stops and two excited children flew off the step and ran to Ivan, followed closely by an equally excited black dog. He fell to his knees and wrapped an arm round each of them. All three of them were crying, and Geordie decided he should be elsewhere and went across to talk to the soldiers emerging from the trucks. He introduced himself and led them around to the front of the cabin, where Jim was just emerging through the door.

"Right, guys, this is the boss, Major Wilson."

Eight hands flew up in a salute. Jim chuckled and raised a hand.

"No need for that, lads. I left the Army weeks ago; it's just Jim Wilson now."

He walked down the open tread stairs and shook hands with each of them before leading them inside and showing them where to leave their weapons. Megan came through from the kitchen area and counted the number of people milling around.

"Is that it? Coffee for eight?"

"Two more outside, bonny lass, and something for the kids. They'll be in any minute, when Ivan has finished saying hello."

A couple of the soldiers were looking at Geordie oddly and he waited for the inevitable question.

"Hey, are you the same Geordie Peters who pulled that bulldozer stunt in Afghanistan?"

Geordie sighed. "Yes, that was me. I wish I could live down that damn day!"

Outside Ivan stood up and, taking his two children by the hand, he walked to the RV. Frank and Emma stepped down through the door and waited for him. He let go of the children and hugged Emma, then took Frank's hand.

"I owe you two everything," he said. "Everything."

Frank nodded. "Happy to do it and now these two have plenty to write about in their term papers. That should get their grades up a bit." He hid a smile as the children's faces dropped.

Marian tapped Ivan on the arm. "Dad, are we safe now?"

"Safe as houses, *cariad fach*."

"Good, so does that mean I can have a phone again now?"

Chapter 76

Herb Durkin stood behind the counter of his hardware store contemplating the neatly laid out shelves. Life felt good this sunny morning. His wife had forgiven him for drinking too much at the VFW last Saturday, his two kids were getting decent grades in school and the Dallas Cowboys were playing well this season.

The phone ringing on his counter top brought all that to a shuddering halt. He picked it up without a care in the world, but that would change in seconds.

"Durkin's Hardware, how can I serve you today?"

There was a second or two of silence. "Good morning, Herb. I just need to remind you about our Potemkin weekend."

Herb swallowed. "I haven't forgotten. I'll be there."

He put the phone back in its cradle and sat down heavily. He had dreaded this call for years, but it had been so long now he thought they must have forgotten about him. The code word sent him to his computer to find the coded email that looked like yet another offer of cheap medicines. He recognised the sender's address. This was something else.

Leaving his assistant to watch the store, he printed out the message and went through into the workshop at the back of his house. The panel in the back wall was invisible, until he pressed on the hidden switch beneath his workbench. The concealed door flicked open and he took out the small book inside, then turned the yellowed pages to the one the first line of the email indicated.

It took him twenty minutes to decode the convoluted code using the one-time pad. He wrote the message out and read it twice. While it and the page of the code pad were burning he stared at the wall lost in his memories.

It had been almost twenty-seven years since he had been Sergei Mihalov Kuznetsov. He had finished only his basic military training in the Red Army when the political officer had sent for him. His facility for languages had been noticed by the KGB and he was to serve the motherland in another way than in the Army. Whisked away from the barracks within the hour, he had been disorientated as they drove him through the gates of the KGB training school.

The training had been long and hard, with very high standards expected. Even he was surprised that he made it. In the end he looked and sounded like an American. His backstory was laid out for him and he adopted the identity of a man who had been killed in a road accident in Illinois. He had arrived in this quiet Texas town, supposedly moving south from Chicago to get away from that crime-ridden city. His friends at the VFW respected that he was one of the ones who didn't like to brag about his military service and the people at the church had made him welcome.

His mission had been to grow a wide circle of contacts that could be used when the Soviet

Union needed them and he had been diligent in doing that. When the USSR collapsed he had thought he was free to continue as an American, but a visit from an FSB officer had put paid to that. Now he was called to action. The email had told him it was a worthwhile task, but what would his family think? They had no idea who he really was and this mission would probably expose him.

Herb was not alone. All across the south and east of the USA, agents were being activated to try and prevent a massive tragedy in their adopted country. Their last service to the motherland would be an important one, but at serious personal cost if they were identified by the Americans.

Chapter 77

It's cold at two o'clock in the morning on the Delaware Memorial Bridge and the I-295 was empty of traffic. Unusual for a major highway leading into Wilmington. The two young police women sat in their cruiser with the radiation detector between them. They knew Philadelphia was one of the targets, but they had been assigned to an unlikely route into that city. It had been a long shift and their eyelids were drooping when the low pinging noise from the detector brought them back to the world.

They looked in front and behind, but there was no sign of any vehicle lights. "Oh shit! Has it passed us? Have we missed it?"

"Damned if I know," said the older of the two as she got out of the car and listened for a vanishing engine noise.

There was nothing on the road in either direction. She stamped her feet to get the circulation going again, then walked to the edge of the walkway and looked down. She saw movement in the darkness and the faintest of sounds. For a moment she was puzzled, then her mind cleared and she ran the few paces to the car.

She grabbed the radio. "Despatch, Despatch, this is car fifty-six, urgent message, Alpha."

The Alpha code word cleared all other traffic from the air in an instant. "Car five six. Understand Urgent Alpha. Send message over."

"Despatch, we are at position Delta Seven. The detector has just alerted and there is a boat going under the bridge heading for Philly. No lights showing. No other traffic."

"Car five six confirm, unlit boat heading north-east of your position on the Delaware."

"Confirmed."

"Maintain position and keep watching. Other units will deal with your target. Out."

All around Philadelphia, police and National Guard units were deployed to preordained positions. Terrorist attacks using the Delaware River to get to the city had been envisaged, but felt to be a lesser threat. The response teams on the river were limited. From the Philadelphia Navy Yard three patrol boats moved down the river in line abreast. Their orders were clear: nothing was to be allowed to pass them.

Along the banks of the wide river, police and army snipers took up positions while heavier weapons were being deployed. Forty-seven minutes after the warning call came in, everything available was in place and waiting. The troops and police officers waited, their breath making small clouds of thin vapour as they scanned across the wide, empty waterway.

Chapter 78

On board the darkened boat, the two men tasked with planting the nuclear device huddled inside the small, unheated wheelhouse. The windows in front of them misted up continually and they wiped the damp glass with whatever rags they had. The helmsman peering into the night through his smeared window saw nothing ahead of him until three searchlights turned his window to a mass of oily streaks.

Dazzled, he raised his arm across his eyes as the amplified voice boomed across the water. "Unknown boat, stop your engines and prepare to be boarded. There will be no further warnings."

The helmsman reached down and pulled the throttle lever back to the idle position and the engine note dropped away as the engine slowed. He turned to his companion, who stood open-mouthed staring at the three armed patrol boats that were emerging from the darkness.

"Go and trigger the bomb. We are close enough for a device of this power to do our work."

The younger man's eyes widened. "I am not a martyr. I was told to position the bomb and set the timer."

"That chance has gone. Now we change the plan and do what we can. Trigger the bomb. I will distract the Americans so you can make it."

The young man looked down to the corner of the small wheelhouse as the helmsman reached to pick up the loaded AK47 rifle that leaned there. He watched in amazement as the older man kept the weapon out of sight as he cocked it and flipped off the safety catch.

"Ready? Now move!" the gunman yelled as he pushed the young man out onto the side deck.

The chatter of the assault rifle sounded loud in the confused young man's ears, as the weapon was swung to send a stream of 7.62mm bullets across the deck of the nearest patrol boat. He heard the scream of pain from the American boat as he staggered uncertainly to the aft end of their boat, where the nuclear backpack had been stowed. He paused as he reached the bomb and looked up at the stars, whispering a silent prayer.

It was a prayer he was never to finish. Two cones of high-speed machine gun rounds from two of the patrol boats slashed across the aft deck of the target boat, just as the third long burst of fire destroyed the wheelhouse and shredded the gunman standing there. The younger man died on his feet and was thrown into the dark cold water by the force of the bullets that ripped his life from him.

The blood was still running in the gunnels as the patrol boats came alongside and men leapt across onto the deck of the enemy boat. They checked the helmsman, but his days of threatening the US were over. Quickly, they searched for the man who had run towards the bomb, but he was resting in the mud at the bottom of the river by then. Lastly, they warily approached the backpack nuclear bomb that rested against the transom rail at the aft end of the boat.

Carefully, oh so carefully, the first man knelt by the backpack and started to unfasten the straps. He opened the flap and peered inside. The timing device reflected back at him in the dim moonlight. The figures were dark and he breathed again. The timer had not been set. This device and the city of Philadelphia were safe. One down and three to find. He waved back to the skipper of his boat.

On the small bridge deck, the skipper sighed quietly, then picked up the ship to shore phone to call in his report.

Chapter 79

"Mr. President, it's time you left here and started using Air Force One as the flying command post."

Randolph Baines looked up from his briefing papers at the Secret Service agent standing in front of the Resolute Desk. "Explain that to me:"

"Sir, the first of the nuclear bombs has been stopped on its way into Philadelphia up the Delaware river. We now know for sure that the threat is credible and we already know that DC is a target. We need to get you to safety now, Mr. President."

"Let me get this straight. There is a threat to the city and hundreds of thousands of people will probably die if the bomb goes off and you want me to run away?"

The Secret Service agent sighed slightly to himself. The good ones were always difficult when it came to times like this.

"Mr. President, whether the bombs go off or not, the country will still need to be governed. We can't evacuate the cities; the panic would be horrendous and obstruct any chance we have of finding these devices. The standard procedure is for you to use the airborne command post so that we can respond if necessary. Sir, it's not cowardice, it's what the country needs."

President Baines leaned back in his chair and looked at the man in front of him. He knew he was right, but it sure as hell felt like running away and sometimes leadership demanded personal sacrifice.

"Where is the Vice President right now? And where are my family?"

"The Vice President is at his ranch in Kentucky, recuperating from his recent illness. Your family are all well clear of the target cities, except your wife who is of course here and will travel with us."

"You know there are times I regret agreeing to stop being a District Attorney and entering politics?"

The agent fidgeted. "Yes, sir, but right now we need you to come out to Andrews. The plane is ready and on standby."

"What about the Congress and the Senate?"

"Most of them are away from the capital during the recess. The few that are still here are being rounded up right now and being moved out of the target areas."

The President put his hands down flat on the surface of the old desk and pushed himself up. He took his jacket down from the coat rack by the door and slipped it on. He took a long slow look around the Oval Office.

"You know, it will be a terrible shame if these people manage to destroy all this. Then again, we can rebuild like we did after the British burned it in 1814." He shrugged. "All right, Mr. Pascoe, lead on. Let's do what we have to do."

Chapter 80

The subdued lighting in the situation room beneath the Pentagon made the illuminated map being projected on the screen painfully clear. The number of possible entry points into the three remaining target cities was unmanageable. Those people who had not considered a waterborne entry were now reconsidering the situation, and it was bad. All three of the cities had navigable waterways that could take a bomb to almost the centre of the city.

The Homeland Security Director chairing the committee was a worried man. He looked slowly around the large oval table. It was obvious he was not alone in his worry.

"All right, everybody, we have deployed as much as we are able and now the Navy is bringing in as many patrol boats as they can to support local law enforcement. As far as I can see, it's still not enough. What else have we got that can be deployed without causing a destructive panic?"

There was a silence around the table and a few shrugs. Everything that could be quietly deployed was already out there. The detectors were working and vehicles were being stopped and checked for minor infringements wherever possible.

A hand raised from the table. "I have something, but you aren't going to like it."

The Chairman looked into the gloom and saw the uniform of a senior officer from the NYPD. "I don't like it now, so how much worse could it get? Speak up. We said at the start of this that no idea is a bad idea."

Patrick Murphy cleared his throat; this was not going to be pleasant. "How about we involve the gangs?"

"Gangs, what gangs?"

"Organised crime gangs. We know who they are and we know who calls the shots. At least, we do in New York."

The small white-haired man at the end of the table leaned forward. The Chairman remembered he was here from the Justice Department to ensure that the legal boundaries were observed. This would be the first time he had spoken since sitting at the table.

"You cannot be serious. You want to drag in criminals and tell them what is going on? How the devil is some pimp or drug pusher going to be of any use at all? This is preposterous."

The NYPD officer looked around the room before he spoke. "I don't hear any other ideas from around the table. Maybe I'm going a little deaf?"

The Chairman held up a hand. "The last thing we need is a spat while three nuclear bombs are on the loose. Run us through the idea and then we can see if it's palatable."

"OK. First off, these people don't have anyone from Justice second-guessing everything they do. Second, they have an intelligence network in their own areas that puts the FBI in the shade. And third, certainly in New York, these people live in the city. It's their town, too, so they care about what happens. If these bastards get in and blow up the middle of New York it's going to be bad for business."

The Justice Department official's flushed face was obvious even in the dimly lit room. "That is just ridiculous. You are treating these people like another arm of government. I can't believe you would even suggest something as outrageous and illegal."

Murphy sat back in his chair and looked around the silent room, then back to the irate man at the end of the table. "Well, since you have contributed just about nothing so far, maybe we can have your pearls of wisdom on how to save the lives of potentially millions of people?"

The Chairman banged his hand down flat on the table. "Ladies and gentlemen, this is way too serious for points scoring, but I agree with Deputy Commissioner Murphy, let us hear what the Justice Department has to offer as a solution."

There was a long pause and all heads swung to look down the table at the white-haired man from Justice. "That's not my function here, as you well know."

The Chairman gave his best charming smile. "In which case let us discuss the suggestion further. What do the police officers from Boston and DC think about it? Could you do something similar? Do we believe the criminals would cooperate? What are the risks?"

Chapter 81

He had driven through the whole of the day before and then slept in the back of the car behind the gas station. He woke to a feeling of fur on his tongue and grit in his eyes. He pushed the jacket off and let it drop to the floor before he opened the car door and struggled out.

The morning sun was in his eyes as he stumbled round to the bathroom to wash his face and try to clear his head. As he expected, the bathroom was filthy with a crack running right across the mirror and a big chip out of the porcelain of the basin. He waited as the water sputtered into the sink and then swilled his face and hands. No soap, of course. No towels either, so he wiped his hands down his rough shirt as he stepped back outside.

Across the street, the fast food place was just opening up, so he walked across and left the car out of sight where it was. He sat in the booth waiting for the waitress to finish setting up the counter and the cook to finish crashing about in the kitchen beyond.

Finally, she came across and took his order. He was sipping at the coffee waiting for his eggs and pancakes when a shadow fell across the table. He looked up into a face he knew.

"Mario? What the hell are you doing here?"

The heavyset man in the surprisingly well-cut suit sat down opposite him. They paused as the waitress came over and took the newcomer's order. Bacon, sausage, hash browns and two eggs over easy.

"That stuff's going to kill you one day, heart attack on a plate. Now you didn't say what brings you out here."

The heavy man sipped his coffee and then added more sugar. "Looking for you, Henry, my friend. We heard you were delivering a special package and the handover was going to be here."

Henry swallowed. "So how did you hear about that?"

"We have our sources. One hand washes another and we hear things. You're the fifth link in the chain, did you know that? No, probably not. So how did it work? You turn up where you are told to, pick up the package and then bring it here to hand it over?"

Henry nodded, but didn't speak until the waitress finished putting the two breakfasts down on the table, none too gently. She refilled their coffee mugs then walked away again.

"Yeah. Just a transport job. A phone call and cash in hand from the guy who picks it up. Nice and simple."

Mario sighed. "Not so simple this time. I need that package."

"Hell, man. You know I can't do that. I have a reputation to protect. Always a reliable delivery, no funny business. Anyhow, it's just an old backpack. Too heavy to be drugs, so why would you want it?"

"Henry. Some good friends of mine want it back. It's property that was stolen from them and if it gets in the wrong hands it could be messy. Real messy. So how about we finish here and you take me across to that shitty car of yours and hand it over?"

"Mario, I'd like to help, but the people I work with take these things seriously. I could end up dead if I don't deliver. You know how it is."

Henry felt a heavy tap on his knee beneath the table. "I know how it is and you should know that my friends don't care about your troubles. What you can feel against your knee is an ex-Army M1911 automatic pistol. If I pull the trigger your kneecap disappears and you probably bleed to death before the 911 call is finished."

Henry put down his coffee carefully and looked at the man sitting opposite him. He saw no sign that this was any kind of a joke and the weapon beneath the dirty table felt very real. He swallowed and kept his hands in clear sight.

"You make a good point. Maybe I should help your friends out. I don't want to be accused of handling stolen property."

"Now you're thinking straight. Tell you what, no hard feelings, I'll buy breakfast."

Mario tossed a twenty on the table and they stood up to leave. The heavy pistol had vanished into the big man's jacket pocket, but since his hand stayed in there with it, Henry felt no need to try anything clever.

They walked together across the street with Mario hanging back just a little. As they rounded the corner of the gas station the rusty green Plymouth came into view, standing next to a white delivery truck with the owner's name down the side panel in blue lettering. The driver saw them through the windshield, slid his door back and climbed out. Mario pulled his heavy pistol from his pocket, but it caught in the lining and as he struggled to free it the van driver brought his MAC-10 sub machine gun up into the aim and sprayed both men. The Ingram MAC-10 is not an accurate weapon, but at that range he could not miss. Henry was thrown to the ground and died in seconds; Mario, badly wounded, lay in the dirt to watch the driver climb back into his van and drive away.

Mario passed out for a few moments and was disorientated when he recovered. His fingers were slick with his own blood as he drew the mobile phone from inside his jacket. He struggled to see the numbers as he dialled the people he needed. The call was answered quickly and he spoke his last words.

"Borscht, borscht. White panel van, blue lettering. Peter's Flower Shop. He's on the I-95 heading towards Springfield."

Mario never heard the reply as the phone dropped from his nerveless fingers. Arkady Alexandrov Belinsky had carried out his last duty for the motherland.

Chapter 82

Geordie sat on the rock at the base of the carved totem, watching the stars dance in reflection on the smooth water in front of him. He could hear the footsteps coming slowly across the rocky beach behind him and turned to watch Janet negotiating her way over the rough ground.

She sat down next to him and he saw her smile reflect the light of the sickle moon. "These people are well overdue some streetlights. It's black as a lawyer's heart out here."

He grinned at her. "But if you have streetlights you never see stars like this."

She looked up where he was pointing and marvelled at the myriad points of light that dappled the night sky. "You're a bit of a romantic then? I didn't think that of you."

"Just because I'm a Geordie doesn't mean I don't appreciate beauty. I was a coal miner when I first left school and you wouldn't believe some of the things the older guys produced. Twisted, scarred hands producing the most delicate paintings and rough throats making the music of the Welsh Valleys. Never underestimate a miner."

She smiled at him and took his hand. "I like it when I learn more about you. You really aren't just the tough soldier you appear to be, are you?"

"Not with you, anyway."

She nodded and he saw the starlight reflect off her hair. "So then, Geordie, what are we going to do about this? You feel it, too, don't you?"

"I think you know I do, but there's not much chance to get to know each other in this place. Far too many people in open-plan rooms."

She looked out across the silvered water. "So what next?"

"So first we make sure you are safe. The boss says the CIA and MI6 are closing down Calanthe's organisation left, right and centre. They haven't run her to earth yet, but once they do we should be able to go back to our lives."

"And where is your life?"

"Back in the Army, I guess." He paused and thought for a moment. "Unless I get a better offer of course."

A cloud passed across the moon and she could hardly see his dark face in the night, though she knew his eyes were on her. "Is that a hint for me to make you an offer?"

"Maybe not just yet. Maybe we should take some time and see if this goes anywhere?"

"I think I'd like that. So before we go back in and warm up, is there anything else?"

He leaned forward and kissed her gently and then more urgently. She kissed him back and he felt the connection between them.

She whispered, "I wish the CIA and the rest would hurry up. So we can be alone."

"Me too. Having a SEAL operator somewhere in the forest with Night Vision Goggles, does cramp a guy's style a little."

Chapter 83

All across Washington DC, and in the surrounding towns, the word was passed rapidly on the secure channels to intercept a panel van that belonged to a flower store. Every available law enforcement officer from every police force was on high alert. The Secret Service, the FBI and the Military Police were providing support with no sign of the panel van reported from anywhere.

Tucked behind the Embassy Suites hotel in Crystal City, the van that was the focus of so much attention was parked under a tree to shield it from any eyes in the sky. The driver sat calmly reading a holy book and biding his time. He needed the chaos of Washington's morning traffic to hide him as he took himself well within range of the White House. He had the spot all picked out and his ride, to get the hell out of the blast zone, was already parked there. They would change over as he arrived. It would be a matter of moments to set the timer, park the van and then vanish in the thousands of cars. They would be well outside the Beltway when revenge came to the capital city of his enemies.

The driver checked his watch and took a look at the Jefferson Davis Highway running behind the hotel. The traffic was building up just the way he needed it. He would join that road and that would lead him to the other roads that would take him across the Potomac on the Williams Memorial Bridge. From there it was a short drive to 15th Street where his comrade waited. They had calculated that 15th Street would be near enough to wipe out the White House and to tear the heart out of central Washington, but not be close enough to encounter the high security cordon they expected.

The flower van left the Embassy Suites car park and drove down the local streets until it entered the major traffic flow of the Jefferson Davis Highway. The driver, in his short white jacket and his white topped cap, attracted no special attention. He checked constantly for extra police cars around him; there was nothing out of the ordinary. He carried on along his planned route and drove up the slip road onto the Williams Bridge. There was still no sign of an increased police presence. Off to his left he could see the white Jefferson Memorial overlooking the Tidal Basin. He smiled. That would not look so white by this afternoon.

He left the bridge and carried on towards 15th Street. The traffic was moving slowly as expected and he did not try to overtake anything. He drove along 14th Street until he came to Constitution Avenue and made a left turn. He could see the next junction up ahead where he would turn right on to 15th Street. He picked up the small handheld VHF radio from the seat next to him and thumbed the transmit button.

"I am coming to the last turn. Are you ready?"

There was a wait of only two seconds before the answer came. "I am ready. Flash your lights as we agreed."

The driver of the van smiled to himself again. This was going to work. He ran through the plan in his mind as the traffic edged forward towards the 15th Street junction. He would keep to the right-hand lane and when he saw his companion's car he would flash his lights and block the traffic so his accomplice could pull out and leave him a space. When he had swung the van into the space, he would throw the switch to start the timer and then leave the van. Once in the car, the two of them would drive and leave the city heading west on Route 66. They would hear of the nuclear explosion on the radio. The plan said they should be near to the town of Front Royal when the blast ripped Washington off the face of the earth.

Chapter 84

Sergeant Gomez of the Metropolitan Police sat in his Crown Victoria with the rookie by his side. He was tired. It had been a long shift with everybody in the force doing extra time to give as much cover to the city as possible. The traffic was crawling as usual as he came up to the junction. He paused at the red signal and yawned, then wiped his gritty eyes.

"Hey, sarge, what colour was that van we were supposed to look for?" the rookie said.

Gomez looked to where his companion was pointing. Across the junction, the flower van was halfway through its turn into 15th Street and waiting for some idiot in a green Ford to get out of the way. His mind clicked into high gear as twenty years of police experience worked its magic. He stamped on the accelerator pedal and powered the big solid police cruiser across the junction. Almost without thinking, he flipped on the light bar and siren as he told his co-driver to brace.

The white cruiser with the red and blue trim lines of the Washington police surged across the junction with other cars slamming their brakes on to avoid him. Gomez had just time to register the startled face of the van driver turned towards him before the cruiser slammed hard into the side of the lighter truck.

The flower van was pushed violently sideways until it smacked into a light pole on the corner of the street. Inside, the driver, who had removed his seat belt in readiness for a quick exit, was thrown hard into his door. His head bounced hard against the side window and then he was thrown across the cab as his vehicle came to an abrupt stop. Dazed, and with blood pouring from his nose and a head wound, he started to struggle off the floor and towards the bomb.

The doors on either side of the driver's cab were wrenched back and two police officers came through, preceded by two police issue automatic pistols. The driver almost made it. His hand was no more than six inches from the firing mechanism when Gomez fired three rapid rounds. The driver was picked up and slammed across the passenger seat with blood gouting from his wounds. Still he tried to reach the bomb. The rookie earned her pay that day by grabbing the injured man and wrenching him out of the truck and onto the sidewalk.

Gomez came around the front of the truck to find the rookie kneeling in the middle of the driver's back. He leaned down and checked the bomber's carotid artery for a pulse.

"You can get up now. He's not going anyplace."

The rookie pointed up the road where a squeal of tires was following a red Chevrolet out of a parking space and up the street. "That guy seems keen to get the hell away from here."

Gomez nodded as he grabbed the personal radio clipped to his jacket. He called in the description of the car and its number. He would not get out of the city. Not in this traffic.

Chapter 85

The straps of the heavy pack cut into his shoulders as he walked slowly through the park. When he had planned this on the map, Central Park did not look this big. Despite the slight chill in the air he wiped the sweat from his forehead again as he checked the small tourist map in his hand.

He was still on track to leave his gift to the imperialists. From here he had to pass the lake and the zoo, then walk along the Avenue of the Americas to 42nd Street. Once there, he had to turn to find Grand Central Station to leave the device he carried in a left luggage locker. The train would take him far away, before the blast put the attack on the World Trade Centre in the shade.

This was a good plan. There was no chance of a car or truck breaking down. He just had to walk through the Americans and tear the heart out of their city. Easy. He shifted the weight on his shoulders again and kept trudging forward.

Nobody paid him any attention. He saw the police cruisers driving up and down the roads alongside the park and he had seen them stopping vehicles all over Harlem as he walked past them unnoticed. He was a ghost in the city; maybe he should call himself that when this was over?

He passed the women with their grizzling brats in pushchairs and the old men playing chess on the tables. He paused for a moment by the small granite memorial to the police and fire officers who had been killed in the nerve gas attack on New York all those months ago. That had been good to watch on the television, with the cameras continuing to film even when their crews were dead beside them. That had been done by brothers, too, but his attack would be better.

He walked along East Drive past the Loeb Boathouse restaurant on the edge of the lake, being passed by panting idiots jogging. It would be good to stop for something cold to drink, but he had no time; his explosion must happen at the same time as the other three. The four major cities of the north-east coast would be destroyed together so the world could see the power of jihad and tremble.

He saw the four young black men lounging on the bench by the side of the road, but paid them no attention as he passed. He walked on, getting closer to the edge of the park now. He could hear the traffic on 5th Avenue through the trees to his left. He heard the footsteps behind him and turned to find the four young men right behind him.

"That's a real big bag to be humpin' through the park, man."

"Yeah, real big, looks heavy. It heavy, man? You want I should help you with it?"

The man shook his head. "I need no help, thank you." He turned to walk on.

One of the young men stood in front of him now, with a smile on his face. "We was wonderin' what you got in the bag, man."

"Yeah, how come if it's so heavy you don't catch a bus?"

The man kept walking. "I need the exercise. Now leave me to walk."

The one in front of him placed a broad hand on his chest. "You don' seem to understand, man. We want to see what you got in that big bag. Right now would be good."

Then the man understood. This was what the Americans called a mugging. He had an answer for that. He reached under his jacket and started to draw out the pistol in the clip holster on his belt. He stopped as the blade flashed in front of his eyes.

"Stay very still, friend, and you may even walk out of the park."

Another of the young men moved close to him and removed the pistol from his hand, then moved clear. The third and fourth men moved up alongside him and walked him off the road and into the trees towards 5th Avenue. With the blade held steadily in front of him, aimed at his stomach, he could do little unless he could reach the trigger of the weapon on his back. The explosion would be early and he would be a martyr, but it would take these street thugs with him.

The men either side of him took hold of the shoulder straps and lifted them off his shoulders. They put the big back pack down on the ground next to a tree. This could be his time.

"If you want to see what is in there so badly, let me show you," he said, taking a step towards the tree.

"Nice try, man, but we know what's in there and you ain't touchin' it."

"How can you know?"

"This is our town, brother, we know everything that moves. You don' walk through Harlem with that thing without bein' seen. And you don' attack our town if we got anythin' to say about it."

The man straightened up to ease his back now the weight was gone. "Who are you? Police? FBI?"

"No man, we ain't five oh. We, what you might call, the opposition. Today though, we workin' with the feds to protect our town and our people."

"You don't understand why I do this."

"We understan' all right. Elroy here is a convert. He goes to the Mosque regular and he pray all the damn time."

"Then you should let me go to avenge our brothers that the Americans have killed."

The one called Elroy looked hard at the would-be bomber. "Is you stupid? If you blow that thing up my brothers right here die, and my sisters, and my aunties. Ain't no way."

The man nodded slowly and half turned. Then he spun back and dived for the backpack. He grappled with the old leather straps that had stiffened with age, trying desperately to open the pocket where the trigger mechanism sat.

Elroy was the first to reach him and plunged the wicked-looking knife between his shoulder blades. He grabbed him by the hair and dragged him back from the bomb, before plunging the knife into his throat and ending his troubles.

"Nice move, Elroy. Is that one they taught you in the Marines before they threw you out?"

Elroy looked up at the speaker. "You say that to me again and I show you what the Marines taught me. Now call the feds and get this damn thing out of here. Tell them 'Canada' when you call."

Chapter 86

"Mr. President, we have the latest update for you."

Randolph Baines looked up from the map he had spread across his desk. "I hope it's some good news for a change. There are just so many ways these devices could be moved into the cities we need to be incredibly lucky." He leaned back. "Have you heard the saying 'The terrorists only need to be lucky once, but we need to be lucky all the time'? Never truer than today."

His security adviser nodded and smiled. "It is good news, sir. The van taking the bomb into Washington was spotted by two bright police officers and they stopped it. The attacker was killed and his accomplice in the escape car is in a police chase right now. The tip-off came from one of the Russian agents. It seems that the device aimed at New York was stopped as well, but the details on who stopped it are a little hazy."

"So with the one heading for Philadelphia already intercepted, that just leaves Boston?"

"As far as we know, Mr. President, yes."

"Good, get this aircraft turned around and back to Andrews. There's no reason for me to skulk up here now the threat to Washington is done."

The aide gave a small cough. "Er, Mr. President, the Secret Service would rather you stay in the flying command post just in case the fourth bomb has been retargeted."

"The intel our people picked up in Cyprus has proved accurate and we know the Russians have only lost track of four of these weapons. That makes it an acceptable risk. So Andrews now, if you please."

"Very good, Mr. President." The aide turned to leave the office.

"One more thing, I want those two police officers on the tarmac when we land. I want to shake their hands."

Ninety-seven minutes later Air Force One touched down at Andrews Air Force Base and taxied around to its allocated parking area. As the President came to the top of the steps down he saw the convoy of armored suburbans waiting for him with armed Secret Service officers around them in a cordon. He looked around slowly and standing quietly in the shadow of the hangar he saw the two police officers. He walked down the steps and through the Secret Service officers who tried to shepherd him into his car.

He reached the two police officers, who looked a little nervous at all the attention. He looked them in the eye and appraised them. The thick-set Sergeant, Jorge Gomez, looked capable and not a man to mess with. The tall slim black woman by his side must be Eloise Jackman, the rookie officer on her second day out of training.

Randolph Baines shook them by the hand. "I want to thank both of you for what you have done for your country and our city. You can't tell anybody what it was really about, but we'll work up a cover story for the press. However, you and I know just how important your actions have been today. I guess it's just another day for you,

Sergeant, but you are going to have to work hard to top this one, Eloise."

The young officer smiled shyly. "Yes, Mr. President."

"Tell me, with having to come out here to see me, have you had your lunch yet?"

"No, sir, but we don't mind," Gomez answered.

The President smiled. "I thought that might be the case." He waved one of the security men over. "This officer is going to take you onto Air Force One. I've asked the chef to stay aboard and make you something to eat. Take a look round while you're there. After all, it belongs to the taxpayers."

He shook their hands again and then walked back to the convoy. "Right now, get me to the Pentagon situation room as quick as you like."

Less than an hour later all the experts around the big oval table stood as the President swept into the situation room. He shook the chairman's hand and took a chair.

"Right then, people. I'm an hour out of date. Tell me what you know."

"Well, Mr. President the first device was …"

President Baines held up a hand. "I know that we've got three of the devices. I don't need to be run through the history. That can come later. Now what about Boston?"

Chapter 87

Boston was swamped with officers from the police and other law enforcement agencies. To avoid any concerns, most of them were out of uniform. The densest concentration of watchful eyes was around the central district all around State Street. A command centre had been set up in the wood-panelled dining room of the Omni Parker Hotel, to ensure that the officers out in the city around them knew that senior officers were sharing their risk. A worried group of those senior officials was coordinating search and surveillance from there.

They knew that the other three bombs had been found and they knew they were the last target. It didn't help. They had no tip-offs and no clues as to how this device was being moved. Setting up the surveillance had been delayed by an interagency squabble about jurisdiction, and the big worry now was that the bomb had been slipped through during this time.

Divers were searching off the wharves all around the huge harbour and officers with radioactivity detectors were posing as building inspectors throughout the city. Closed circuit TV cameras were being monitored closely and recordings of the last few days were being trawled through in darkened rooms. Hotel registers were checked and receptionists quizzed about anyone arriving with a large backpack. The students on their gap years were rousted out of bed in a number of YMCA buildings and their large backpacks were searched, ostensibly for drugs, although any that were found were quietly flushed and a warning given.

Calls were coming in from agencies in other cities offering help and the Governor offered the National Guard. They were all politely declined. Putting more personnel on the streets would only worry and panic the people of the city and the damage done by a mass panic would be extensive.

As the day drew down to a close and night crept through the streets, the command team were at a loss. They had searched everywhere they could think of and nothing had been found. The detectors had identified nothing of interest and now they were rapidly running out of ideas.

Down on Clinton Street, Patrolman Ted Casey was walking his usual patrol route. One of very few police foot patrols in the city. He turned into North Street and then cut through by the McCormick and Schmicks restaurant towards Faneuil Hall. He knew he could rely on a coffee from the night janitor around now. He took a stroll through one end of Quincy Market and accepted a couple of small samples from the food stalls before he walked across Merchant's Row to the side door of the hall. He knocked on the door and it opened almost immediately.

"Hey, Ted."

"Hi, Al. Coffee on?"

"Always. Still, I wasn't sure you'd be coming with all the extra heat walking the streets."

"Ah, you noticed that, did you?"

"Hard to miss. All those extra tourists taking a look in the garbage bins and not looking at the girls. What's going on? Anything to worry about?"

Ted sipped his coffee and looked out of the window. "Could be. You see anyone leave anything laying about that they shouldn't?"

Al put his chipped blue coffee mug down on the scarred table. "Sure did. You want to see it?"

"Yeah, why not? Where is it?"

"Just round here in my storeroom. It was upstairs in the main hall. How anybody could forget a damn great pack like that I'll never know. Still, you see some strange things left in here. I remember one time …"

Ted spilled his coffee and swore when he realised what Al had just said. "Wait. A pack? You mean a backpack? A big one?"

Chapter 88

Sergeant Merv Kowalski had been defusing bombs for a while now. Most of them were the IEDs left by insurgents in Iraq and Afghanistan, but this was his first nuke. He stood by the narrow doorway to the janitor's store and looked at the pack that had been tossed onto the rough concrete floor. Access would be a problem with all the heavy bomb disposal protective equipment he was wearing and he could not afford to make a mistake with this baby.

He stepped back into the corridor and started to strip off the protective equipment. His assistant ran up and grabbed his arm.

"What the hell are you doing? You know you have the wear this stuff."

Merv turned and smiled at her. "Jay, if I make a mistake and this goes off, then it's going to be like the centre of the sun in here and no Kevlar padded jacket is going to help. I need to be able to get in there and deal with it without knocking a pile of cleaning gear on top of it."

Jay looked at him and nodded, then she started to help him take the heavy protective clothing off and laid it on the floor. "So did you read the manual they gave us?"

"I looked at the pretty pictures. The Russian text was not a lot of use and the interpreter is still on the way."

"Then why don't you wait?"

"Because according to the intel this should be going off anytime now. The timer is probably running already. We're out of time."

"OK. Remember the rule, if the timer hits zero put your head between your legs and kiss your ass goodbye."

"I'll remember, and you put your fingers in your ears. Six kilotons of instant sunshine is going to be noisy."

"That's the last of it. Are you ready?"

"I'm ready. And Jay, if this goes right I'll buy you a clam chowder across the road there."

She smiled at the handsome soldier and winked. "It's pronounced chowdah and you can buy me a damn steak after this one."

Merv picked up his small roll of tools and walked slowly back to the janitor's store. He stood and sized up the situation again and then moved carefully inside. The backpack lay on its side and he could see no sign of lights or exposed wires. He very slowly started to open the cracked leather straps of the first pocket, where the immediate trigger was supposed to be, as far as he could tell from the diagrams he had seen. With both straps unfastened, he gently lifted the pocket flap and peered inside.

The immediate trigger was there and the red catch that held it in the safe position was still in place. He breathed a small sigh of relief. He now had to find the timer trigger and that should be in the pocket the device was laying on. He took a firm grip on the two shoulder straps and gently pulled the heavy pack upright until it stood on its flat base. He wiped the sweat from his forehead and paused for a moment or two to let his racing heart slow down before he moved to the next part of his plan.

He shifted his position to put himself directly in front of the timer pocket and moved his tools within reach. There were three straps holding this pocket closed and he undid them carefully with a pause after each one. With the third strap unfastened he whispered his own superstitious prayer.

"For what we are about to receive, Lord make us thankful."

And then he lifted the flap of the pocket. There was the timer with a row of red numerals flashing at him. They were all on zero: the timing countdown sequence had completed. He thought about running, but the timer lights kept flashing and nothing happened.

He sat back on his heels and thought about his next move. Then with a surgeon's scalpel he cut around the pocket until he could see the whole of the timing mechanism. He looked beneath the rectangular box and smiled to himself. One of the multi-pin connectors hanging beneath the timer was not connected. Judging by the rust inside the connector body it had never been connected. Thank god for Soviet quality control.

Chapter 89

Geordie and Janet came through the door of the cabin carrying brown paper sacks from the grocery store. They put them down in the kitchen and turned to go and get the rest.

"You've missed all the excitement while you were out," Simon told them.

"Oh, I wouldn't say that," Geordie said as he smiled at Janet. "Why, what happened?"

"Uncle Jim got a phone call from the President. The real one down in Washington."

Geordie looked across the room at Jim with a raised eyebrow. Jim nodded and walked towards him.

"I'll give you a hand with the groceries."

They walked outside and down the steps from the veranda. Geordie leaned against the side of Megan's pickup truck and waited for Jim to reach him.

"Come on then, boss, what's excited young Simon so much?"

"He took the call and I think he was turning cartwheels after speaking to President Baines himself. He was like a puppy with two tails when he gave me the phone."

"So what gives?"

"It seems, my friend, that the President has been advised that the American alphabet agencies, mostly the CIA, the Russians and everybody who wants to be friends, with either of them, have dismantled Calanthe's organisation. They have emptied all their weapon stores and arrested virtually all of her people. He thinks it's all sorted out now and we can all go back to our lives. They just have Calanthe herself to find."

Geordie lifted two of the grocery bags out of the bed of the pickup and handed them to Jim. "That sounds good to me. Really good. If I can get Major Irwin to give me a couple of weeks' leave, I've got an invitation to visit Spain."

"Janet? Good for you. In fact, good for both of you. I haven't told anyone else yet. We could do that over dinner. May be our last dinner before we all shoot off back to wherever we need to be. Is it true you're going to make that three-alarm curry of yours?"

"It surely is. We scoured the stores all over town to get all the right ingredients."

"That's good. I haven't had one of your curries for ages. But don't call me Shirley."

Geordie grinned at the old joke and walked up the steps and into the cabin. Jim looked around before following him in. It would be good to go back to normality.

Over dinner, Jim waited until everyone had their bowl of curry in front of them before he made his announcement. He saw there was a little sadness mixed with relief. Living here on the edge of Canada in the pristine conditions of the British Columbian coast had been good for most of them.

Ivan was the first to put a damper on things as he took his first forkful of the beef curry. "All good as far as it goes, boss, but that damned contract will still be out there, on the dark net for any thug who needs cash to have a try at us. Even if they aren't going to get paid, they won't know that."

"I can help with that, Uncle Jim," Simon said. "I've been talking with Rashid and the others on line and he thinks he can send an electronic message to everyone who has looked at the site to tell them that there's no money for killing us anymore."

Jim nodded. "That could work nicely …"

"No, it won't, Jim."

Jim turned to look at Sandra. "Why not?"

"You're going to get one chance at this. If you tell all the scum of the earth that the contract is finished, that's fine, until Calanthe goes on her website and tells them all it's still going. If you send another saying it really is cancelled then about half of them will still think it's there and still live. That's human nature when greed is involved."

Jim looked at Sandra steadily. His sister was back. The old intelligence she had hidden during her marriage to Brian was back in place and so was her confidence. He wondered if he had a certain SEAL operator to thank for that.

"So we are still on the hook until Calanthe is found. That could be a while, even with all these agencies looking for her."

Chapter 90

The morning had dawned crisp and clear with only a little snow during the night. It was the perfect day for a little fishing. Jim and Ivan picked up the rods and walked down to the waterside with Geordie who just wanted to sit and talk. Geordie sat at the base of the totem again and watched as his friends baited their hooks and cast their lines out into the waterway.

"No sign of your hairy friend today, boss."

Jim looked round at Geordie. "He hasn't been here for a couple of days now. Megan thinks he has probably gone off to hibernate somewhere warm and dry."

"Reckon he'll be back next year?" Ivan asked.

"We're not sure about that. Judging by the grey around his muzzle and all the scars he's carrying, he's pretty old for a bear. This might well have been his last summer."

"Do you think you'll miss him?"

"You know, Geordie, I think I just might. It's pretty special having a massive bear come down and watch you fish, then just wait for you to chuck him his breakfast."

Geordie heard a twig snap in the woods to his left and turned to see if the bear had arrived. It wasn't the bear.

"Well, well, just the three people I was looking for and all in a group waiting for me."

Ivan and Jim turned to see Calanthe standing behind them with a sub-machine gun held at the ready and pointing in their direction. Strangely, Jim could not help but notice how beautiful she looked in the morning light. Even the heavy jacket couldn't disguise her dancer's physique, and the way the dark hair hanging down to her shoulders shone in the sunlight.

Jim put his fishing rod down slowly and straightened up. The Webley revolver was tucked into its holster on the back of his belt. Any move to grab it would be too obvious. He moved slightly to his left so that he covered Ivan, in the hope that the big Welshman might be able to grab it.

"So what happens now?"

"So now, Major, I take my revenge for my father. I just wanted to make sure you knew who shot you. I want to see the fear in your eyes as I pay you back for all you have done to me."

Geordie stood up slowly with his hands in clear view. "Hang on, bonny lass, these two had nothing to do with shooting your Dad. That was me and it was payback for him getting a Spanish girl killed. We should be even."

"No, we are not even, as you call it. My father was worth a hundred of your Spanish whores. I am glad you told me it was you. I shall kill you last so you can see your friends die."

As she raised her weapon towards Jim there was a deep cough behind her. She spun round to see the huge bear rising up on its back legs right behind her. The massive left paw swung across her and ripped the gun from her grasp. The power of the blow sent the weapon spinning out across the waterway. Calanthe seemed frozen with fear as the right paw swung and the vicious claws ripped across her stomach, throwing her back against a tree.

The old bear dropped down to all four paws again and his great head swung round to look at Jim and his two friends. He huffed once, deep in his throat, and turned away. As he did so, he seemed to nod to Jim and then ambled slowly into the gloom of the forest.

Ivan was the first to recover his wits. "God Almighty," he said as he started towards the young Greek girl.

Calanthe lay up against the tree where she had landed. The massive blow from those huge claws had ripped her stomach wide open, disembowelling her. The three men looked down in horror at the entrails splattered on the stones of the beach, knowing there was nothing anybody could do for her. She looked up at them for a second or two and then the light faded from her eyes as her life ebbed away.

Chapter 91

The three men were still standing by the torn body when Simon ran from the cabin. He stopped when he saw what had happened and then went pale and turned away to vomit onto the rocky beach. He turned back towards the scene of horror and wiped his mouth with the back of his hand.

"Simon, we'll deal with this. You go back in the cabin."

"In a minute, Uncle Jim. I need to do something first."

Simon drew the digital camera out of his pocket and turned it on. Jim was disgusted by what he saw the boy doing.

"Simon! You can't. That's awful,"

"Uncle Jim, trust me on this, I know what I'm doing and it's not being ghoulish."

Jim looked at the boy and slowly nodded. He owed him that trust after all he had done and been through. Simon moved forward and took a picture of the savaged body, then he move to one side and took another, then yet another. He raised his pale face to Jim and nodded, then walked unsteadily back to the cabin.

Geordie found a piece of old tarpaulin in the aircraft hangar and they covered the body, but left it where it was for the authorities to deal with. Together they walked slowly back into the cabin and went to sit around the log burning stove.

Megan and Sandra walked across the room to join them. "Was it bad?" Meagan asked.

All three men nodded silently. "Bear attacks usually are," she said. "A good thing they are so rare around here."

Sandra was standing behind her son looking at the work he was doing on the laptop computer. "Oh my God!" she whispered as she stared at the screen.

The three men walked across and stood behind Simon. The photograph of Calanthe on the screen looked, if anything, worse than the real thing outside.

"What are you doing, Simon?" Ivan asked quietly.

"You wanted the contract closed down? Well, that's what I'm doing. We cracked the security protocols on the website, so now my friend Rashid is sending a message to everyone who has visited the site, telling them that there is now nobody to pay for the contract. What I'm doing is posting the photos of the body to prove that what he says is true."

"Can we have a look at it?"

"Of course," Simon said and turned the screen towards them. There were the three photographs of Calanthe's torn and mangled body. Somehow her face was still beautiful and sad.

They looked at the pictures in silence and then read the caption Simon had put beneath them in larger letters.

"It's Over."

Twelve Lives – Factual Content

One of the reviewers of my first book commented on the anomaly of using US spellings and terminology in a book with British heroes. My previous publishers and I debated this point and we decided that we would use US standards. I hope my readers who are more used to the Queen's English will forgive me and I hope it did not affect your enjoyment.

As with all my books I try to be as factual as possible and this one is no exception. This chapter will give you the facts I have used, so that you can make a judgement about whether my story is credible.

The Beaver is a single-engine high-wing monoplane built by De Havilland of Canada from 1947 to 1967. When production ended, 1,657 had been built and hundreds of them are still flying today. It was designed to be a reliable bush aircraft and has proven to be exactly that. Many of the variants in use in Canada today are floatplanes due to the remarkable number of lakes and waterways that can be used as landing fields. Its outstanding short take-off and landing capabilities make it ideal for hauling cargo and passengers into and out of wilderness areas usually only accessible by foot or canoe. Wheeled versions were used in other parts of the world and various militaries used these for a range of tasks for many years. The engine is a large, reliable nine cylinder Pratt and Whitney

Wasp, although later versions have been given a turbine engine.

The village of Guadalest in Spain does exist and is reputed to be the most visited village in that country. The ruined castle (*Castell de San Josep*) dating from the year 719 stands on top of an impressive rock outcropping and dominates the surrounding countryside. The entrance to the castle and the older part of the village is through a gated tunnel (*Portal de San Jose*) carved through the rock. There are various cafes and museums as well as numerous shops catering to tourists. The boutique hotel known as Cases Noves is there and is extremely well run by its owners, Toni and Sofi, who very kindly allowed me to use their names in my story. Sofi insisted on being portrayed as bad, although she is actually a very nice person and produces exceptionally good meals..

The John Browning-designed Winchester Model 1894 is the most prevalent of the Winchester repeating rifles. The Model 1894 was first chambered for the .32-40 cartridge, and later, a variety of calibers such as .25-35 WCF and the .30-30. Winchester was the first company to manufacture a civilian rifle chambered for the new smokeless propellants, and although delays prevented the .30.30 cartridge from appearing on the shelves until 1895, it remained the first commercially available smokeless powder round for the North American consumer market. Though initially it was too expensive for most shooters, the Model 1894 went on to become one of the best-selling hunting rifles of all time. It has the distinction of being the first sporting rifle to sell over one million units, ultimately selling over seven million before U.S.-production was discontinued in 2006. In the early 20th century, the rifles designation was abbreviated to "Model 94". See http://www.winchesterguns.com/ or Wikipedia for more details.

I have tried to describe the mass of coastal islands and waterways on the coast of British Columbia to be found north of Vancouver. This area is sparsely settled and really does have very few roads. The people there are hardy and self-sufficient, as they need to be. Many of the smaller settlements are still populated to a great extent by the original inhabitants of Canada, now commonly known as First Nations or First Peoples, although they often refer to themselves by their various tribal names. They do tend to have two names, one for dealing with other Canadians and then their own tribal name. Of all the Canadian provinces, British Columbia has the largest concentration of these fascinating people, many of whom make their living in the logging industry or hunting and fishing in the rich waters off this coast.

In the coastal area where I have set my story, one of the major groups of native people are the Heiltsuk. Originally there were many of these people, who have lived in the area for at least 10,000 years, although recent archaeological evidence shows they may have been here for more than 13,000 years, probably the oldest settled community in the world. In 1793 they made contact with Europeans and more importantly with the diseases the Europeans carried. The population was killed in droves by these diseases, mainly smallpox, and by 1919 the population had been reduced to about 225 individuals. Happily, the population is now recovering. Interestingly and understandably, after their huge length of time living in the area, these people believe the land is theirs and that Europeans have stolen it from them. They are famous for using their considerable woodworking skills which are evident in the construction of ocean-going canoes called 'Qatuwas'. They oppose the excessive logging and mining that they believe is doing considerable damage to the forests and poisoning the ocean. They also object to the rampant over-fishing of the waters that have supported them for millennia. Go to http://www.firstnations.de/fisheries/heiltsuk.htm for more information about these first Canadians.

The wooden weapon that is known in English as the "Face Splitter" does exist and the statement that First Nation peoples of the Pacific North West used to take heads as war trophies is also true. Although these people live in harmony with their environment, it should be remembered that the environment of this area can be extremely difficult. The treatment of these peoples by previous Canadian governments was harsh and abusive. Their ceremonies were banned by law and their children were forced to go to Residential

Schools, where their treatment was often extremely unpleasant, yet still they kept their rich culture alive and now that they are being treated better by the government that culture is thriving.

The Holiday Inn on Wisconsin Avenue in Washington is much as I have described it. As with most American hotels from the big chains, it is well run, clean and the food is pretty decent. It backs onto a small area of scrubland that does have paths that lead through as a shortcut towards the British Embassy.

The Resolute Desk stands in the Oval Office of the White House and is used by the President. It was made from the timbers of HMS Resolute and was a gift from Queen Victoria in 1880. It is less well known that HMS Resolute was one of five ships in a Royal Navy search group which was sent out to try and find the ill-fated Franklin Expedition, which had been searching for the North-West Passage. She was abandoned in the Arctic ice and recovered some years later by the USA. She was refurbished in the Brooklyn Navy Yard and sailed across the Atlantic to Britain where, in 1856, she was presented to Queen Victoria as a gift. The generosity of this gift by the United States went a long way to repairing relations between the two countries that were at a low ebb at the time.

The Colt Python revolver is arguably one of the finest weapons of this type. Chambered for the .357 Magnum round, it comes with a range of barrel sizes. The six-inch barrel is said to be the most popular size. It was manufactured from 1955 to 2005, but discontinued when it started to fall out of favour with law enforcement agencies.

The Armscor M200 .38 Special Revolver is a much lighter weapon than the Python and so is more suitable for most women who, without being sexist, generally have a lighter build and will therefore find the lighter weapon more controllable. Developed in the 1980s, the three versions of this revolver are still in production at the time of writing.

Pickett's Charge was the final act in the three-day battle of Gettysburg during the American Civil War. It involved thousands of Confederate soldiers walking up an open slope towards the rifles and cannons of the Union Army who held Cemetery Ridge. I have stood at the top of that ridge and looked down the approach. The courage it must have taken to make that attack is almost inconceivable, with nowhere to take cover and a long way to walk while under heavy fire.

The Gettysburg Park is remarkably well maintained as befits a site of such historical significance. The open-topped bus ride around the park is an enjoyable experience. The Park Rangers are well informed and helpful. The RV Park set in the woodland just outside the town is also a reality and I found it very comfortable and welcoming when we stayed there. All in all, this is a fascinating place, particularly for those interested in the history of the Civil War.

Niagara Falls spans the border between the USA and Canada. Canada has arguably the best views of the falls, although the view across the Horseshoe Falls from Terrapin Point in Goat Island is worth the effort of visiting. The restaurant I have described called "The Top of the Falls" is there and has some great reviews online, so you don't just have to take my word for it. Below the falls it is possible to take a boat ride on "The Maid of the Mist" and this, too, is something I would recommend while you are there.

Ivan's description of Jim's .38 Webley revolver is essentially correct. This caliber of pistol was issued to the police, while the armed forces were issued with the more powerful .455 caliber weapon until 1947. The various marks of this pistol stayed in use with the British Army from 1887 to 1963, when it was replaced by the 9mm Browning Hi-Power. A CO2 powered version of the Mark VI Webley, made from the original drawings, is available at the time of writing.

RAFSA, or more formally the Royal Air Force Sailing Association, does keep a set of 5.8 meter Ribcraft RIBs, or RhIBs. They are used to teach powerboat handling skills and to support various water-based sporting activities. The RAF generously allows them to be used to support significant civilian sporting events as well. Their crews are well trained and very experienced.

Northern Exposure Rescue is a charity group that also provides safety cover for water sport activities in the UK at minimal cost. Most of the boats are privately owned and the crews give their time and the use of the boats for free. They have provided safety cover for a number of major events, including the annual Great River Race through London and Her Majesty's Diamond Jubilee Regatta on the Thames. I was a member of this group until I retired and moved to Spain. Chris and Moira are leading members of the group.

The M1911 pistol is considered by many gun collectors and veterans to be the greatest self-loading pistol ever made and the grandfather of the modern handgun, which despite its age is still used alongside modern pistols today. Designed by John Moses Browning in 1910 with patent dates going as far back as 1897, the .45 caliber pistol was adopted into the US military arsenal on February 14, 1911. For more information visit (www.imfdb.org). It has been superseded by a 9mm pistol, but is still used by some Special Forces operators who value the stopping power of the larger round.

The British Challenger Armoured Repair and Recovery Vehicle (CRARRV) is built on a Challenger 1 chassis and was developed in the 1980s to recover damaged Challenger 1 Tanks. The vehicle has remained in British Army service since the introduction of the Challenger 2 and is operated by the Royal Electrical and Mechanical Engineers (REME). It weighs in at 61200 kg and has a maximum speed of 59 kph driven by its 1200 bhp Perkins-Condor CV12 engine. The British Army has had 75 in service since the late 80s. It has been deployed with both the Challenger 1 and Challenger 2 in several wars, including the 91 Gulf War, 2003 Iraq War and during Operation Moshtarak in Afghanistan during February 2010 in counter-Taliban operations where it was stationed in a Danish base. For more details go to - http://tanknutdave.com/the-challenger-armoured-repair-and-recovery-vehicle/

Soldiers and officers employed within the Royal Electrical and Mechanical Engineers (REME) are the technicians, mechanics and fabricators that consistently inspect, repair, modify and maintain the large array of equipment that the British Army operates. Wherever the British Army are, whatever the unit is, there you will find REME. Within REME, Recovery Mechanics have the job of racing into the field, recovering an immobilised vehicle and getting it back to somewhere safe where it can be properly fixed. All this makes them popular soldiers in the eyes of marooned vehicle crews. They have a tendency to be tough, no-nonsense individualists who identify a problem and solve it on the spot. For more details see - https://www.army.mod.uk/reme/reme.aspx

In the story I mention the British Army rank of ASM. More correctly this should be WO1 (ASM) or Warrant Officer Class 1 (Artificer Sergeant Major). This is the highest rank for noncommissioned soldiers in the REME and is only reached after considerable training and experience. I have to say that, I used to be one, many years ago.

The brown bear has the widest habitat of all the bears. There are some 90 sub-species with quite a remarkable amount of variation due commonly to different locations providing different food. The largest of the brown bears live along the Pacific North-West coast of Canada and Alaska and males can grow to 680 kg (1,500 lbs.). In North America they are often called grizzly bears, while the larger coastal population are known as Kodiak bears. On average there are two fatal attacks per year on humans in North America. Brown bears seldom attack humans on sight, and usually avoid people. They are, however, unpredictable in temperament, and may attack if they are surprised or feel threatened. Females with young are particularly aggressive if they feel their cubs are under threat.

The Nuclear Backpack Bomb, or more correctly the Special Atomic Demolition Munition, does exist. They were developed by both the USA and Russia during the cold war and they were intended to be infiltrated into enemy territory by Special Forces troops to attack key targets. For the US version, the bare warhead package was an 11 in by 16 in (28 cm by 41 cm) cylinder that weighed 51 lbs (23 kg). The explosive yield of such a device would usually be in the region of six kilotons. There are presently strong concerns that the Russian devices are not under close enough control and even that a few may have been "lost". Strategic nuclear weapons are under control by heads of state, but by their nature small devices that can be carried by one man can also be detonated by that one man.

The Javelin is a medium range anti-tank guided missile developed by Javelin, a joint venture between Raytheon and Lockheed Martin. The missile is currently in service with the US forces and has been combat tested in Iraq and Afghanistan. The Javelin is considered the world's best shoulder-fired anti-tank weapon and 12 nations currently operate the missile under foreign military sales from the US. Each missile weighs 11.8kg, while its command launch unit (CLU) and round weigh 6.4kg and 15.9kg respectively. The Javelin employs a long-wave infrared (LWIR) seeker for guidance to destroy tanks, bunkers, buildings, small vessel and low-speed helicopters with a high hit probability. It can also be fired from tripods, light armoured vehicles, trucks, and remotely piloted vehicles. It carries a tandem-shaped charge enabling a maximum range of 2,500m. For more details see - http://www.army-technology.com/projects/javelin/

The FIM-92 Stinger is a personal portable infrared homing surface-to-air missile (SAM), which can be adapted to fire from ground vehicles or helicopters. Developed in the USA, it entered service in 1981. Used by the militaries of the

United States and by 29 other countries, it is manufactured by Raytheon Missile Systems and under license by EADS in Germany. Some 70,000 missiles have been produced. It is classified as a man-portable air defence system (MANPADS).

The current US inventory contains 13,400 missiles. It is rumoured that the United States Secret Service has Stinger missiles to defend the President, a notion that has never been dispelled; however, US Secret Service plans usually involve moving the President to a safer place in the event of an attack rather than shooting down the plane, in case the missile (or the wreckage of the target aircraft) hit innocent people.

During the 1980s, the Stinger was used to support different US-supported guerrilla forces, including the Afghan Mujahidin, the Chad government against the Libyan invasion and the Angolan UNITA. For more details see - http://military.wikia.com/wiki/FIM-92_Stinger

The Intelligence services of the United Kingdom are divided into two distinct elements, MI5, the Security Service, and the Secret Intelligence Service, commonly known as MI6.

MI5's mission is to work internally to keep the country safe. For more than a century they have worked to protect the UK's people from danger, whether it be from terrorism or damaging espionage by hostile states. They work under the auspices of the Home Office and answer to the

Home Secretary. For more detail visit - https://www.mi5.gov.uk

At the Secret Intelligence Service (SIS) – otherwise known as MI6 – their mission is clear. They work secretly overseas, developing foreign contacts and gathering intelligence that helps to make the UK safer and more prosperous. They help the UK identify and exploit opportunities as well as navigate risks to its national security, military effectiveness and economy. They work across the globe to counter terrorism, resolve international conflict and prevent the spread of nuclear and other non-conventional weapons. They are here to help protect the UK's people, economy and interests. They work under the auspices of the Foreign Office and answer to the Foreign Secretary. If he existed, this is the service that James Bond would belong to. For more detail visit - https://www.sis.gov.uk

The British Army training base known as BATUS at Suffield in Alberta, near the town of Medicine Hat, does exist and does provide facilities for training personnel in armored warfare, in a way that is not possible in Europe. There are large tank sheds there for maintaining and storing the vehicles through the savage Canadian winter. The story about the local wildlife starting to turn white is correct. I observed this personally when I served at BATUS. It is also true that winter comes suddenly on the prairies. I went to work one morning in the normal summer uniform of the

British Army and had to draw a winter parka from the stores to get back to my billet through the snow that afternoon.

Type 23 Frigates of the Royal Navy (Duke Class) are an effective weapon system, commonly commanded by a Lieutenant Commander who is addressed with the courtesy title of Captain. There is no HMS Huntingdon, but there is an HMS Lancaster, so Huntingdon would be a possible name for this class of vessel. Ships of this class carry a range of weapons, including various missiles, a Lynx helicopter and a 4.5 inch naval gun. With a firing rate of twenty-five rounds per minute and a reputation for accuracy, the modern 4.5 inch naval gun fitted to many Royal Navy warships is a formidable weapon, particularly at close range.

The idea of a magazine-fed grenade launcher may seem far-fetched to some people, but it is actually a reality today in US service. The M32 is a handheld grenade launcher that carries six 40mm grenades in a rotating magazine. The Mk19 grenade launcher is a large, heavy, belt-fed weapon that deploys 40mm grenades of various types. It has powerful recoil so can be difficult to deploy when off a vehicle. The XM307 is a modern weapon due to replace the Mk19. It is lighter and has a less powerful recoil, making it much more comfortable for the two-man crew. It fires 25mm air bursting smart rounds that are programmed to explode at the right place by the computerised sighting system. It has a range of approximately 2000 meters.

GSG9 (Grenzschutzgruppe 9) was formed after the debacle of the terrorist attack on the Munich Olympics in 1972. Germany at that time had no units that specialised in anti-terror operations. Unlike other nations, these Special Forces were formed as part of the police border guards rather than the army. Hence the name, which translates as Border Protection Group 9. They were modelled to some extent on the British SAS and the Israeli Special Operations unit. They are known to be highly effective and have been used on numerous operations, mainly in Germany, but also overseas, when the occasion demanded it, to protect the lives of German citizens.

Hermannsdenkmal is a massive monument to Arminus, a tribal chieftain who defeated three Roman Legions in the year 9 AD. Including its huge plinth, the statue stands some 53 meters tall (175 feet). It is mounted on top of a 386 meter hill just outside the town of Detmold in the district of Lippe. The riveted copper plates of the outer covering give it a distinctive green colour. The figure shows Hermann (or Arminus) wearing a winged helmet and holding a sword aloft. Set in a wooded park, it is well worth the walk through the forest to reach it and the viewing gallery around the top of the plinth gives fine views across the surrounding area.

Mexico has a number of battalions of Special Forces troops. Of these the veteran soldiers of the *Grupo Aeromóvil de Fuerzas Especiales del Alto Mando* (GAFE High Command) appear to be the most likely to undertake the sort of Black Ops mission that I describe in my story. Much of the work of Mexican Special Forces is targeted at the drug cartels that are making life in that country such a misery for its people.

Is a tunnel from Mexico under the US border realistic? Sadly, yes. Tunnels have been found that are big enough for small trucks to drive through and at least one has been found with rail tracks laid. These are used by criminal gangs for drug and people smuggling, as well as moving US manufactured weapons south to equip those gangs for their fight with the Mexican authorities.

The I-35 Interstate Highway does run north from Laredo to San Antonio. From there, there are four Interstate routes that a criminal could take, as well as any number of other routes.

The National Nuclear Security Administration (NNSA) exists and provides expertise, practical tools, and technically-informed policy recommendations required to advance US. nuclear counterterrorism and counter proliferation objectives. It executes a unique program of work focused solely on these missions and builds partnerships with US government agencies and key foreign governments on these issues.

Borsch is a classic Russian and Ukrainian soup based on beetroot and sausage. To make it vegetarian just miss out the sausage. For one of the recipes go to:- www.simplyrecipes.com/recipes/borscht

The Crown Victoria Police Interceptor is the classic American police car. Designed by Ford, specifically for law enforcement, it has been adopted by police departments across the USA. It is used by the Washington DC City Police, who are known as the Metropolitan Police. Uniquely, this police force is under Federal rather than local jurisdiction.

Central Park in New York is a remarkably attractive green space in the middle of that busy city. It can be very tranquil to walk through, but it is surprisingly large if you are not ready for it. There are problems with crime in the park. Although these incidents are mainly at night, travellers should be careful, as in most big cities.

Faneuil Hall in Boston was built in 1742. It has served as a marketplace and meeting hall ever since. It is sometimes referred to as the Cradle of Liberty. Located near the waterfront and Government Center in Boston, it is a well-known stop on the Freedom Trail. The ground floor contains shops and eating establishments. The second floor is a meeting room. The third floor contains the museum and armory of the Ancient and Honorable Artillery Company of Massachusetts.

Faneuil Hall Marketplace also includes three long granite buildings called North Market, South Market, and Quincy Market. It operates as an indoor/outdoor mall and food eatery. It was designed by Benjamin Thompson and Associates. For two centuries the symbol of Faneuil Hall has been the gilded grasshopper weathervane on top of the building. It was created by Deacon Shem Drowne in 1742. It is the only totally unmodified part of Faneuil Hall today. For more details see:- http://faneuilhall.com/

The Omni Parker Hotel in Boston does exist and is very comfortable. It has been in School Street since 1855 and has quite a history. The dark wall panelling in the public areas give it a European feel that is quite unusual. My wife assures me they make an excellent dry martini.

Jim Wilson and his men have now been promised by the most senior politicians that they will never be called on again, so they can settle down to a quieter life. But then these are politicians' promises, so …

This book is the sixth in a series so Jim, Ivan and Geordie will put their lives on the line again.

I hope you have enjoyed this book and if so an honest review on Amazon, or wherever you bought the book, would be very much appreciated.

For more information about my books please visit my website.
http://www.nigelseedauthor.com/

Photograph "Courtesy of Grupo Bernabé" of Pontevedra.

<u>Nigel Seed</u>

Born in Morecambe, England, into a military family, Nigel Seed grew up hearing his father's tales of adventure during the Second World War which kindled his interest in military history and storytelling. He received a patchy education, as he and his family followed service postings from one base to another. Perhaps this and the need to constantly change schools contributed to his odd ability to link unconnected facts and events to weave his stories.

Nigel later joined the Army, serving with the Royal Electrical and Mechanical Engineers in many parts of the world. Upon leaving he joined the Ministry of Defence during which time he formed strong links with overseas armed forces, including the USAF, and cooperated with them, particularly in support of the AWACS aircraft.

He is married and lives in Spain; half way up a mountain with views across orange groves to the Mediterranean. The warmer weather helps him to cope with frostbite injuries he sustained in Canada, when taking part in the rescue effort for a downed helicopter on a frozen lake.

His books are inspired by places he has been to and true events he has either experienced or heard about on his travels. He makes a point of including family jokes and stories in his books to raise a secret smile or two. Family dogs make appearances in his other stories.

Nigel's hobbies include sailing and when sailing in Baltic he first heard the legend of the hidden U-Boat base that formed the basis of his first book some thirty eight years later.

The Other Books by this author

Drummer's Call

Revenge of a Lone Wolf

Simon Drummer is on loan to a bio-warfare protection unit in the USA when the terror they fear becomes real. A brilliant Arabic bio-chemist is driven to bring an end to the suffering of his countrymen. He believes that the regime that oppresses them could not exist without the support of the US government and the weapons they furnish. He needs to bring the truth to the American people in a way that will grab their attention. So begins his journey to bring brutal death and understanding to the USA. And now Simon must help to find him and stop him.

The Minstrel Boy

A Future History

Billy Murphy minds his own business and sings his songs in the pubs around Belfast. Then the IRA decides that he can be useful to them in preparing to restart the armed struggle for Irish unity. He finds himself caught up in their plots and learns the truth about the Troubles that he had never been told. But there are others who watch and take revenge for past atrocities. Billy must be careful not to come under suspicion and find his own life at risk from the terrorist killers he is working for.

The Jim Wilson Series

V4 – Vengeance

Hitler's Last Vengeance Weapons Are Going To War

Major Jim Wilson, late of the Royal Engineers, has been obliged to leave the rapidly shrinking British Army. He needs a job but they are thin on the ground even for a highly capable Army Officer. Then he is offered the chance to go to Northern Germany to search for the last great secret of World War 2, a hidden U Boat base. Once he unravels the mystery he is asked to help to spirit two submarines away from under the noses of the German government, to be the central exhibits in a Russian museum. But then the betrayal begins and a seventy year old horror unfolds.

Golden Eights

The Search For Churchill's Lost Gold Begins Again

In 1940, with the British army in disarray after the evacuation from Dunkirk, invasion seemed a very real possibility. As a precaution, the Government decided to protect the national gold reserves by sending most of the bullion to Canada on fast ships that ran the gauntlet of the U boat fleets. But a lot of gold bars and other treasures were hidden in England. In the fog of war, this treasure was lost. Now, finally, a clue has emerged that might lead to the hiding place. The Government needs the gold back if the country is not to plunge into a huge financial crisis. Major Jim Wilson has been tasked to find it. He and his small team start the search, unaware that there is a traitor watching their every move and intent on acquiring the gold, at any cost.

Two Into One

A Prime Minister Acting Strangely and World Peace in the Balance

Following his return from Washington the Prime Minister's behaviour has changed. Based on his previous relationship with the PM, Major Jim Wilson is called in to investigate. What he finds is shocking and threatens the peace of the world. But now he must find a way to put things right and there is very little time to do it. His small team sets out on a dangerous quest that takes them from the hills of Cumbria to the Cayman Islands and Dubai, but others are watching and playing for high stakes.

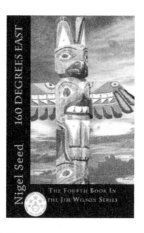

160 Degrees East

A fight for survival and the need to right a terrible wrong.

Major Jim Wilson and his two men are summoned at short notice to Downing Street. The US Government has a problem and they have asked for help from Wilson and his small team. Reluctantly Jim agrees, but he is unaware of the deceit and betrayal awaiting him from people he thought of as friends. From the wild hills of Wales to the frozen shores of Russia and on to the mountains of British Columbia Jim and his men have to fight to survive, to complete their mission and to right a terrible wrong.

One More Time

A Nuclear Disaster Threatened By Criminals Must Be Prevented At All Costs

Jim and Ivan have retired from the Army and are making their way in civilian life when they are summoned back to the military by the new Prime Minister. Control of two hidden nuclear weapons has failed and they have been lost. Jim must find them before havoc is wreaked upon the world by whoever now controls them. It is soon apparent the problem is far bigger than originally envisaged, and there is a race against time to stop further weapons falling into the hands of an unscrupulous arms dealer and his beautiful daughter. The search moves from Zimbabwe to Belize and on to Norway and Spain, becoming ever more urgent and dangerous as the trail is followed.

Twelve Lives

A Threat to Millions But This Time It's Personal

During a highly classified mission for the British Government, Jim Wilson and his two companions make a dangerous enemy. A contract has been put on their lives and on those of their families. Jim moves the intended victims to safety and sets about trying to have the contract cancelled. However, his efforts to save his family uncover a horrendous plot to mount a nuclear terror attack on the United States and the race is on to save millions of lives.

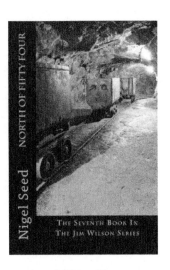

North of Fifty Four

A Crime Must Be Committed To Prevent A War

Jim Wilson is forced to work for a Chinese criminal gang or his wife and child will be murdered. While he is away in the north of Canada, his wife manages to contact Ivan and Geordie for help. The two friends set out to save all three of them, but then the threat to many more people emerges and things become important enough to involve governments in committing a serious crime to prevent a new war in the Middle East.

Short Stories

Backpack 19

A Lost Backpack and a World of Possibilities.

An anonymous backpack lying by the side of the road. Who picks it up and what do they find inside? There are many possibilities and lives may be changed for the better or worse. Here are just nineteen of those stories.

The Michael McGuire Trilogy

No Road to Khartoum

From the filthy back streets of Dublin to the deserts of the Sudan to fight and die for the British Empire.

Found guilty of stealing bread to feed his starving family, Michael McGuire is offered the "Queen's Hard Bargain", go to prison or join the Army. He chooses the Army and, after training in Dublin Castle, his life is changed forever as he is selected to join the 'Gordon Relief Expedition' that is being sent south of Egypt to Khartoum, in the Sudan.

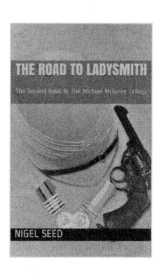

The Road to Ladysmith

Only just recovered from his wounds Captain McGuire must now sail south to the confusion and error of the Boer War.

After his return from the war in the Sudan, McGuire had expected to spend time recovering with his family. It was not to be, and his regiment is called urgently to South Africa to counter the threat from the Boers. Disparaged as mere farmers the Boers were to administer a savage lesson to the British Army.

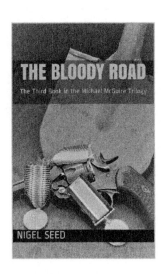

The Bloody Road

Michael McGuire has left the army, but as the First World War breaks out his country calls him again.

At the start of the war the British expand their army rapidly, but there is a shortage of experienced officers and McGuire is needed. He is sent to Gallipoli in command of an Australian battalion that suffers badly in that debacle. He stays with them when their bloody road takes them to the mud and carnage of the western front.

If you have enjoyed this book a review on Amazon.com would be very welcome.

Please visit my website at www.nigelseedauthor.com for information about upcoming books.

Printed in Great Britain
by Amazon